ONE
HOT
SUMMER

rayo *An Imprint of* HarperCollins*Publishers*

ONE
HOT
SUMMER

[A NOVEL]

CAROLINA
GARCIA-AGUILERA

HarperCollins books may be purchased for educational, business, or sales promotional use. For information, please write: Special Markets Department, HarperCollins Publishers Inc., 10 East 53rd Street, New York, NY 10022.

FIRST EDITION

Designed by Shubhani Sarkar

Printed on acid-free paper

Library of Congress Cataloging-in-Publication Data
Garcia-Aguilera, Carolina.
    One hot summer / by Carolina Garcia-Aguilera.—Rayo 1st ed.
    p. cm.
    ISBN 0-06-000980-2
    1. Cuban Americans—Fiction.   2. Female friendship—Fiction.
    3. Women lawyers—Fiction.   4. Miami (Fla.)—Fiction.   I. Title.
    PS3557.A71124 O54 2002
    813'.54—dc21
                                2001057878

02 03 04 05 06 BVG/QW 10 9 8 7 6 5 4 3 2 1

To my daughters, Sarah, Antonia, and Gabriella

The loves and passions of my life

And, of course, as always, to my beloved Cuba—

you are forever in my heart and soul

ACKNOWLEDGMENTS

This novel, *One Hot Summer,* was a departure for me from the genre in which I am used to writing. Having had six detective novels published before this one (three bodies per book, or your money is refunded), I have to admit, writing a love story presented a whole different set of challenges. For example, I had to train myself to write scenes in which two people were in bed simultaneously and both were still breathing. I have to express my gratitude to several very special individuals who had faith in me and who believed I could accomplish that.

I would like to thank my agents at International Creative Management, Richard Abate in New York, and Ron Bernstein in Los Angeles, for their unwavering support and belief in me. I am very grateful to Rene Alegria, my editor at Rayo, so aptly named, for his unbridled enthusiasm and joie de vivre, which made writing this novel so much fun. Quinton Skinner, as usual, deserves a special thanks for his special talents, but especially for his uncanny ability to morph himself into yet another Cuban woman.

As always, I owe debt to my family: my mother, Lourdes Aguilera de Garcia; my sister, Sara; my brother, Carlos; and my nephew, Richard, for all the years of encouragement and support they have given me. It gives me great comfort to know I have their backing in my literary efforts.

Sarah, Antonia, and Gabriella, my precious daughters, thank you for blessing me with your presence, for being with me as much as possible, for having stood by me at all times, good or not so good. Every day I am in awe of my unbelievably good fortune, and for the blessings that have been bestowed upon me. Even though I do not have a clue as to what that might be, I am positive that I must have done something right for God to have given you three to me. However, I don't question too much, I just happily accept my gifts and enjoy them to the fullest.

I have to acknowledge the importance of my friends, recognizing I have been blessed in that aspect as well. Beginning with my childhood friends from Cuba, to the gang on South Beach, all of you plus many others, *gracias*. Thank you for being my friends, which, I suspect, is not easy at times. For the friendship you have given me throughout the years, I owe you all a debt I can never repay.

But, finally, I must thank the men who have played such an important part of my life, for without you I would not have been able to write a book such as this.

ONE
HOT
SUMMER

 I was in an unusually upbeat mood, riding that luscious high a woman comes by when she knows she's looking particularly fine and that she has a good time ahead of her. Earlier in the day I'd run over to Saks Fifth Avenue at the Bal Harbour Shops and picked up a new dress, a simple Armani sleeveless black sheath that fit me perfectly. I knew I would get a lot of use out of it. My previous black dress, reserved for trips to the Caballero Funeral Home, had been getting overexposed, I figured, since I'd worn it to more than a dozen wakes and funerals. It needed replacing with a fresher and more stylish model. My husband claims that I'll jump at any excuse to go shopping. I guess he's right.

Well, what of it?

In Cuban Miami, going to a wake at a funeral home isn't necessarily the depressing social trial it would be anyplace else. A wake doubles as a social setting where old friends get together and reconnect before setting out for the night. And that was Miami for you—not even death can get in the way of the pursuit of a good time.

It was seven o'clock on a hot sultry early July night. I was driving on the MacArthur Causeway with the latest Marc Anthony CD blasting. The speed limit on the causeway was fifty but no one—except maybe for tourists and old ladies—ever drove that slow.

I had just left Miami Beach, where I live, heading for Coral Gables to meet my best friends—Vivian Mendoza and Anabel Acosta—at the wake for the great-aunt of Maria Teresa Martinez, another of our friends. Neither Vivian nor Anabel nor I had ever so much as exchanged pleasantries with the octogenarian lady who had passed away peacefully in her sleep earlier that day, but because of our friendship with Maria Teresa, our attendance was mandatory.

I hoped it would be a closed-casket viewing—however oxymoronic the concept. It gave me the creeps to make small talk with a dead body lying a few feet away. I could never banish the thought that the deceased was listening to us discussing what restaurant we preferred for dinner that night. It just wasn't seemly, and, now that I was thinking about it, I realized that this entire train of thought was threatening to dampen my mood. So I pushed it away. I really wanted, no, I *needed*, to have a good time that night.

In Cuban circles, wakes are actually considered a great place to pick up dates—if not in the viewing room, definitely at the cafeteria behind the building. The quality of the pickings rose in proportion to how well-known the deceased might have been, or whether he or she came from a big family. When we were teenagers, Vivian and Anabel and I would check out all the boys at viewings and discuss their physical traits within earshot of the deceased. Not exactly proper behavior for three Catholic girls—maybe my guilt over my actions lay behind my distaste for open-casket viewings now that I'm an adult. The worst part when we were girls came when the priest started to recite the rosary. It took forever, and there was no escape—no one could possibly leave the room while the rosary was being said, that was one of the few rules that could never be broken. We used to try to time our visits to avoid encountering the priest.

I have countless memories from wakes throughout my life, and every so often my friends and I reminisce about all the viewings we've attended together. Of course we only remember as pleasant the wakes that involved an elderly distant relative and not someone we were close to—*those* evoked a different kind of memory altogether. The wake that night was in the former category: None of us knew the departed, and we were looking forward to having dinner together afterward. Since two of the three of us were married, there was no need to check out the scene. It was a night out for us, something we hadn't enjoyed in at least a few weeks. Maybe longer, after I thought about it.

Driving always clears my mind. I watched Biscayne Bay shimmer like spun silver. There was some kind of regatta going on, boats with bright sails stretched taut against the wind, their masts almost touching water. They skimmed the surface, headed north in tight formation. Farther along I saw a Sealand container ship so heavily loaded that it lay low in the water; it was pulled by two tugboats through the narrow channel, almost visibly yearning for the open seas.

There were three cruise ships, so enormous they looked like floating apartment buildings, docked in a line at the Port of Miami for service before heading south to sail the Caribbean. I'd never taken a cruise, and every time I saw one of these ships I fantasized about drifting off on one, removing myself from daily life and going completely incommunicado. My temptation, or desperation, had never built to the point where I was compelled to buy a ticket and go. Still, I read the Sunday *Miami Herald* travel section every week from cover to cover.

I passed the bridge that led to Palm and Hibiscus Islands, taking my eyes off the road for a second to look for one of the dolphins that could sometimes be seen cavorting in the distance. But it was not to be. I might have been a sophisticated thirty-five-year-old woman who'd seen plenty of dolphins in the wild before, but the sight of one of those majestic animals still always made my heart race. It wasn't such a bad thing to maintain some shred of innocence inside my soul. It wasn't easy, not in Miami. And for a lawyer, it was almost impossible.

With the *Miami Herald* building on my right, I pulled the wheel to merge two lanes left for my exit onto I-95 south, which would take me past downtown and eventually to U.S. 1 and the final leg of my voyage. My first impulse was to get off at the Biscayne Boulevard exit, the normal route I would take to my office at the First Dade Corporation Building. That is, if I were still working there. No, I thought, I *was* still working there. Until I decided otherwise.

I drove onto the overpass and glanced up to check out the top three floors of the building where our law offices were located. It was almost seven thirty, but all the lights were still blazing away. No surprise there. The brutal hours were one of the reasons I'd taken a year-long leave of absence from the firm. The support staff—secretaries, paralegals, clerks, assistants—pretty much kept to a nine-to-five lifestyle. But there was no such thing for the attorneys. There was really no room for a personal life for the lawyers at Weber, Miranda, Blanco and Silverman. Many times I had heard the big clock in the hall outside my office chime twelve strokes for midnight while I was anchored to my desk racking up the billable hours. And that was the core of the business, the crux of the attorney's existence: *billable hours*.

It wasn't all drudgery. I had made good, close friends there. We went out together and partied hard, like soldiers on leave. I had accepted the firm's work ethic without complaint for five years. But once I got married the long hours became a problem. And when the baby came, well, my fate was pretty much sealed. For a Cuban woman—professional or not—husband and children are supposed to come first, with work placing a distant third.

And that's the way it was.

It had been ten months since I took my leave of absence, and the maximum time allowed by the firm was one year. So I had difficult decisions to make and, so far, I had done a pretty good job of avoiding them. But the time was approaching to make a choice, and the pressure was intensifying. From all sides.

The Marc Anthony CD finished up just as I-95 blended onto U.S. 1. An old Gloria Estefan disc came on next—*Mi Tierra*, one of my favorites. The songs were all about Cuba, which would put me in the right mood for the wake. After all, I was about to enter an all-Cuban zone. Who better to prepare me than that quintessential Cuban, Gloria Estefan.

I turned west onto Douglas Road and a couple of minutes later I was searching for a spot in the lot behind the funeral home. It wasn't easy. The Cadillac Escalade was a big car that took up a lot of space. That was what I loved about it, but parking spaces that could accommodate it were few and far between.

Cruising slowly, I passed up three or four spaces that a smaller car could have easily squeezed into. I tried to block thoughts of my husband, Ariel, from my mind: He had warned me that the Escalade was going to bring me nothing but headaches. Oh, but it was such a badass car, a huge black SUV with tinted windows. How could I resist? I knew at the time that Ariel was giving me good advice when he counseled me against buying the beast, but I had fallen in love with it the moment I spotted it in the Cadillac showroom.

When I fall in love with something, I must have it. And damn the consequences. It wasn't exactly the best character trait for an attorney, but my great passions had fortunately been very few. Otherwise I might have ended locked up in jail instead of visiting my clients there. Going to jail, even as a visitor, is an education. You realize how one little act, one single mistake, can land you on the other side of a steel door that isn't going to open. It's sobering, and it makes you appreciate what you have.

Finally. I found a big enough spot in the farthest row, right next to the security wall. I inspected my makeup in one of the many mirrors conveniently arranged every few inches inside the car, checked my lipstick to make sure my teeth weren't stained red, gave myself a final squirt of perfume. I reached up with a practiced hand and did a quick tease of my shoulder-length hair to achieve that naturally tousled look that costs me hundreds of dollars every month. Now I felt adequately prepared to pay my respects to Tia Esther, a fine lady, to be sure.

I swung my legs around and tried to step out of the Escalade with as much ladylike grace as I could manage, careful not to twist my ankles. I was wearing a reasonably new pair of "limousine shoes," backless sandals with high heels that made walking more than a block impossible, thus requiring the services of a limousine. The car was so high off the ground that I had to make use of the running board under the door to get me halfway down to earth.

I was walking as stiffly as a Chinese woman with bound feet as I scurried through the parking lot toward the main entrance. It wasn't far, but by the time I got there it felt as though I had navigated the length of Pro Player Stadium. I looked around and saw that both Vivian's Lexus and Anabel's BMW were there. Good. There was nothing worse than going to a wake without knowing anyone there. It had happened to me in the past, when someone died who merited our family's respects and Mamá would insist that someone go to Caballero's to represent us. As the only daughter, that task more often than not fell to me. If Vivian and Anabel hadn't been there, I would have been forced to make awkward conversation and offer condolences for someone I never knew. Maria Teresa would be there, but she would be occupied with the responsibilities of grieving grandniece.

One thing I knew about wakes—always sign the guest book on the table outside the viewing room. It's like having a receipt that proves your attendance in case the grieving relatives don't remember who they saw and who they didn't. I was always careful to print my entire name as legibly as possible: Margarita Maria Santos Silva. I definitely wanted full credit for my efforts.

Before I went inside, I checked out the small crowd milling in front of the entrance, scanning faces for someone I knew, but they were all unfamiliar to me. There were about a dozen men of all ages, dressed either in formal dark suits or white guayaberas—the stiffly starched white shirts that were a traditional dress-up uniform for Cuban men—with dark trousers. There were two women, dressed all in black, gesticulating wildly and talking in animated spitfire Cuban Spanish. Just about everyone was holding a cigarette or a cigar, the trails of smoke ascending over their heads toward heaven in the yellow lights on either side of the front door. I adjusted my black pashmina shawl around my shoulders, which I wore as protection against the fierce air-conditioning inside, ran my fingers through my hair, and steeled myself for mingling with the A list of Miami's Cuban exile society. No thinking about work, no thinking about Ariel, I told myself. Lately I hadn't been able to carve out enough time for myself and to be with my friends. I was damned well going to enjoy myself.

And then tomorrow I was going to sort everything out. I promised myself I would.

 "Margarita!" a familiar voice called out to me. Vivian was waiting just inside. She hurried over and kissed my cheek. I was enveloped in the scent of her Carolina Herrera perfume. "Anabel is in the bathroom," she volunteered, gesturing vaguely. "We were waiting for you!"

A moment later Anabel emerged from the ladies' room. Anabel was severely near-sighted, and I saw that she wasn't wearing her glasses. It would take her a while to recognize me standing next to Vivian.

Anabel was almost legally blind and, to make it worse, her eyes rejected contact lenses. She refused to wear her glasses in public unless she had no other option, such as when she wanted to drive without being charged with vehicular homicide. I had gone with her to the Florida Department of Motor Vehicles when she was issued her first driver's license; I still remember how outrageously she flirted with the officer who tested her, in a futile effort to keep him from marking the "needs corrective lenses" box on her license. Anabel's particular form of vanity made her feel that her condition made her imperfect, and, for her, having it branded on an official document meant all the world knew her shame.

I knew it. Anabel was right next to me when she finally recognized me. She stepped closer, misjudging the distance between us. I hopped back and yanked my feet out of her way just in time; a little slower and my limousine shoes would have been history—and both my feet would have been in casts.

"Margarita!" Anabel puckered her lips to give me a kiss. Then she aimed her mouth in the general direction of my face and lunged toward me. I cringed as she connected with my cheek, knowing that she had left a blood-red streak.

Within seconds, Vivian was searching through her purse for a tissue to wipe away Anabel's lipstick. This was part of being friends with Anabel—she routinely rearranged our makeup. I just wished she would wear her glasses. It would make life easier for everyone—or, if not easier, then tidier.

I waited quietly for Vivian to clean me up, taking in the scene. My friends and I were dressed essentially in widow's weeds—the appropriate attire for a Cuban wake—and looked as though we were prepared to throw ourselves on the deceased's funeral pyre. This was the custom: Even those who didn't know the dead person at all were expected in theory to behave as though they were suffering deeply. Unwritten rules mandated proper dress that was reserved strictly for trips to Caballero's—conservative clothing, in black, covering the knee, nothing too fashionable or trendy. Viewings were the only occasions that didn't require a phone call in advance to plot what we were going to wear. We all knew. That night I recognized both Vivian and Anabel's outfits, since I had seen them a few times before.

I waited for my friends to notice my new dress, but they were focused on my shoes. Anabel had to practically crouch down in order to see them. I considered taking one off and handing it to her, but it would have strained the boundaries of propriety. I glanced over and saw the wheels in Vivian's mind turning as she estimated how much my Manolo Blahniks cost. She knew I only paid retail, a practice that filled her with anxiety and loathing.

It was fairly crowded inside, with people milling around the reception area and the viewing rooms. I read a notice posted in the foyer and saw that Tia Esther was laid out in Room 2, the largest of the five inside. That meant they were expecting a big turnout. This was good news for us; we could each sign the book and do a quick run-through. We could express our sympathies to the receiving line stationed in front of the casket, then spend a few minutes with Maria Teresa purely out of form, since she barely knew her Tia Esther any more intimately than we did. Then we'd be free for a quick exit and on our way to dinner.

The fact is, we were pros at the Caballero experience. The three of us didn't need to consult about strategy—we all knew intuitively how things would play out and how long it would take. We were in lockstep with one another.

Vivian, Anabel, and I didn't go to school together. But we'd been friends since the second grade when we played soccer on the same YWCA team—our parents had all independently decided we needed some exercise in addition to our schoolwork and enrolled us against our will on the squad. Our team was one of the best in Dade County, and was nearly undefeated in the five years we played. Which sounds impressive, as long as you never saw us play. It was sheer dumb luck that my friends and I were assigned to such a good team.

The three of us played defense. Our offense was so strong and aggressive that almost all the action took place around the opponent's goal. Anabel was our goalie, in spite of the fact that she couldn't see more than a few inches in front of her face. Vivian and I were simply hopeless athletically. We basically hung out around the goal and talked trash about our teammates. Then, when we got a little older, the talk turned to boys. We would break huddle to clap and cheer every time our team scored a goal—although not too loudly, since we didn't want to attract our coach's attention. The rest of the team thought we were great, since they were all ball hogs and we never wanted to see the thing.

The games were on Saturday mornings; Tata, my family's nanny, would drive us to wherever they were held. We discouraged our parents from ever attending, since they might have objected to our nonparticipation strategy. After the game we would spend the afternoon together at one of our houses and, depending on how much home-work we'd been assigned, often spend the night. We developed the kind of friendship that can only be cemented by sleepovers and a shared promise to never keep secrets from one another, which we've managed to maintain into adulthood.

All three of us were Cuban Americans, born in Miami of Cuban parents and growing up less than two miles apart in Coral Gables, an upscale residential district of Miami. I always thought the fact that we went to three separate schools—all the way from elementary school through college—kept us close. We were never in competi-tion with each other, and we never fought over the same prizes, hu-man or otherwise.

Vivian Mendoza was a lawyer like me, but we were in different specialties. I was a business immigration lawyer, and she was a solo practitioner in criminal defense. At thirty-five, she was one of the few women in Miami with a thriving criminal-defense practice. She was also still unmarried—she'd had plenty of relationships with men, but none that lasted. Her last man had been married and, after months of playing second fiddle to the wife, she'd ended the affair. In her personal and professional life, Vivian had to be number one. All the same, I knew she was still hurting from the last one—the fact that she hadn't yet found another man confirmed it. Vivian was not a woman to go without male companionship for very long.

Although Vivian claimed to be perfectly happy staying single, Anabel and I suspected that she longed for the traditional route of husband and children. It wasn't something that we could talk about much with her. We had to pretend to believe that she was happiest playing loving aunt to her nieces and nephews. Vivian gave off an aura of self-sufficiency and independence that I thought alienated a lot of men. The killer instinct that worked for her in court didn't al-ways achieve the same result with men, who, let's face it, have to be made to feel stronger than their women whether they are or not. Men might say they liked their women strong, but most of them found Vivian overpowering or devouring. Recently she had alarmed me and Anabel with her comments about her dates' bone structure and brains; it was as though she viewed them as sperm donors rather than love interests.

It wasn't that Vivian wasn't attractive—she was tall, leggy, and a real blond with a knockout figure, the best that money could buy. She owned a small house in Coconut Grove, a glorified bungalow that she'd had decorated by one of the hottest designers in town. She had a legion of friends, and had to maintain a separate calendar just to keep her social life straight. Still, though, there was no husband and no real prospects.

Maybe prospective boyfriends were put off once they heard about the bomb that had once been planted in the undercarriage of her Porsche Boxster. If that were true, my feeling was that those guys lacked big enough *cojones* and didn't deserve her. Anyway, the police had found the bomber and he'd gotten twenty-five to life tacked on to the two sentences Vivian had been unable to get him acquitted of. It turned out that the mobster had hired Vivian to represent him because she was a Cuban woman—he figured she'd be able to connect with a jury in an overwhelmingly Latino city. Vivian is a very good attorney, but there are limits to ethnic sympathy. This client had been pulled over on a routine traffic stop that led to the discovery of two bodies in the trunk, prints lifted off the .357 Magnum that was used for the execution, and the victims' blood on his clothes. Not even O.J.'s dream team could have kept him out of prison.

When a lawyer takes mob clients and is unable to produce the desired results, these things happen. Vivian took the attempt on her life with surprising equanimity. She said it was the cost of doing business. My mamá agreed. She said when you lie down with dogs, you get up with fleas.

That was one of the few times in my life I've actually agreed with my mother.

Anabel Acosta, on top of her vision problems, was also mildly color-blind—a condition usually associated with men. Somehow she managed to work as an architect, a successful designer of upscale homes. The great tragedy of her life was her inability to ever fully view any of her creations, even with the help of the strongest lenses on the market. She was happily married to her high school sweetheart, with three kids—triplet five-year-old girls. Vivian and I thought she cruised through the day blissfully unaware of the world around her, but of course we would never tell her that. In fact, I always admired the way she organized her life. Anabel lived in a grand home in Coral Gables—she designed it herself, and it had been featured in glossy magazines. She was a partner in a three-person architectural firm that she founded along with two of her fellow graduates from the Yale School of Architecture. She was so naturally talented that she was able to overcome the daunting obstacle posed by her faulty eyes.

For the past few years Anabel and her partners, all Cubans, had become increasingly involved in restoring historic buildings in Havana that were in a process of rapid deterioration. Anabel got a lot of satisfaction from the work—she got to save Cuban treasures that might otherwise be lost, and she became intimate with the city that loomed in every exile's dreams.

Anabel's terrible vision dictated many aspects of her life, but the most obvious was how it influenced the way she dressed. Sometimes she turned up looking like an upscale bag lady, with mismatched shoes and a riot of clashing colors. She wore expensive designer clothes, but they looked as though they'd been mixed in a blender. I wouldn't have been surprised if she were banned from certain shops—the way she looked sometimes gave designers a bad name.

She was tiny, barely over five feet, and weighed about a hundred pounds soaking wet. Still, Anabel commanded attention. She had naturally red hair that she helped along, usually to a flaming result. Her hair came halfway down her back, and she wore it loose. Her bright blue eyes were always open wide—as though that was going to help her see better—and so she always seemed to be in a state of perpetual amazement. That night at Caballero's she had managed to select such different shades of black that the colors actually clashed. Vivian, of course, looked perfect down to her jewelry and could have won the prize for Best Dressed. As usual, I was someplace in the middle.

"Well, *chicas*, let's sign the book and go pay our respects," I suggested. "I'm hungry."

The three of us circled the small table on which the condolence book had been placed. We dutifully and carefully printed our names and addresses, made our final adjustments, and entered Room 2. We took our place at the end of the line making its way toward the family and the coffin, which I now saw was mercifully closed. My eyes had barely adjusted to the dim light when Vivian stiffened and grabbed my arm, gouging my skin with her long pointed nails.

"I have to get out of here," she whispered to me. "Now!"

With that, she turned around and headed back toward the door. In the same moment Maria Teresa spotted us and raised her head in recognition.

Anabel, in line in front of me, looked around confused. "Where's Vivian?" she asked. "Did she get sick or something?"

"I don't know," I said, shaking my head and stepping out of line. "I'm going after her."

Anabel took a moment to consider. "Me, too," she said.

We were close enough to the front of the line for our exit to create a noticeable scene. The only person not shocked by our display of insensitivity and bad manners was Tia Esther. We walked out with our heads down and caught up with Vivian in the reception area.

"What happened?" I asked her. "Tell me why we just embarrassed ourselves in front of the whole Martinez clan."

It was my turn to grab Vivian's arm. She looked miserable, her eyes were filling up with tears.

"He's here! He was in the line ahead of us." Anabel and I exchanged worried glances. "Him! Luis! With his wife!"

Now it all made sense. Vivian was talking about her married lover, the one she had broken up with. I had noticed a good-looking man ahead of us, but I'd thought it wasn't appropriate to check him out in front of Tia Esther. Vivian still had feelings for him, that was obvious, and it must have been a nasty shock to see him there with his wife. The bastard. It probably wasn't his fault, but still: the bastard.

The reception area was full of people, and conversations stopped when Vivian began openly sobbing. It wasn't unusual to see people crying in a funeral home, but no one thought a woman as tough as Vivian was broken up over Tia Esther's passing. This scene was taking on real meltdown potential.

A moment later the ex-lover appeared in the doorway to Room 2; he paused, his face turning white when he spotted us. His wife simply looked confused. I couldn't have him witnessing Vivian in this state, so I looked around for a quick escape route. I steered her in the other direction.

"I know a back door out of here," Anabel told us. "Let's go."

Vivian and I followed her down a hallway until we reached an unmarked door. Anabel stood there blinking.

"Here it is," she said. "This leads out to the parking lot."

We opened the door and stepped into pitch darkness. "Anabel, are you sure about this?" I asked. I wrapped my pashmina tight around my shoulders, feeling a sudden chill.

"I'm sure. I recognize the way." Anabel spoke with such total certainty that I knew we were in trouble.

"*Mierda!*" Vivian cried out. "I stubbed my toe! Where are the damned lights in here?"

"Anabel, are you sure this is the way out?" I asked.

"Thank God," Vivian said from somewhere ahead of me. "I found a light switch."

"*Fuck*, Anabel," I said when the lights came on. "You must not have been wearing your glasses the last time you went out the back way. Because this sure isn't the way to the parking lot."

We were standing in an icy-cold room filled with bodies lying on gurneys. One look around, and facing Luis and the missus didn't seem so bad. I'll take a married ex-lover over a dead body any day.

"I know you're a liberated woman and everything, Margarita, but you're a traditionalist at heart, right?" Ariel, my husband, gently teased me as he stroked my hair. We were lying in bed with only the moonlight illuminating our bedroom, enjoying the quiet peace after making love.

"Mmm," I murmured.

"We can try all these different ways, but you really like the old-fashioned way best, right, *mi amor?*" he whispered in my ear.

Since that had been an observation rather than a question, I burrowed my face deeper into his chest instead of answering. I could never tire of the smell of him. It was late, and I knew we should go to sleep because our mornings started early. But I was reluctant to end the day without analyzing everything that had gone on. It was a lifelong habit. I lay there in our king-size bed listening to Ariel's breathing become deeper and more regular as he drifted off to sleep.

After our unexpected encounter with the temporary—and rather frigid—guests at Caballero's, Vivian, Anabel, and I had gone to dinner. We opted for Versailles, the Little Havana restaurant that was the epicenter of all things Cuban in Miami. Vivian's painful experience definitely called for comfort food, and lots of it. We had thought about going to a fancy Italian place in Coral Gables, but it wasn't the kind of atmosphere where we could discuss the situation. When in crisis mode, Cuban exiles turn to Versailles.

We overate and drank a little too much sangria, which is what you do at Versailles. Even visiting the morgue at Caballero's had failed to dampen our appetites. It takes more than a room full of corpses to make a Cuban pass on a meal, especially the bounty of hot, tasty, cheap food at Versailles.

The place was packed, as always, so we had to park in the lot across the street. Knowing parking would be at a premium, we had all gone together in Vivian's Lexus. We crossed the road and went in through the main door on Eighth Street. Within seconds the maître d' led us to one of the tables set for four against the long mirrored wall in the main dining room.

Following my friends, I caught sight of us in the mirror. We were dressed in black from head to toe, and it brought back vivid memories of recent wounds suffered by the exile community that had yet to heal. If this had been a couple of years earlier, during the Elian situation, we would have been taken for women from Mothers Against Repression, an organization of Cuban women who dressed exclusively in mourning black.

God, what a tumultuous five months, from Thanksgiving to Good Friday. The child's fate had fluctuated wildly, and those dedicated women could be seen daily at Versailles sitting quietly, taking a break from their round-the-clock demonstrations in front of the family home in Little Havana just a few blocks away. They were a constant presence, unwavering, always standing in a circle praying unceasingly for Elian. Versailles was at the center of the controversy. The news crews—local, national, international—took up residence outside Versailles, where they interviewed patrons and tried to gauge the exiles' reaction to whatever had happened that day. Anytime a Cuban crisis erupted—which seemed to happen about every five minutes these days—you could count on turning on the TV and seeing Versailles featured in an exterior shot.

The restaurant had been around for decades, ever since Castro came to power. It was open almost twenty-four hours a day, closing only for the brief time it took to clean the place. It didn't matter what time of day it was, the dining room was always packed. It was named, of course, after the Palace of Versailles outside Paris and decorated in a knock-off of the Hall of Mirrors but with a definite Cuban twist. The decor featured an equal measure of Havana in the fifties, with lots of Formica and plastic.

Versailles had two menus, one in English and one in Spanish, and the waitresses instinctively knew which to hand their customers. I had never seen them err, although it wasn't so surprising, since the clientele was overwhelmingly Cuban. The few Americans who came there had read about the place in guidebooks and were pretty easy to spot. I always smiled inside when I heard young Cubans—second generation—ordering their meals in accented Spanish, using atrocious grammar and lapsing into Spanglish when they couldn't come up with the right word. Still, I was proud of them for trying to speak the language of their parents, and for eating at a real Cuban place instead of opting for Olive Garden or TGI Friday's.

Versailles had featured prominently in our lives ever since we were teenagers. It was where we went to plot and maneuver our love lives, and it was where we had confessed our secret dreams and humiliating secrets to one another. But maybe the real reason Versailles had always been so important to us was that it was invariably our final stop after a night of carousing, a place to eat a gargantuan meal in a frantic shot at sobering up before returning home. With enough food in our bellies, we figured, we could avoid our families' wrath and endless lectures about standards of proper comportment for young women.

Well, that's not entirely right. The lectures were really about the expectations laid out for young *Cuban* women of a *certain class*.

Vivian calmed down after a couple of sangrias; she always did. She shook her head and bit her lip.

"God, I freaked out. I hope he didn't see the way I acted," she said. "I don't want him to think he mattered that much to me."

"He didn't see anything," Anabel said, trying to comfort Vivian. Vivian and I shared a glance. There was no way Anabel had any idea what Luis had seen or not seen.

"I know it's hard," I said. "But it'll get better. You just have to let time pass. The wounds are too fresh right now."

"Margarita's right," Anabel added. "That situation just wasn't going to work out for you."

"You said he would never leave his wife," I added.

Both Anabel and I seemed to realize at the same time that we should stop offering advice. Since we were both happily married, our words had a hollow ring.

"You're right," Vivian sighed. "He couldn't handle me, anyway. He was always making little remarks about how *strong* my personality is. You know what that means. Be a nice little Cuban woman. Listen when I talk. Don't come on so strong."

There was nothing much to say. Vivian was right. Few Cuban men could handle her. Maybe few men could handle her, period, but that was an ugly question that no friend would raise at a time such as this.

I surprised Ariel by coming home a little earlier than expected. He was in the den watching about ten TV shows simultaneously. He barely looked up when I came in, so I walked down the hall to check on the baby. I loved to watch him sleep. I was still getting used to the idea that I had produced such a creature.

I had been pretty wild in my youth. Nothing I was terribly ashamed of, but I had done some things I still blush to think about—and which would definitely disqualify me from consideration for a high-government appointment (Okay, so I thought about such things. It wasn't out of the question). Getting older, I had a vague idea that God might have kept a running score of my conduct in order to hold me accountable. Guilt is like a stone-solid foundation in any Catholic's view of the world. My sense of guilt and shame is very well developed, and has been finely honed through the years. In my weaker moments I dread the possibility that my family might be affected in some way by my past sins.

When I was pregnant with Marti I had a morbid fear that something would be wrong with him as God's way of punishing me. I started going to Mass every week, sometimes more, in a frantic try at atoning for my past. I even went to confession for the first time in years, but the priest told me off when I explained the reasoning behind my sudden rush to piety. He told me in no uncertain terms that God does not punish people in that fashion.

And that He doesn't bargain.

I thought about it and realized that I was taking a lawyer's approach to the situation. God was not a prosecutor with whom I could plea bargain to obtain a favorable deal for my client—in this case, the baby. It finally hit me that I'd been working too hard, so I concentrated my energy instead on trying to take better care of myself and not being so crazy. That would do more for the baby than cutting deals with God.

I paused for a second outside Marti's room. God hadn't punished me. For reasons I couldn't fathom he had given me a husband who adored me and a child who was a joy.

What else could I want?

Marti was a month shy of his third birthday. We'd named him after the Cuban patriot José Martí, and he was the spitting image of his father both in looks and character. He was built solid, with his father's dark hair and shining black eyes. Sometimes it was disconcerting to look at him and see a mini-Ariel staring back with the same intensity as his papa. It was like a window in time, a glimpse back to my husband's childhood.

I went in on tiptoe and spied on Marti sleeping in his bed. He even looked like his father when he slept—blissful, completely relaxed. I remembered the first time I ever saw Ariel, ten years before, at the University of Miami law library. Ariel had been comfortably ensconced in a study carrel—I soon learned he went there because he could never get peace and quiet at home. Ariel still lived with his family in those days; his mother and three brothers shared the same crowded two-bedroom Miami Beach apartment they had had for years. The father had left the family when Ariel, the youngest, was a baby. He was never heard from again, and money was always tight.

From what little I had heard about Ariel's father, though, they were better off without him. Better no father than a bad father.

At the time, I was a first-year law student at Duke. I had gone to the UM library because I had to do some research for a legal writing class paper that was due after Thanksgiving. All the carrels were occupied, and I was on a tight schedule. In desperation I began asking each occupant if they were planning on leaving any time soon. Ariel was the fourth person I asked, and the last. We struck up a conversation about what I was working on. It turned out Ariel was ranked first in his class. He helped me out without making it seem like a big deal.

I had to go back to Durham in two days, so we made open-ended plans to see each other over Christmas vacation. I had just started to date a classmate back at Duke, Luther Simmonds, an American from New York, so I wasn't particularly eager to get involved with anyone else. It's funny to think about it now, but I had a feeling that things between Luther and me might work out on a permanent basis.

Since Ariel was from Miami Beach, he hung out with a completely different crowd than mine growing up. Dade County is really several cities, and people stayed within their orbit, but our never meeting before was more than a fact of geography. We came from different social classes and, to be frank, we wouldn't have been comfortable with each other and didn't share much of anything in common. For the older generations, it's an accepted fact of life that Cuban exiles of different classes don't interact socially, but for the younger that's slowly changing. We interacted for business reasons, of course; that was accepted and encouraged. But, for now, it was also pretty much the full extent of class mixing. The fact that we're all exiles isn't enough to make us overlook social status. There were strong memories of who was who in Cuba, but as the older generation died out, so did the individuals listed in the *Chronica de la Vida Social*—the Cuban social register.

I liked Ariel, though, and we saw each other a few times during various vacations when I was back home in Miami. Our friendship developed very slowly, as we really weren't at ease with each other. We knew about our differences, thus made a conscious effort to overcome them, but at times it almost felt as though we were speaking different languages. We had our studies to fall back on, though, and because Ariel was such a sharp legal mind I enjoyed talking to him without the competitive pressure I felt from my go-getter classmates.

After he graduated Ariel went to work for a five-person personal-injury firm in northwest Miami; the firm was housed in a one-story ramshackle building owned by one of the partners. Ariel took me there one day when I was home for Christmas vacation my second year at Duke. I remember that I had to hide my shock—I always envisioned lawyers working in glamorous offices, and this was anything but. The building was wedged between a mom-and-pop grocery and a tire store painted the most garish yellow ever imagined. Ariel's office would have had a terrific view of the Orange Bowl, if it weren't for the thick iron bars over his window. At the time Ariel was living in a garage apartment a block from the office; I visited there once and actually considered calling the health inspector on the landlord.

For a couple of years Ariel's clients were mostly neighborhood types; they'd come in and tell him about getting hurt or incapacitated on the job in falls, burns, electrocutions, car crashes—all sorts of accidents and assorted malice. Ariel helped them with their workmen's comp cases and took his fee from a percentage of recovery. Since he worked steadily and methodically, his client list grew until he was a trusted presence in the community.

As the top student in his class, Ariel would have had his pick of white-shoe law firms in Miami. But his instincts had sent him elsewhere, to get experience with the people he knew and who needed him most. A lot of people questioned his judgment and I have to admit I was one of them. But then The Case walked into his office. Ariel was proved right, silencing his critics forever.

I looked around Marti's room. It was decorated with Disney characters and the best baby furniture available. Probably none of it would have been there if not for an August day when Señora Matos walked into the firm's office and described Ariel's appearance, saying he was the lawyer she wanted. Once Ariel was produced she sat down across from him and explained that she had a personal-injury case involving her son. Ariel's office was on Señora Matos's daily route to her job as a seamstress at a dry cleaner; many times she'd walked home late at night and seen Ariel at his desk through the security bars on the window. She figured anyone who worked as hard as Ariel would do a good job for her son. And her instincts could not have been more sound.

A truck owned by one of the biggest private construction firms in Dade County had jumped a curb on Flagler Street—one of the busiest thoroughfares in Miami—and struck Señora Matos's son. Alfredo Matos was a married father of five, and the accident had paralyzed him permanently from the neck down. This might have been considered a tragic but unavoidable accident, were it not for the fact that the driver of the truck was legally drunk with three prior offenses on his record. The construction company knew about the driver's history, but he had kept his job because his brother-in-law was the home office dispatcher. Alfredo Matos was a pillar of his neighborhood, a bookkeeper for his church, and an active volunteer along with his wife, Esmeralda.

Ariel took the case like a dog takes to a bone, and in the end the jury couldn't award the Matos family enough money to compensate for their loss. The award was the largest ever granted by a Dade County jury for a personal-injury case. A year later the ruling held up on appeal; Ariel, with his thirty percent of recovery, was set for life. He was twenty-seven years old, and he could have retired then and there.

The standard recovery for attorney's fees was forty percent, but Ariel declined to take that much—he thought a lower figure was more fair, and said that the family needed the money more than he did. Imagine that—a lawyer refusing to collect his full fee. That gesture earned Ariel even more publicity than the case itself. After that, Ariel's phone never stopped ringing. I sometimes wondered what his motivation for that had been, as Ariel had never been particularly altruistic. He had been born and raised poor, and every dollar to him had always been precious. It was not like him to give a poor mother a break, but, whatever his reason, it had helped propel him into the limelight of the Miami legal community. Ariel could be cold and calculating to reach his goals, and he was a master at cost/benefit analysis, characteristics I lacked. But then, I had to acknowledge that I was brought up in a wealthy family, so I had not faced what he had.

Marti stirred in his bed, sensing my presence. I carefully adjusted his blanket and crept out of the room. I lingered a little in the hallway, looking over the framed photographs that covered almost every inch of wall. I reached out and touched a couple of my favorites.

The oldest picture was of my parents in Miami, taken early in 1960—the year they left Cuba. They left in a hurry, with no time to pack any photos, so my family's visual history started here. That void must have affected us pretty strongly, because we had shot pictures with a vengeance in the forty years since—thousands and thousands of them. Sometimes I thought we did it because we had no visual evidence that we had, indeed, enjoyed a full and successful life in Cuba. So, damn it, we would prove we had one here in America. My two brothers and I were all avid picture-takers, so we had a thorough pictorial chronicle of the Santos clan. My walls, desks, and dressers were all packed with framed photos. Someday I was going to run out of room to display them.

I returned to the den to check out how serious Ariel was about his TV viewing. The moment he heard me come in, he switched off the set and stood up.

"The baby's okay?" he asked, walking toward me. "I checked on him right before you got back."

"Sleeping soundly," I replied. "Sweet and innocent."

Ariel put his arms around me. "I missed you tonight," he said in his deep voice. "Jacinta fixed me a tray. I had dinner in front of the TV."

He kissed me below my ear, one of my most sensitive areas. He knew all my shortcuts.

"You look sexy dressed all in black like that," he purred, then kissed me on the mouth. "Garlic. All in black, coming home from a funeral smelling like garlic. I feel like I have a Sicilian wife. Very sexy."

He started working on the other ear. Soon we were in the bedroom. For all our differences, this was one area where we were always in tune with each other. And that was what was important.

 "Margarita, *mi amor*, I know you've been avoiding the subject. But I'm here if you need to talk about it."

Ariel carefully folded the *Miami Herald* and put it on the table.

"Time's getting short," he added. "You have to let them know."

We were on the terrace behind our house, breakfast behind us, watching the waters of Biscayne Bay. The effects of last night's lovemaking were still with me, making me relaxed and languorous. But now Ariel was jolting me back to a reality that I didn't want to confront.

I fought off the impulse to groan. It was a beautiful morning, why should I deal with any pressure? It was eight in the morning, a perfect temperature, with no trace of humidity and just enough breeze to drive away thoughts of the stifling heat that would set in when the day progressed.

Ariel was looking good that morning, his hair still damp from the shower, his skin glowing after a close shave. He wasn't storybook handsome; his features were rough and sort of meshed together. He looked a little tough; in jeans and a T-shirt he could be taken for a street fighter. The toughness was no act—without it, he wouldn't be where he was. He also had a certain undefined charisma that, I had to admit, surfaced after he won the huge Matos award. It proved that money was indeed an aphrodisiac, and that large amounts of it were orgasmic.

That morning he was dressed in a white shirt and dark suit pants, his jacket and tie draped over a free chair at the table. From this point it would take him only a minute or so to get ready to leave for the office. Several months ago I would have also been wearing a suit, prepared to take on the world. This morning, though, I was still wearing my nightgown and a bathrobe.

From where I was sitting on the terrace, I could watch all the recreational and commercial fishing boats setting off to try their luck on the Atlantic. For some reason I felt jealous of them. I picked up the binoculars off the table and focused on a few sailboats anchored in the calm waters of the cove nearest our house. The people who lived out there on the boats seemed to hardly ever come ashore; at times they disappeared for a few days then reappeared one morning as though they had never left. One of the men who lived out there was a Robinson Crusoe look-alike, with wild sun-bleached hair and beard; he usually wore nothing more than a loincloth, and always had a beer in his hand. On another boat lived two stocky butch women with short spiky hair; these lovers demonstrated their ardent lust for each other in private, if the waves that they generated when they went below were any indication.

We lived on North Bay Road, a street along Biscayne Bay just north of South Beach. It was a long, winding, tree-lined street favored by the rich and famous; the houses were set back from the road in hopes of affording privacy from prying eyes.

We bought our seven-thousand-square-foot home the year we were married. The place used to belong to a salsa singer from Puerto Rico who hadn't had a hit record in five years. It was built in the old colonial Spanish style, with enormous public rooms—the singer used to give wild, memorable parties there, we learned from our neighbors. The house was too big for us at first—a couple with no children—but the terrace in the back had sold us. Who wouldn't want to have their morning coffee while taking in a sea breeze and watching the sun-kissed waves of the bay?

I had lived in Coral Gables all my life and never really considered living in Miami Beach, but Ariel was determined to make his home there. He specifically wanted one of the houses on North Bay Road. When he was a boy he delivered the *Miami Herald*, and his route had taken him there every morning at dawn. He used to promise himself that someday he would own one of those houses. I actually cried when he told me about his boyhood dream, and I immediately agreed to live there. Our only regret was that Ariel's mother hadn't lived long enough to see her boy make good in such a spectacular fashion.

Marti was playing on a little rug next to the table, occasionally sipping juice from his plastic cup, happy and oblivious to the scene around him. He shared his father's ability to focus on one thing to the exclusion of everything else; just then he was concentrating on a wooden puzzle while Jacinta cleared away the morning's dishes.

Ariel wasn't pressing me to talk, but I could sense him closely watching me as I looked out over the water. He had learned the hard way that there was no use hurrying me to discuss things I didn't want to talk about. However, I knew him well enough to know that unless I was careful he could maneuver me into where he wanted me to be. He had the ability to manipulate me in such a subtle way that I was unaware he had done it until it was too late. I had to be careful in this instance, as I knew what he wanted.

"I know I have to tell them what I'm going to do," I finally said. "I know."

My firm's policy was that a leave of absence could last up to a year, but it wasn't fair for me to keep withholding my plans from them. I was the only lawyer there who specialized in immigration, and I knew that some of my work had been farmed out to other firms. So far my partners had been supportive of me, but I knew it was only a matter of time before their attitude changed. Business was business, and personal goodwill was only going to take me so far.

Weber, Miranda, Blanco and Silverman, P.A., was the only place I had ever worked as a lawyer. They had hired me as a summer associate after my first year at Duke, then picked me up for a second summer a year later. After I graduated they offered me a job contingent on my passing the bar. I became their business immigration lawyer by default, really. During my second summer the firm got a commercial litigation case that involved a major immigration factor—not central to the case, but important enough that it needed to be thoroughly researched. The attorney to whom I had been assigned was given that aspect of the case, and I was told to work on it. That had been my first day on the job that summer, and I really wanted to prove my worth. So I threw myself completely into the task.

When I was through with my research I gave my boss a report that could have been submitted to the Supreme Court. Immigration law was interesting to me, which was a good thing—once I came on full time, all those kinds of cases were assigned to me. I must have done a good job, because I was made partner five years after graduation, the first woman at my firm to have done so.

Most of my Duke classmates had gone on to work for big firms in New York, but I returned to Miami. I had been away for seven years, including my undergrad period at the University of Pennsylvania in Philadelphia, and I felt like I was losing touch with my inner Cuban. There had been only a few Cuban students at Penn, and none at Duke Law, so my infusions of Cubaninity came via care packages of Cuban food that my tata sent me, and from the boxes of supplies I carried with me after vacations home. I had an off-campus apartment where I threw parties and served Cuban food, but I think I always knew I wouldn't be able to stay away forever.

My parties were great. Food, music, and rum drinks—mojitos, Cuba libres, mango daiquiries. I was a professional Cuban in those years, with a framed poster of José Martí in the living room and a floor-to-ceiling Cuban flag next to my bed. I had Cuban books scattered everywhere, and usually a Gloria Estefan CD was playing in the background. I worked out in the gym wearing a T-shirt that said, "All this, and Cuban too."

The men I dated in school were always American—not by design, but because they were the ones I came into contact with in class or through my sorority. My only serious entanglement was with Luther Simmonds, during my second year at Duke.

I used to think he was my soul mate. He told me he felt the same.

In the winter of our last year at Duke we started talking about marriage, discussing the different places we might live and practice law. But later something happened that I still don't understand. The bond between us drifted away in a weird haze of expedience. After we graduated, Luther took a job at a major civil-law firm in New York when they made him a big money offer he felt he couldn't refuse. Not wanting to live in New York just then, I went back to my firm in Miami. Our phone bills were outrageous. At first, we talked about how we were going to work things out, then a day passed without us talking. A week later, it was two. We were both so busy that it was almost six months before we actually managed to see each other again.

I hadn't considered dating Ariel because of Luther, but soon he asked me out to dinner and I accepted. And that was that. I still thought about Luther. Part of my heart would always be his, especially in the early morning before dawn broke—that was always our best time together.

But some things weren't meant to be.

I worked hard all my life. In school I took the hardest courses, and gave them my all. My parents had lost everything after the revolution in Cuba, where they owned and operated a nationwide chain of pharmacies. They told their kids again and again: The one thing they can't take away from you is your education.

But I found out the truth later, that their advice was really directed at my brothers instead of me. The rules for sons and daughters in Latino families are very different. Unfortunately, the twenty-first century has yet to arrive for us.

I knew early on that I wanted to be a lawyer; order and precision appealed to me. My family was appalled when I told them my decision, figuring I would turn into a frump or a bitter career woman, and never get married as a result. I was bound to be an old spinster, a dried-up prune, unfulfilled and alone; most importantly, I would never produce grandchildren. They told me that no woman in my family had ever done a man's job. Hell, the truth was that no woman in my family had ever graduated from college before, much less earned an advanced degree. For upper-class Cuban Miami, college was a waiting room where girls from good families spent a couple of years before they walked down the aisle.

My female cousins had all majored in the course of how to marry well. I had to admit, they were overachievers and made the dean's list. Cuban girls of my class might graduate from college and even take jobs, but never anything serious that might cause them to look old and tired. It was understood that they would drop everything and raise the kids once their boyfriends were established enough to marry and buy a home. It wasn't as restrictive as the fifties, but we really hadn't left Havana too far back.

There was almost a sense of collective pity directed at Cuban women who were successful; the assumption was that success always came at the expense of a good personal life. And a personal life always, always, meant a husband and children—the only true road to happiness and fulfillment. The only reason for a woman to work was economic necessity, the thinking went. Beside the fact that I loved them, I think one of the reasons I was so close to Vivian and Anabel was because they, too, had rebelled against the fate that had been set out for them by the accident of their birth.

And now I had to decide what I was going to do with the rest of my life. I had worked so damned hard to get where I was. At thirty-five, I was a partner in a successful firm with several national offices; however, I was also a wife and a mother, with a small child at home and a husband making noises about having another one soon.

Going back to work meant long days and major stress, but it was all mine: my satisfaction from making a major difference in my clients' lives, my office, my own world. I liked the people I worked with; they were my friends. I liked meeting with clients, the intellectual work of analyzing their cases and plotting a strategy. I relished the euphoria when I did good work on a case; I got off on the feeling of doing well. I loved the fact that I had a reputation as a thorough, sharp attorney.

It had been ten months since I took my leave of absence. I loved all the time with Ariel and Marti, but the truth was that I also missed the office. About ten times during the day I glanced at my watch and wondered what I would be doing if I were at my desk instead of at home.

My job paid very well, but, honestly, we didn't need my income, not with Ariel working and the investments we made after the Matos case, a fact that Ariel kept repeating to me, so often that it had almost become his mantra. I almost wished that wasn't true, since it would have made my decision easier.

Don't get me wrong—I knew that many women would have traded places with me in a heartbeat. I kept in mind all the women raising children on their own, with no money or, even worse, having to deal with some alcoholic battering scumbag for a spouse. I wanted to take a deep breath and count my blessings, but my personality just wouldn't allow it. I had to obsess over this dilemma until I reached a resolution.

It was like a voice was repeating over and over: *Give in, leave the job, have more kids.* But what would that mean? That I never took my professional life seriously in the first place? All the time, effort, and money invested in me by the firm would go to nothing—and I knew what that would mean for the next young Latina lawyer. For better or worse, I represented an image in the legal community. And people were watching.

I loved Marti more than anything in the world. I treasured being able to watch his daily changes, going swimming with him, teaching him manners, and helping him make his way in the world. And as for Ariel, it was a nice change for us both to be home at the same time in the evening. I must have spent more time with him in the last ten months than in the previous eight years of our marriage.

In this, my family was no help. There was no use going to them for advice, because I knew in advance what they thought. *A woman's place is at home, with her husband and children.* Mamá was already making noises about Marti needing a little brother or sister. This is the same woman who had been violently opposed to my relationship with Ariel in the beginning. He was from the wrong side of the tracks or, as was the case in Miami, from the other side of the causeway. The more they came to know him, though, the more they began to warm to him.

And, let's face it, the Matos award didn't hurt. Cubans are nothing if not practical, with a healthy respect for money and success, and the better Ariel did, the more attractive he became.

When I was still at the firm, Mamá told me that I was courting disaster with Ariel, that although he was a fine person he was still a man who wanted his wife available to him at all hours. If I wasn't there waiting for him when he got home, then he would eventually find another woman who would be. *Guaranteed,* she said. *It's just a matter of time.*

Thanks, Mamá.

Just before I took my leave, Mamá started telling me how tired I looked, how worn out, that I was losing my looks. Pretty soon Ariel was going to lose interest and take up with a younger, fresher, sweeter woman. I was playing with fire, trying to have a life of my own. So no, I wasn't going to my mother for advice.

Vivian and Anabel, God bless them, told me that my family was full of shit, that they were trying to guilt-trip me into giving up everything I had worked so hard to achieve. Sure you can have it all, they told me. You can be a good wife and mother and still be a successful and fulfilled working woman.

The only party involved who had yet to voice a firm opinion was Ariel himself, but it was crystal clear what he thought. He was proud of me and my accomplishments, but he felt that I had proved what I had set out to prove. Now it was time to devote myself to my family. He just wanted me to arrive at the same conclusion on my own, without feeling pressured. I had to keep in mind that he loved me, and that he trusted me to do what's right for our family.

Still, in spite of his reassurances, I could not help but suspect that he had ulterior motives. He knew I was more independent when I was working, with responsibilities and interests that excluded him. He claimed he was happy that I did well and was successful on my own, but, as a Cuban man, he felt that having a working wife diminished him in the eyes of his contemporaries. Also, if he was working, and making money, and I was not, I would be financially and emotionally dependent on him, something I felt he wanted and needed. I told myself not to be mean-spirited, that Ariel was a good man who wanted the best for me, but these suspicions crept up from time to time.

And there he was, still sitting there and waiting for me to say something. He shook his head, a wry expression on his face.

"I can see you don't want to talk about it," he said. "Just so long as you're giving the matter thought."

"*Gracias,*" I replied. "And thanks for being understanding. Believe me, I'm thinking about it. I really am."

Ariel stood up, stretched, reached for his jacket and tie.

"I'd better get going or I'll get stuck in traffic." In Miami, leaving five minutes too late could make a huge difference in how long it took to reach a destination. He leaned over to kiss me, then bent to kiss Marti on the head. Marti barely noticed; he was still engrossed in his puzzle.

I watched Ariel walk away, then turned my attention back to the water. I watched a dark shadow in the waves, thinking it might be a manatee, when the phone rang. I reached for the extension on the side table, annoyed by the interruption.

"Hello?" I said.

"Daisy?"

It was a man's voice. A voice I knew. I almost dropped the phone. Only one person has ever called me "Daisy," the English translation of Margarita.

"Luther?"

 A Cuban waiting for an American. Now that was a switch. I sat glancing at my watch at a table in the courtyard of Nemo's, one of my favorite restaurants on South Beach.

It had been nine years since I last saw Luther Simmonds, but somehow speaking with him on the phone that morning and agreeing to meet for lunch a few hours later seemed perfectly normal. Maybe I should have heard alarm bells ringing, but I didn't. Mostly I was thinking about how I was going to look to him. I had given birth to a child since I last saw him, after all, and although I worked out religiously at the gym I knew my figure wasn't the same as before. *Ay, vanity. Thy name is Margarita.*

Luther and I had agreed to meet at one, and now it was a quarter past. I remembered that Luther used to exemplify the annoying American proclivity for punctuality. I was starting to wonder if something had gone wrong, and I could have kicked myself for not giving him my cell phone number.

After a quick look around to make sure Luther wasn't nearby, I opened up my purse and took out my little silver pocket mirror. I studied my reflection, trying to imagine what Luther would see when he finally arrived.

At thirty-five, I considered myself neither old nor young, although I knew I looked a few years younger than my age. Maybe it was in the genes. I always thought Latino women held out better against the ravages of time because of our olive-colored skin. As a teenager I'd railed against my oily complexion, but now I blessed it because I was virtually wrinkle free. I used to swear under my breath when my mother refused to allow me to bake in the hot tropical sun with my friends, but now I was glad she had kept me inside. And, yes, prepared to admit she was right about something.

Luther was going to meet a woman with shoulder-length dark brown hair, wavier now than in Durham because of South Florida humidity. It was a few shades darker than in years past, but that wouldn't surprise Luther—I'd been experimenting with hair color since before my Duke days, and I used to change shades as often as I could without my hair actually falling out. My eyes were the same, light blue bordering on gray. Now I knew more about makeup, and how to accent my best features, so I concentrated on bringing out that gray tone.

I always dressed fairly conservatively, and still did—although now, of course, I wore better outfits. And the higher quality the clothes the better the fit, so hopefully Luther wouldn't notice that my hips had widened a bit. Dressing for this lunch, I'd pulled out, inspected, and tried on nearly everything in my closet. At one point it looked as though Hurricane Andrew had hit my bedroom; it took almost an entire hour to hang everything up again. I finally settled on a fine-cotton khaki shirtwaist dress by Yves St. Laurent that fit me perfectly even though it was a couple of years old. I matched it with black open-toed snakeskin sandals and a Chanel bag. I thought I passed inspection, but just to be sure I chose a seat with the sun at my back. I might have looked good for my age, but there was no point pushing the envelope and exposing myself to the cruel midday light.

I replaced my mirror in my purse. *Why so much preparation, why so much worry about what he's going to think?*

And more to the point, why was I meeting my old flame? I hadn't told Ariel that I was having lunch with Luther. Ariel trusted me—

and with good reason, because I'd never given him reason to do otherwise. But I knew he wouldn't be at all pleased if I had informed him of my lunch plans.

Which meant I was keeping a secret from my husband.

My conversation with Luther had been very brief. After the how-are-yous he told me that he was in Miami working a case and that he'd like to get together, if that were possible. He said he'd called my firm and learned that I was on an extended leave of absence. Since I knew the firm wouldn't give out my home phone number, and we were unlisted, Luther had called up Duke Law School to find out how to reach me. Knowing all the trouble he went to secretly pleased me.

I didn't know much of anything about Luther's life, whether he was married, or ever had been. After we broke up we pretty much ceased to communicate, although I heard a few snippets about him now and then from mutual friends. Gradually even those friends dropped off. I exchange an occasional e-mail with an old classmate, but I don't really keep up on their lives. I was the only person in my class from Miami, so I didn't socialize with anyone who could keep me posted on the latest gossip.

For the first time I wondered what Luther would look like. The years must have had some impact on his good looks. Luther could have had his picture in the dictionary under WASP. He always gave off an air of confidence that only sometimes verged on cockiness, and generally acted as though he belonged wherever he was, not surprisingly, since his ancestors had arrived in this country on the *Mayflower*. He moved with a natural athlete's grace, smooth and fluid as though gliding to some internal rhythm. Luther was a couple inches over six feet, thin but muscular and strong, with light-brown almost-blond hair that was always in need of a trim. He had blue eyes and freckles, and usually sported a two-day-old beard years before it was fashionable. He wore tortoiseshell glasses that made him look intellectual, but in a sensual sort of smoldering-romantic way.

At Duke, Luther had always dressed casually, in jeans, T-shirts, and tennis shoes. Whenever he needed to upgrade his look, he pulled out a navy-blue blazer that had seen its prime in the early years of the

Reagan administration. But somehow no matter what Luther wore, he gave the impression of being dressed appropriately while everyone else was either over- or underdressed. Now that he was working for a big New York firm he would have to wear a suit every day. Luther dreaded wearing suits. I wondered how he was taking the change.

I looked at my watch again. One thirty. I had been sitting at the table for a full half hour. The waiter had stopped refilling my water glass. At least I didn't have to feel guilty about occupying one of the choice outdoor tables because the restaurant was almost empty. No surprise there: The locals knew to sit inside, in air-conditioned comfort. Tourists loved to sit outside, but there were few to be found in July. Maybe it had something to do with the heat, humidity, and hurricane season.

I made up my mind to order. The hell with it. If I was going to be stood up, I was at least going to eat before leaving. Then I felt a shiver run down my back. A man materialized out of nowhere and stood across the table from me. It took me a good ten seconds to realize that it was Luther.

"Daisy! Great to see you." Luther came around and kissed me on the cheek. I could see his eyes on me, checking me out. He had once known every corner and curve of my body. By the way he was looking at me, I could see he was going over old notes in his mind.

"You, too, Luther."

"So sorry I'm late," he said. "I missed the exit on I-95 and had to double back. I hope you didn't get too angry waiting for me."

With the self-confidence that I remembered well, he pulled out the chair next to me and sat down. He knew I had never been able to get upset with him, and saw no reason for that to change.

"It's all right," I managed to say. I simply couldn't get over the way Luther looked. This wasn't what I had expected. Not at all.

Luther had definitely learned something from his colleagues at that big-shot, overpriced New York law firm. I guess if lawyers are going to charge clients five hundred dollars an hour or more, then they have to dress the part. And to look at Luther, he might have broken the thousand-an-hour mark.

In spite of the heat and humidity, not to mention an hour spent in Miami traffic, Luther looked fresh and clean. Well, he'd always been that way. At Duke he'd been able to emerge from the library after a marathon study session looking as though he'd just stepped out of the shower. This was in contrast to me; after a couple hours cracking the books I looked so beaten up that my friends asked me if I needed a ride to the hospital.

Gone were the glasses. Contacts, I guessed. The hair had finally gotten a trim, and the scruffy beard was gone. The blue jeans and sneakers had been replaced by a beautifully cut tan poplin suit with a blue shirt that brought out the tone of his eyes. This was also the first time I could recall seeing Luther in a tie. He looked . . . really good.

Seeing that I hadn't been lying about expecting a guest, the waiter came over. Taking in Luther's air of definite prosperity, the waiter became positively solicitous and handed Luther a menu plus the extensive wine list. I looked at Luther's hand as he took them. No wedding ring.

"Red still good with you, Daisy?" Luther asked, then ordered a bottle of the best Barolo on the wine list. I knew the wine prices at Nemo's, and I was impressed with Luther's choice. No iced tea for us.

Business was taken care of, and now we had no choice but to inspect each other. I tried not to wilt under his gaze, hoping that Luther would think I'd held up as well over the past decade as he obviously had.

"You look more beautiful than ever, Daisy," Luther said fondly. "Life has been kind to you, hasn't it?"

I felt my face and neck turn warm. Oh, no, I was blushing. Just then—thank God—the waiter showed up with the Barolo and two glasses. Luther waved away the silly ritual about inspecting the cork and tasting the wine and, with a dismissive gesture, let the waiter know that he would take charge of the situation. I could tell the waiter smelled a fat tip if he handled our table properly; he told us he would wait for our order, then withdrew.

"You look good, too, Luther," I said.

We tipped our glasses and sipped the wine. Almost instantly I felt warmth coursing through my body. For a fleeting moment I saw myself sitting in a restaurant with an ex-lover, my old soul mate, drinking wine in the middle of the day. I would have to pace myself; drinking on an empty stomach during the hottest part of the day in the dead of summer was a sure way to get drunk.

"That's nice of you to say, Daisy." Luther seemed genuinely pleased by my compliment. "If you don't mind my asking, why have you taken a leave of absence from your firm?"

I didn't want to explain about Ariel and Marti and my reasons for taking a leave. I just didn't. I didn't want my real life to intrude upon sitting there next to Luther sipping wine. My first glass was almost gone. I knew I needed to stand up and get out of there. But I couldn't. It simply felt natural to be there with him.

"I've just been working too hard," I replied. "I needed to take some time off, get some breathing room."

It was time to direct the conversation away from me. "And you," I said, "what are you doing in Miami?"

"My firm's working a huge commercial litigation case," Luther said. "There are about a dozen corporations involved and one of them has a Miami connection. So here I am."

"Here you are," I said. I couldn't read what he was thinking. I had always been able to before. Luther had gotten tougher somehow, his skin had thickened. It was an added aspect to his old self-assurance, more attractive than intimidating.

Luther looked me right in the eyes. No glasses like in the old days, just his eyes and mine a couple of feet apart.

"Actually, any one of the other three attorneys on the case could have come down here," he said. "But I insisted it be me."

Now I knew for sure that I should be getting out of there. Something deeper than the red wine was hitting me.

Instead I picked up the menu. "Shall we order?" I asked sweetly.

6

"*Chica,* you're playing with fire and you know it." Vivian was so livid her words were coming out in sputters. "What the hell are you doing, meeting your ex like that? Are you *loca?*"

Before I had a chance to reply, Anabel raised a finger to interrupt me. "You didn't tell Ariel, did you?" she asked, ever practical.

Vivian, Anabel, and I were huddled around a tiny table at Starbucks in Coconut Grove, right next to Cocowalk. It was eleven the next morning after my lunch with Luther. I had called both of them and explained my need to meet with a single word: *Luther.* This wasn't a conversation we could have on a speaker-phone conference call. I'm not sure which alarmed them more—the fact that I had seen Luther, or that I suggested we meet at Starbucks. They knew my strongly held opinion that no self-respecting Cuban would voluntarily drink the watered-down liquid Starbucks passes off as coffee and serves in cardboard cups.

We were sitting at one of the indoor tables, far away from the counter for as much privacy as possible. I chose Starbucks because it was doubtful we'd see anyone we knew there, but I certainly wanted to make sure no one overheard us just in case. Miami might be a city of three million people, but it was still a small town in many respects. The last thing I needed was for malicious ears to hear what I was saying.

When I had telephoned my friends Vivian told me she had a one o'clock court hearing downtown; Anabel said she had to pick up her triplets from playschool a few blocks away at twelve thirty. Starbucks might have been the heart of enemy territory but it was geographically central to all our needs. Also, there was parking nearby. There is no way to overemphasize the importance of parking in daily life in Miami. I knew individuals, especially on Miami Beach, who wouldn't date anyone who didn't have a parking space allotted to them by City Hall. It was too much trouble otherwise, with all the parking tickets and towing charges.

Anabel had heard me out so far, but now she put on her glasses. This meant she was serious. Anabel only put on her glasses in public when it was a matter of life and death.

"Margarita, have you thought through the implications of your meeting Luther?" Anabel asked in a gentle voice. I could tell from her tone that she was trying to give me the benefit of the doubt.

"He caught me by surprise," I explained. "But when he asked to meet for lunch, it just seemed natural to accept."

I looked at my two friends and felt a sudden rush of misery, knowing I was opening myself up to insult and criticism, both of which I deserved. I knew Vivian and Anabel would spare my feelings only to a point. One of the reasons our friendship had survived so long was because we were capable of brutal honesty with one another.

"It was almost as if I was waiting for him to call, actually," I added.

This was too much for Vivian; she sighed in disgust.

"You're so weak, Margarita," she said. "You have a great life, a husband and a child. And now this gringo you haven't heard from in about ten years picks up the phone and calls, and you go running to him. One call and you drop your drawers."

"You're such a slut, Margarita," Anabel flatly concurred.

"I have *not* been to bed with him," I sternly reminded them. I wasn't about to be crucified for crimes I hadn't committed.

"Not yet," Vivian and Anabel said at the same time.

The three of us looked at each other and, despite the seriousness of the situation, howled with laughter. We knew each other too well, that's for sure. I believed the reason none of us had ever been to therapy was because we had each other. Well, that and our innate Cuban distrust of going to a stranger for help when we were too arrogant to acknowledge we had any kind of flaw. God knows we probably could have used some help somewhere along the line.

Laughing like this broke the tension, and I felt less defensive.

"Really, *chicas*, help me out with this," I said. "I need to talk about it and figure it out."

Vivian leaped to cross-examination. "So you had lunch and nothing happened. Is that right?"

"It was all pretty innocent," I answered. "He told me about the case he's working. It's a commercial litigation with—"

"Just the facts, ma'am," Anabel interrupted. Neither Vivian nor I pointed out that her Joe Friday impression was pretty pathetic. She sounded like Ricky Ricardo tripping on acid. We would tell her, though, if she kept it up. "What about personal stuff? What did you talk about?"

"We really didn't get into personal matters," I said.

My answer didn't convince them. Vivian and Anabel both frowned and inched their chairs closer to mine so they could watch my reactions in order to gauge the truthfulness of my replies.

"I promise," I insisted. "We really didn't talk about anything personal. I would tell you if we had."

Vivian paused, reconsidering her approach. "How did you feel about him? Any vibes?"

It was a few seconds before I could speak.

"Yes, I did find him attractive," I said. "Remember, I was thinking about marrying him at one point in my life."

I took a sip of my lukewarm coffee and nearly gagged. Steaming hot it was barely tolerable, but tepid it was atrocious.

"To tell you the truth, he looks better than ever." I then went on to describe Luther as best I could. I guess I went overboard because Vivian started to nod knowingly and make a clucking sound.

"You're in heat, *chica*," she said. "That gringo is in your system."

"Well, he can't be all bad," Anabel said, "if he's still willing to talk to you after the Elian fiasco."

Anabel lowered her voice for that comment. Cuban exiles still felt like we were viewed as pariahs by most Americans. We were right-wing zealots and nut cases who went to extraordinary lengths to keep that boy from being reunited with his father. The whole thing had been incredibly painful and heartwrenching. The six-year-old boy had seen his mother drowned and eaten by sharks in the Florida Straits three days after the rickety motorboat they'd used to flee Cuba had capsized. Before she died she had placed the boy in an inner tube in a desperate hope that he might survive. On Thanksgiving Day he'd been picked up by a couple of fishermen and brought to the United States. The symbolism of his rescue wasn't lost on anyone, especially Fidel Castro—after the seemingly miraculous rescue, Fidel demanded instantly that the boy be returned to Cuba. The whole thing erupted in a firestorm of publicity.

Elian had relatives in the U.S.—his great-uncle and the uncle's wife and daughter. They took the boy in and gave him a home. Once press interest waned, Elian's story would have been just another one of thousands had it not been for Castro's personal involvement. Soon the whole thing was front-page news and then started the lawsuits, the allegations, the court orders.

Even before Elian, Cuban exiles had been perceived differently from other immigrants to America; rightly or wrongly, we enjoyed special immigration status and were able to bypass a lot of restrictions other groups faced in establishing residency. As a result, there was always resentment. During and after Elian, public opinion vilified and attacked Cubans in a way that truly shocked us. Not all Cuban exiles believed the boy should be kept in America, away from his father, but it was definitely a minority opinion. It didn't matter what an individual thought, though—we were all tarred with the same brush.

The fact is, Americans never really understood the Cuban exiles' side of the story. They didn't want to hear about the fact that one and a half million Cubans had left the island, abandoning everything they knew and loved because of political persecution. For most exiles, it was unthinkable that a boy who succeeded in escaping should be ordered to return. Few in America wanted to consider what awaited Elian after he got back to Cuba. His life would change in very real ways—and not simply because he would no longer have access to Disney World and Toys "R" Us, as was portrayed in the press.

Under Cuban law, a child didn't belong to his family. He belonged to the *patria,* and the government made final decisions concerning his welfare. Parents' wishes were secondary. As a teenager, he would be removed from his home and sent to work in the countryside. He would live in camps and coed dormitories, where sexually transmitted diseases were common and the rate of pregnancy was sky high. At age seven his rationed provisions would start limiting his diet—he wouldn't be eligible for the milk, beef, and proteins that he'd gotten used to. And, of course, the first order of business upon his return would be to openly denounce his mother as a traitor. *That* was required of everyone who came back. However, these realities were not portrayed in the press, which saw it simply as a father being kept from his son.

Elian's great-uncle was a mechanic, his wife worked in a factory sewing garments, and the daughter was a bank clerk. They were unsophisticated people and had absolutely no media savvy. They made a big mistake when they picked as their spokesman a political operative, a slickster who did them a disservice with the decisions he made on their behalf. There were no winners in the Elian Gonzalez family. The little boy had to return to live under Castro's regime, and the Cuban exiles were cast in a harsh, negative light. Miami was incredibly polarized. Americans and Cubans who had been friends, neighbors, and business partners broke off relations. Some thought that the divisions had always been there, and that the Elian disaster simply brought them to the forefront.

Cubans used to enjoy an image as industrious good citizens and, believe me, it was an impression that we worked hard to project. It had evaporated in the space of a few months, and it was devastating. I knew of deep personal relationships that had been permanently and completely severed because of rancorous arguments about Elian.

"What would Ariel do if he found out you met with Luther?" Vivian asked me.

"He wouldn't like it," I admitted. "But Ariel has always let me do pretty much whatever I want."

"Margarita, Ariel might be liberated and all that, but *chica*, he's still a Cuban man," Anabel pointed out. "He might have trained himself to be open-minded about women—or you might have trained him, I don't know—but you can't change what's in the genes."

"You know, I think what's troubling me is that I don't feel like I'm being unfaithful to Ariel." To make sure my friends didn't get the wrong idea, I hastened to add, "I mean, I've done nothing wrong and I have nothing to hide. I've been to lunch with plenty of men in my life without anything happening."

I could tell from Anabel and Vivian's expressions that I was protesting too much.

"Margarita, this is us you're talking to. You don't have to rationalize your behavior." Anabel fixed her gaze on me; her eyes behind the Coke-bottle lenses reminded me of fish swimming in an aquarium. "But none of those men you had lunch with was your lover for three years, were they? And none of them made your toes curl—now did they?"

Leave it to Anabel to nail me. She might not be able to see a thing, but nothing important ever got past her.

"How long is Luther going to be in Miami?" Vivian asked. "Did he say how long his case is going to take?"

Vivian took out her cell phone, checked it for messages. Time was running short.

"Somewhere between two and three months," I told her.

Vivian and Anabel looked at each other, shook their heads, and rolled their eyes. Anabel looked at her watch and started to gather her things.

"So how did you leave it?" she asked me.

Just then my cell phone rang. I grabbed it, intending to shut it off. I had thought it was set for voice mail, so I wouldn't be interrupted while talking to my friends, but obviously I had forgotten.

I looked down at the screen to see the caller's number displayed. From the exchange I could tell it was coming from downtown. I felt my heart start beating a little faster.

What the hell, I picked it up.

"Daisy?"

The second I heard Luther's voice I tried to turn away from my friends to talk in private, but it was not to be. They could both tell who was on the line. Both Vivian and Anabel pointed at their watches in a secret code we'd established twenty years before. It meant *Hey, chica, it's just a matter of time.*

Listening to Luther, feeling what I was feeling, I had to admit my friends were right. After all, they knew me best.

7

After I left Vivian and Anabel, I went straight to my parents' house in Coral Gables. Though it had been just a few days since I'd been there last, it had been an eternity by Cuban standards—behavior that could cause serious friction, and for which I would pay dearly in one form or another.

I had told my mother that I would arrive around lunchtime, which had triggered a ten-minute digression into what I might like to eat that day. I knew that Mamá would assume I was bringing Marti, and that she would be disappointed when I showed up alone. I would have ordinarily brought my son along—if nothing else, he was a good buffer against my mother—but I didn't think it was appropriate to discuss the situation with Luther at Starbucks in front of him, even though he wouldn't have known what I was talking about. Just because I was contemplating having an affair with my former boyfriend didn't mean that I lacked all moral consideration. And, on the practical side, it's impossible to have any kind of serious conversation with a three-year-old running around.

The truth was, I was loath to expose Marti to Starbucks. He might have been born in the United States, but the blood that flowed through his veins was definitely Cuban.

The traffic from Coconut Grove to Coral Gables that time of day was light, and I made the trip in less than fifteen minutes. Mamá and Papa's house was in northern Coral Gables, near the Biltmore Hotel. My parents bought the place in the mid-sixties, just before I was born, because they and my two older brothers had outgrown the place they'd rented during the tumult and uncertainty following their arrival from Cuba. Our lives were so ingrained in the Coral Gables house that it was almost impossible to imagine that they had ever lived anyplace else.

My parents were among the few Cubans fortunate enough not to have arrived in the United States penniless and destitute after leaving the island. The bulk of their wealth remained back home, but they had some investments outside of Cuba, primarily in the American stock market. As was the case with many other Cuban families of our class, our ties to America were longstanding and strong.

My father's side of the family had always been staunchly pro-American: My paternal grandfather had studied at Yale, my father at the University of Virginia. All the men in my family had studied for their MBAs at Columbia in New York City. They had been sent to America for the educational opportunities, but perhaps more important they were to learn about American business practices and to make American friends. Still, no matter how much they came to love and admire the United States, they always knew that Cuba was their home. That was a fact that was never in question.

The Santos family, like many other upper-class Cubans, had money in the American stock market that was out of Castro's greedy reach when he began confiscating private property on the island. This was the money my parents used to start their business over again from scratch after fleeing their homeland. The Americans hadn't disclosed any information on Cuban holdings to the Castro government, so many exiles were able to retain at least a part of their wealth. Canadian banks, incredible to my mind, cooperated with the Cuban government—they granted Castro access to their records, and those Cubans unfortunate enough to have placed their trust in Canadian banks saw their deposits confiscated along with their holdings back home.

When Castro began his wholesale theft of private enterprise, my family owned the largest chain of drugstores in Cuba. Santos Pharmacies had been founded more than a century before, by my great-great-grandfather Don Emiliano Santos, the very year Cuba gained its independence from Spain. Until 1960, when we were forced to leave Cuba, the pharmacies remained a family-owned and -operated business in which all of Don Emiliano's male descendents worked, all the way down to my father and his three brothers. And, although the Santos family had some money in the U.S., the vast majority of its wealth stayed behind in Cuba. My family owned all the land on which the drugstores stood—prime, valuable real estate throughout the island. The last we heard, a Spanish hotel chain had built some resorts on our land in Varadero.

After landing in Miami, a couple of years passed before a harsh realization descended on my father and his brothers: Castro wasn't going anywhere in the near future. Many Cubans had arrived in this country with the assumption that their exile was only going to last a few months, perhaps a year or two at the most. Surely, they thought, word would leak out about the atrocities and injustice perpetrated by the Castro regime and he would be removed from power. This mistaken belief delayed implementing plans to make America into a new home, and a lot of families burned through their money without making plans for the future. If only they'd known what was in store.

The Bay of Pigs fiasco killed off all hope that the exiles would be returning home any time soon. Not only did many exiles lose relatives in that ill-fated military operation, but, more important, they learned the cold fact that they couldn't rely on the United States to help them return home. It was a sobering moment. So many exiles felt that America had helped put Castro in power and that the country had a duty and obligation to get rid of him. They soon learned that history does not follow the law of justice.

The Bay of Pigs was the turning point for the Santos family.

Instead of concentrating on how to regain what was taken from them in Cuba, my father and my uncles decided to think about how they were going to succeed in Miami. The drugstore business was all any of them had ever known, and they decided to play to their strengths. A week after the Bay of Pigs, Santos Pharmacies started over again in the United States. Papa and his brothers sold off all their holdings in the stock market and leased a building in Little Havana; with the last of their cash they bought inventory to stock the shelves. They invested every penny they owned in that first drugstore, and they knew that failure was not an option.

They were fortunate to have established credibility with American suppliers they had dealt with in Cuba, who extended my family a line of credit and extended favorable rates in inventory. Papa soon realized he was reaping the benefits from decades of paying his bills on time. He and his brothers worked hard, and adapted to their new market. They figured that, since conditions were getting worse in Cuba, there would be a continued influx of new exiles who would need pharmacy supplies. They would cater to this group which, although penniless at the moment, would eventually establish itself into a loyal customer base. They extended credit to fellow Cubans, and payment plans with no interest. Sooner or later, every single customer paid his or her bill in full.

Many a parent left the Santos Pharmacy with medicine for a sick child that they had taken on good faith. That kind of compassion didn't go unrewarded. Even now, more than forty years later, the same customers come to Santos—only now, they pay with American Express platinum cards. No one would ever go broke from counting on the Cuban work ethic.

Things went so well that my family opened a second pharmacy within a year of the first; within the decade, there were several more. Papa and my uncles have since retired from working full time, but they maintained an office in the original building and stopped in at least once a week. My cousins were now in charge, and still upholding the family tradition of increasing profits. As a result, the Santoses were one of the wealthier exile families.

Lately my brothers and cousins had contracted a chemist to start research into developing our own line of pharmaceutical products and, from initial reports, it looked as though we were going to be expanding our business yet again. We had already established a bilingual Web site—one of the first in the country—from which customers could order products to be delivered within twenty-four hours.

I tried not to take our success for granted. After all, I was born in the United States, and I had no real notion of how much they had lost when they left Cuba. There were no photographs to provide me with a mental picture of their old life, so I had to rely on the verbal descriptions my parents offered up on the few occasions they chose to talk about life before exile. My parents, in a sense, left their souls behind on the island. Mamá and Papa were talkative by nature, but they rarely spoke about Cuba to my brothers and me. It was too painful, even after four decades. Time clouds memories, and leads to exaggeration, but from what little I knew I imagined them living a golden existence in a breathtakingly beautiful land that had nurtured our family for generations. I felt the loss of a country in which I had never set foot.

My parents' house was on North Greenway Drive, in an upscale part of Coral Gables. The place was two-story, light pink, built in the old Spanish style with lots of balconies and wrought-iron embellishments. In the devastation of Hurricane Andrew, in 1992, most of the beautiful old trees that shaded the place were lost—pulled from the ground by the force of the winds. Papa and Mamá had had new ones planted, but they couldn't match the majesty of their predecessors. Rather, they were a raw reminder of a late-August dawn a decade past when the skies opened up over South Florida.

I waited for the light to change at the intersection of Le Jeune Road, so I could turn left for the final stretch to my parents' house. This was the point at which, like clockwork, it struck me how much my life had changed since I married Ariel and moved to Miami Beach. My life in Coral Gables seemed tainted with conformity and convention. Since moving to the Beach I felt freer and more in touch with my true self. When I took the causeway to Miami Beach and crossed the waters of Biscayne Bay, I left behind more than just the city of Miami. I shed the more restrained, traditional side of myself. It was liberating, and I liked it more and more.

I thought of Luther just then. The old me never would have.

I spent the first two-thirds of my life in Coral Gables, but now whenever I went back I felt like a visitor to a place that was only vaguely familiar. I had no bond with the stately tree-lined streets, or the homes of my friends in which so many scenes of my life had been played out, or the parks where I had spent the sun-bleached afternoons of my childhood. I was little more than an observer now of a place that had once been everything to me.

This detachment almost frightened me. If I could feel this was about the place where I was born and raised, it might mean I could shed other crucial components of my life, too. There could be another new self inside me, waiting to come into being, which was capable of abandoning the places and people that made up my life as I knew it.

But I was probably getting way ahead of myself.

I wasn't an unfeeling person. If anything, I was feeling too much. Luther's reappearance in my life had showed me that my sense of equilibrium was more delicate than I had imagined. I warmed at the thought of our lunch at Nemo's the afternoon before; when we parted, I had promised Luther that we would see each other again. It was a quiet, civilized parting, but the undercurrents had been deafeningly loud.

That lunch at Nemo's had taken almost three hours—time I knew that Luther, on the clock for billable hours, could scarcely afford to take. I'd even had to come up with a viable explanation for my disappearance, vaguely alluding to a shopping trip with a friend at Sawgrass Mills, a discount mall in Fort Lauderdale that was a notoriously long trek and in a well-known black hole for cell phone reception. Thankfully, Ariel was preoccupied with a case going to trial in a week or so, and we had barely spoken the night before.

I'd never lied to Ariel before. A half-ass story about Sawgrass Mills was one thing, but not telling him about meeting with Luther made me burn with guilt. Nothing had happened between us, but I knew that on some level I was leaving the door open for the possibility that something might. As long as Ariel knew nothing about Luther's presence in Miami, then he would have no reason to be suspicious.

I almost ran a red light when the thought hit me: I was acting just like an adulterer. But I wasn't getting the great sex.

I was brought back to reality by the screeching sound of tires; I had hit the brakes at the red light, and a Mercedes, assuming I was going to run it, had to stop fast to keep from rear-ending me. His assumption hadn't been without basis—red lights in Miami mostly serve as decoration. Only old people, Canadians, and European tourists ever obeyed them.

With a look in the mirror, I offered a hard-hearted wave of apology to the driver in the Mercedes. He was a Latino guy in his twenties, with slicked-back hair and gold chains around his neck. He just shrugged, looking faintly disgusted, his manner broadcasting his opinion that old women like me had no place on the road. Waiting at a red light was probably an insult to his manhood.

Then I looked back and saw Marti's car seat. I had almost just caused an accident because I was thinking about Luther. That was what my life had suddenly become.

Luther wanted us to meet again. Having dinner with him was out of the question; it wasn't as though he could walk up to the front door and pick me up for a date. And another three-hour lunch wasn't likely, either. When I last spoke with Luther, I was sitting at the table with Vivian and Anabel, so the matter of our next meeting was left up in the air.

I executed the final turn onto North Greenway Drive without causing an accident—it was never a good idea to think about major life issues while negotiating Miami traffic—and drove the long block up to my parents' house. None of the kids lived at home anymore. My brother Sergio and I were both married. My oldest brother Emiliano—Micky—was still a bachelor at forty and lived in an apartment on Brickell Avenue. But my parents had never moved into a smaller place, and they kept our rooms decorated as though we were still living there. Going upstairs was like walking into a time warp, a sort of museum to our childhood.

As I turned off the motor and got out of the car, I realized that if I were still single and living at home, then there would be no ethical problem with Luther picking me up for a date. The only issue would be explaining to Mamá and Papa that I was dating an American.

 Mamá greeted me with a smile on her face when she looked up and saw me come into the living room. Then she looked all around me.

"Where's Marti?" she asked.

"I didn't bring him," I blurted out, dutifully kissing her proffered cheek. "He stayed at home."

My mother stiffened, her smile vanished. "Why? Is he sick?" She stepped away from me, looking me over as though searching for lies.

I tried not to shrink away from those laserlike eyes. I was a grown woman of thirty-five, but my mother could still make me feel like a child who had committed some grave infraction. She made me feel guilty for thoughts that had yet to pop into my mind.

My mother used to tell me about one of our ancestors in Cuba at the turn of the century. His father whipped him ten strokes with a belt every morning before breakfast. He hadn't done anything wrong yet, the father explained, but he would slip up at some point during the day. Best to get the punishment out of the way early was the rationale. I still thought about that.

My mother and I were exactly the same height, so she was able to stare right into my eyes. It was the perfect angle to make me feel like she was inspecting my soul. My friends' mothers' eyesight had worsened with age, but not Mamá's; if anything, it had gotten sharper. I shouldn't have been surprised.

She wasn't conventionally beautiful, or even very pretty, but Mercedes Santos was a stylish woman who knew how to make herself look attractive. She was sixty-eight, but carried herself like a much younger woman. Even taking into account her three face-lifts, the liposuctions, the standing appointments for Botox injections, and various nips and tucks, her youthful appearance was due more to her iron will than to surgical intervention. My mother was one of the early adherents to the "my body, my temple" philosophy.

I suppose it would be hard to look too shabby in her designer clothes and beautiful jewelry, not to mention the massages, facials, weekly hair appointments, and personal training sessions. But Mamá took full advantage of all these things. She was a poster child for the battle against the ravages of aging.

Needless to say, I was my mother's worst nightmare. She had tried, I had to give her full credit, but vanity about my looks has never been high on my list of preoccupations. I was no bag lady, and I was no stranger to the cosmetics counter and hairdressing salons, but I never defined my identity by how I looked. My mother thinks I've turned out to be a tough American broad, a militant for equality who lets her looks go as a political statement. It's just one of many things she fails to understand about me.

Besides, I was no frump. I was even a member of the elite Saks Fifth Avenue First Club, open only to individuals who spent a sufficiently ridiculous amount of money in the store. I worshipped at the altar of the Saks shoe department, and had toyed around with the idea of stipulating in my will that my wake should be held there, with my body displayed amid the pumps and high heels. Hey, compared to alcoholism, smoking, and drug addiction, a little shopping fetish was nothing.

Great, I thought. One minute in my mother's presence and I was already defending myself inside my head.

My mother's motto could have been "I look good, therefore I

am." It took me decades to get used to her vanity, and to resist the temptation to look down on her shallowness. Vivian and Anabel were walking encyclopedias on the subject of Mercedes Santos, after listening to me rant and rave about her for decades. They offered me advice and support but, most important, they always backed me up in my fights and disputes with Mamá. I was eternally grateful to them, in no small part because they had probably saved me hundreds of thousands of dollars' worth of therapy.

Mamá was dressed for my visit as if the queen of England were coming over for tea, in a yellow Escada linen suit, a flowery silk blouse, and cream-colored pumps. Her brown hair had subtle highlights, giving her a golden glow. Her porcelain-white skin—her best feature—was accentuated by the light blush on her cheeks, making her look as though she had just emerged from smelling the blooms in some idyllic rose garden.

Whatever the occasion, I knew I was underdressed for it in my pink Gap capris, white T-shirt, and striped espadrilles with matching tote bag. My hair was pulled back into a ponytail, and I wasn't wearing makeup. I looked like an overgrown escapee from a prep school. As I stood there, trying to figure out how to explain Marti's absence, my mind was flooded with one distracting thought: My pants were too tight. Mamá's eyes had narrowed a fraction when checking me out. She hadn't said anything, but I had failed to escape her judgment.

"I didn't come here directly from home, Mamá," I explained. "I stopped at Starbucks in the Grove, to talk to Vivian and Anabel. I didn't want to take him there."

Mamá slowly digested what I had just said. Then she nodded slowly. "You're right," she said. "Starbucks is no place for a Cuban baby."

I sighed. At least we found something to agree on. "I'll bring him soon," I said. "I promise."

Thank God I had slipped in a mention of Vivian and Anabel without getting a reaction. Mamá never approved of them, even when we were young girls. Now that we were full-grown women

Mamá thought they were filling my mind with what she called "women's lib ideas." I had made it clear that my friends were off limits, but Mamá couldn't resist getting a jab in now and then.

Mamá glided over to one of the three-seater sofas by the window, sat down, and nodded for me to sit at the other end. The cushion between us would remain a buffer zone. We weren't a touchy-feely family.

Mamá was a complex person. She mystified me even when I was a little girl. She could be petty, vindictive, and decidedly difficult even with her own children. But if any of us were ever in any kind of trouble, she was there to protect us and help us out. She had never been one for long talks over milk and cookies in the kitchen. For her, nurturing meant making sure we weren't starving and that we had clothes on our backs—once those were taken care of, we could make our own way in the world. It was almost as though she felt strong maternal feelings were a sign of weakness, and that she had to use iron discipline to stave off her natural tendencies. Maybe leaving home and going into exile had made her that way, or maybe it was just the way she was. In her world, sentimentality was a character flaw, one that would inevitably exact a price. My brothers and I knew we would never learn what was behind her coldness. Her advice to me on managing my emotional life was that crying stretched the fragile skin under the eyes and caused wrinkles, not to mention runny mascara.

The maid, Yolanda, materialized from out of nowhere bearing a small silver tray with a glass of iced tea for me. She was dressed in a blindingly white uniform, so heavily starched that it could have set off sparks as she moved. Despite the season she wore white nurse's stockings, and ballerina slippers. Her black hair was pulled from her face in a braid, and her nails were short and unpainted. All our maids always looked and dressed that way; in a closet off the kitchen was a rack of white uniforms in sizes from two to twenty, reminders of former employees.

I thanked Yolanda quietly while my mother watched with eagle eyes as the maid put the glass and a white, crisply ironed linen napkin on the table in front of me. Mamá said nothing to her. That was, according to my mother, the way it should be. Yolanda was the latest in a long line of maids who had worked for our family. In the beginning, the women were always recent Cuban exiles, but as time passed they had been replaced by Central Americans—mostly Salvadorans, Nicaraguans, and Hondurans. I could always tell which countries were having economic and political problems at any given time by the nationalities of women looking for domestic work.

No one in our family was going to be able to run for political office, because none of these women ever had proper immigration papers. Checking documentation before hiring a maid was an abhorrent idea to my parents, almost as bad as withholding Social Security money. My parents would rather have paid a fine to the INS than pry into their employees' personal lives. And none of these women was going to retire in the United States; their plan was always to work in America, save money, and return home to buy a house. They would never see a penny of Social Security money, so there was no point in their paying into the system.

My parents never took advantage of the maids' illegal status, or exploited them in any way. In fact, they paid better than most Miami households. Mamá, no matter how difficult and demanding, remembered what it was like to live in a strange country. She helped the maids with unexpected bills, and paid for their children's education. She understood how hard it was for them to find work without papers, with little education, and little knowledge of English. She paid them in cash, with no questions asked and little information volunteered. My parents believed that the government had no place intervening in private, household matters, and that these women could make their own decisions and spend their money in the way that they saw fit.

I took a sip of iced tea. Mamá watched me expectantly.

Our house had been professionally decorated, and it showed— not, to my mind, in an always flattering light. My parents hadn't had much money when they first bought the place, so Mamá had furnished it herself. It had been great in those days, homey and welcoming. Then, every time the family's finances improved, my mother redecorated—with an increased budget. My brothers and I called these major overhauls Mamá's five-year plans.

The most recent decorator had been a very fancy, socially connected descendent of the Spanish Grandees. And he had definitely gone overboard. The couch in the living room was modeled after one in the Velázquez painting *La Maja Desnuda,* on which a nude woman was being served by a Nubian slave. I really didn't want to think about what this said about my mother's self-image.

All the furniture in the room was upholstered in silver brocade, with fringed tassels hanging from every corner of the massed pillows artfully arranged to convey a contrived image of casual ease. The window treatments used up at least a week's production from a factory in Seville. And the silkworms must have worked overtime on the sofas. I think the decorator must have been on Ecstasy. And my mother must have been on Valium when she agreed to the plans.

When the latest living-room decor was being installed, my mother was filled with so much pride that she refused to let anyone see it until it was finished. On the final day, the decorator's assistants had put in twelve hours seeing to the finishing touches. Then Mamá invited us all over to admire her choices. My brothers and I still wince to think of the monumental hangovers we incurred from that night—the only way we could hold our tongues was to drink our way through the unveiling.

The place had been converted to Madrid East. Well, I didn't want to be the one to remind Mamá that our ancestors had lost their lives fighting in the revolution seeking independence from Spain. The place looked like the palace built for the Spanish Infanta, and it had left my brothers and me with post-traumatic stress disorder toward anything Spanish. Forget Spanish restaurants and Almodovar movies. It had taken me six months before I could even contemplate drinking a rioja.

In the ensuing year I'd grown accustomed to the decor—although I was still a wreck every time I brought Marti there with his three-year-old's dirty hands. I thought of my mother as a tasteful woman, but this latest decorating scheme shouted out "refugee done good."

"Your father is in the office," Mamá said. "So he won't be able to join us for lunch."

"Well, I—"

"It's just as well," she interrupted, "since Marti's not here, and it's just you."

Dios mio. Mamá and me, alone over lunch. How were we going to get through it?

We had just finished off the gazpacho, the first course, and were awaiting the next, when I heard the faint melody of "Jingle Bells." That was the music I had programmed my cell phone to play when a call was coming in, so that meant it was coming from my tote bag in the next room. Mamá didn't approve of cell phones, and insisted they be turned off in her house. Usually I obeyed her rule, but that day I had forgotten. I had plenty of other things on my mind.

I glanced up at Mamá, hoping she hadn't heard. Thankfully, she was well into a long and intricate story about how the surgeon had botched my Tia Norma's latest face-lift. A sure way to distract Mamá was to ask her about any of our relatives—she could gossip about them for hours. She was pleased to think I was interested in her stories, and I was happy not to listen to her free advice about how to run my life. I had learned long ago that the best defense was offense, and that asking about one of my aunts guaranteed the topic wouldn't turn to my conduct.

I looked around the dining room, as if ignoring the sound of "Jingle Bells" was going to make it go away. It wasn't my favorite tune, by any means, but I had never heard anyone else use it, and I figured it would make my phone stand out from the millions of others in Miami. Where else could you hear "Jingle Bells" in July?

Our lunch was Spanish style—what else?—and served in a room where Don Quixote might have been faithfully attended by Sancho

Panza. The table was massive, big enough to seat a dozen guests, with fabulously uncomfortable wooden chairs upholstered in red brocade. The mustard-colored walls were painted in a faux scrolling black ink pattern that was supposed to look elegant and sophisticated. Instead, it always made me think a horde of insects were crawling their way up to the ceiling. The French doors leading out to the garden were covered in yards of black velvet, and the lighting was provided by a massive black iron chandelier that hung over the table and swayed like the sword of Damocles whenever the air-conditioning came on. An enormous gilt mirror was placed over the wooden sideboard—Mamá claimed it was from the times of Columbus and Queen Isabella, but I thought the decorator must have found it in a brothel. Whatever the case, eating in that room made me feel as though it was me facing the Spanish Inquisition. I rarely escaped without indigestion.

"Jingle Bells" began to sound again just as Yolanda came in with plates for the main course. For some reason Mamá hadn't heard the sound, or else she was so pleased to have a captive audience for her savaging of Tia Norma that she was just going to ignore it and expect me to do the same.

I waited for a break in Mamá's description of Tia Norma's neck—suffice it to say the skin was reminiscent of a chicken's—and broke in before Mamá could get started on the too-tight muscles around my aunt's mouth.

"I'm so sorry," I said. "But I have to go to the bathroom before we begin the next course."

I vaguely pointed to the empty iced tea glass in front of me as an explanation for my breach of etiquette. At Mamá's table, getting up during a meal was forbidden.

My mother sighed deeply to demonstrate how wounded she was, and shook her head slightly from side to side as she reached for the silver bell on the table. Yolanda dutifully appeared seconds later.

"Please wait a few minutes before the main course, until Señora Margarita has returned," she ordered. Yolanda nodded.

I ignored my mother's look of annoyance and sprang out of my chair, racing toward the bathroom and grabbing my bag along the way. The phone was still ringing, and as soon as I had closed the door behind me I pressed the button to answer. I had thought that this was an important call, and my instincts were on target.

"Daisy," Luther said.

"Luther," I said, trying to keep my voice calm. My heart beat in my ears.

"Can you talk?" he asked.

"Just for a minute." I tried not to think of Mamá sitting at the table, fuming and checking her watch every fifteen seconds.

"I know I was supposed to wait for you to call me," Luther said. He paused. I could tell this wasn't easy for him, so I waited for him to continue. "Look, I really need to talk with you as soon as possible."

"We're talking now," I said.

"You know what I mean. In person."

I didn't consider the implications of what Luther was saying, or the gravity of his tone. Instead, I started to think of ways to get together with him.

"I'm at my mother's house having lunch right now," I told him. "But I'll be done in about an hour."

Luther thought for a moment. "If I know my Miami geography, you have to pass by Coconut Grove to get from Coral Gables to Miami Beach. Right?"

So Luther remembered that my parents lived in Coral Gables. It almost felt as if the years hadn't gone by at all, like it had been a dream.

"Right."

"I'm still downtown at the office," Luther said. "But I could get out of here and meet you in the Grove someplace. Would that be all right with you?"

There was a hesitance in Luther's voice I had never heard before.

"Well, how about meeting at the Dinner Key Marina, across from the Grand Bay Hotel?" I suggested. I didn't know what was going on, or what I was doing. I was following a logic I didn't understand. "There are some benches there where we could talk. It's reasonably private."

I was about to give Luther better directions, but he cut me off.

"I'll find it," he said. "See you in an hour."

He hung up before we could say good-bye. I put down the toilet seat and sat down. As the reality of what had just happened set in, I panicked. I didn't know what I had just agreed to. And I wished I had dressed better, washed my hair, and put on makeup that morning. Maybe Mamá was right. Maybe a woman should always look as if she had just stepped out of the pages of *W*.

Well, one hurdle at a time. I had to get back and finish lunch before Mamá sent out Yolanda as a search party. The real question was how I was going to be able to eat a single bite of food.

 I had instinctively suggested meeting Luther at Dinner Key Marina because I needed to be near the water for what I knew was going to be an important encounter. I liked to make all the big decisions in my life in the presence of water. I was like most Cubans in this regard—the ocean was best, but a lake would do in a pinch. We're island people; water surrounds our thoughts and souls, it gives us life and protects us.

But there were other reasons. The marina would afford us privacy, and it was highly unlikely that I would encounter anyone I knew there at two in the afternoon on a weekday. And it was a public place, which meant nothing physical could transpire between us. Not that I was planning on anything, but having a deterrent in place seemed like a good idea.

After I had finished talking to Luther, I had shut off the phone and ran water in the sink, then flushed the toilet for good measure. There was no harm in covering my tracks. Then, cell phone back in my tote bag, I left the guest bathroom.

I was deep in thought and preoccupied by the meeting an hour away, and I walked slowly back to the dining room. I dreaded returning to the table, knowing that Mamá would be angry that I had interrupted lunch. It was a mortal sin to have left her there, seated and alone at the table. She probably wouldn't say anything, but her attitude would convey everything she wanted me to know. I was already in her bad books by not bringing Marti, and getting up from the table would have sealed my fate.

The instant Mamá saw me come into the dining room, she rang her silver bell to summon Yolanda. I might have been imagining things, but it felt as though the temperature in the room had dropped about twenty degrees since I left.

"Señora Margarita has returned," Mamá told the maid as I slipped into the seat. "We will continue with lunch, please."

"Sorry again," I said. *"Perdoname, por favor."* I knew what sort of groveling would at least partly appease my mother.

Yolanda returned with a huge silver tray on which two portions of fish lay majestically on a bed of parsley surrounded by white rice and peas. I waited for Mamá to serve herself, then did the same.

My mother took one bite of the grouper and laid down her fork.

"Dry," she announced with profound disappointment.

Her implication was clear to me. Had I not left the table to go to the bathroom the fish would have been served at the proper moment and would not have dried out in the oven for those extra minutes. Subtlety wasn't Mamá's strong suit, but payback was.

I took a bite. I thought the fish was cooked just right, but there was no point getting into a pissing match with Mamá about it. I had learned well over the years that it was no use contradicting my mother. And since I had to be out of there within the hour, I didn't want to get into a prolonged discussion with her about the damned fish.

Instead I turned the conversation toward a subject I knew Mamá would like: my other aunt. Tia Veronica, and her liposuction. I knew I was selling out, but I was on a tight schedule. And who was I to stand on principle? I was scheming how to get out of the house to meet an old boyfriend.

I ate everything on my plate, accepted a serving of flan for dessert, and topped off the meal with coffee, even though I feared it would spoil my breath for my meeting with Luther. The tin of Altoids in my bag, I hoped, would take care of that problem.

As soon as lunch was finished, I kissed Mamá good-bye and mumbled something about having a few errands to run before I went home. I sprinted out to my car, giving her no chance to comment on my horrid manners. If I had hung around I would have been on the receiving end of a major lecture.

Actually, if I thought about it, Mamá had been on her best behavior that day. It must have been painful for her to suffer in silence what she must have thought were so many social gaffes on my part. It was too much to hope that she was mellowing with age, but she might have been moving gradually, slowly, in that direction.

Mamá's attitude, never entirely easy for her family to deal with, took a sharp downturn three years before when, completely by accident, she discovered that my father had been having an affair for ten years with Ofelia Carrera, a Cuban woman who worked as a bookkeeper for Santos Pharmacies. If my father had been a womanizer, his behavior would at least have been understandable if not excusable. For Cubans, it was almost expected that men cheated on their wives at some point in their lives—again, it might not be excusable, but it was chalked up to the appetites of the male of the species. But this hadn't been a one-night stand. Papa had been involved deeply with one woman for a very long time, and that was what made the situation so upsetting for the entire family.

To top it off, the manner in which their affair came to the surface was uniquely tawdry. Papa suffered a heart attack while visiting Ofelia in her apartment—which, it turned out, he had bought for her. When she realized how seriously ill Papa was, Ofelia had been forced to call up my brother Mickey and tell him that paramedics were on the way to the apartment and that Papa was lying down and having difficulty breathing. She told Mickey that she wasn't sure Papa was going to make it, and that the family should be prepared for the worst. And there was a practical matter—as a nonrelative, she would be unable to consult with doctors about his treatment. Papa needed one of us right away.

Until that phone call, my brothers and Mamá had thought of Ofelia—when we did, which was rarely—as the competent and reasonably attractive bookkeeper at Papa's office. Unlike others who worked in the executive office, Ofelia generally kept to herself and was very circumspect about her personal life. Now we knew why.

Once he got over the shock of getting a call at home from Ofelia, then hearing what she had to say, Mickey added two and two and came up with the right answer. Papa wouldn't be at Ofelia's apartment to discuss bookkeeping, after all. Mickey hung up and raced over to her apartment, which was just a mile away from his place. He knew for certain that his father was having an affair. What he didn't know was whether Papa would live long enough to be confronted about it.

Mickey arrived just in time to see the paramedics lifting Papa from the king-size bed in Ofelia's bedroom onto a gurney. They were taking him to Mercy Hospital, the closest to Ofelia's apartment. Mickey identified himself to the paramedics, who said the situation was touch and go. Papa was barely conscious as they slammed the ambulance doors shut. Mickey stood in front of Ofelia's apartment, his blood turned cold by the sound of the siren receding into the distance.

A few nights later, when Papa was out of danger, Mickey took Sergio and me to a bar in the Grove for drinks after leaving the hospital. It was then that he told us all the details of what happened. He told us how Ofelia had sat in a chair in the corner of her bedroom, dressed only in a tatty bathrobe, silent as she watched the paramedics working on Papa. Though it was her home, she seemed to know she was pushed to the margins of Papa's life. Miami might be a freewheeling place, but it hadn't reached the point at which mistresses were considered on a par with blood relatives. Mickey wasn't particularly sensitive, but he said her expression had broken his heart when he left her there with a hollow promise to call later. She knew her days with Papa were over.

As soon as he got in his car to follow the ambulance to Mercy Hospital, Mickey got on his cell phone and patched through a conference call with Sergio and me. I don't know which was more shocking—the news that Papa had suffered a heart attack, or the fact that he'd had it in his lover's bed, like a character in a telenovela. I knew it wasn't unusual for men to cheat on their wives, especially Cuban men, but I didn't think Papa was like that. I had never really given my parents' marriage much thought, I realized. The fact that they were still married after all they had been through meant they were still in love, I figured. They had three children, so they must have had some sort of sex life. I realized that their marriage was a mystery, just like everyone else's. No one knows the full truth, save for the two people involved.

Sergio and I had immediately gone to the hospital, where we met Mickey outside the emergency room and went into full crisis mode on the issue of what to do about Mamá. Obviously we had to notify her, but we weren't sure what we should say. It was possible, we realized, that Mamá knew about Ofelia, or at least suspected that Papa had a mistress. She was, after all, a Cuban woman married to a Cuban man.

We agonized for half an hour while we waited for her to arrive. Then, rightly or wrongly, we decided to concoct a story about Papa falling ill while delivering some documents for Ofelia to work on. We simply couldn't deal with giving Mamá the sordid details. But we were spared having to lie when Mamá arrived. Mamá identified herself at the front desk before she saw us, where a triage nurse handed her the paramedics' report. It was all there: Ofelia, the bed. Mamá didn't need to know any more.

Mamá never discussed Papa's heart attack with me or my brothers except as it related to his physical health. Mickey, Sergio, and I talked about it for a while, but soon they grew bored with the subject. For them, it simply wasn't all that interesting that Papa had a mistress. They were Cuban men, and deeper explanations were unnecessary.

For my part, I felt that I understood Mamá a little better. I wish I had known earlier, because it would have made a lot of things easier to understand. My opinion of Papa didn't change much because the truth was that I had never really known him very well in the first place. Cuban men, especially of his generation, weren't very involved with their children's lives, especially that of their daughters. I was at least able to view him as a complex person, with human needs and desires, and not simply the ultimate authority at home, the breadwinner and decision-maker.

I was then thirty-two years old, and I hadn't begun to sort out the truth of my parents' private lives. After Papa's heart attack, I realized that all of my thoughts about marriage were filtered through my parents' relationship. They weren't exactly great role models, but they were all that I knew. I hoped they were happy, though a lot of the time I feared they weren't.

And now I was driving to meet Luther. I had a flash of my mother's face in the emergency room, ashen, reading the paramedics' report with a black expression. She was a lady at all costs, even in the face of catastrophe. I couldn't have said what she was feeling in that moment.

It wasn't an image I wanted, or needed. Not when I was minutes away from meeting an old love who said it was urgent that we talk right away.

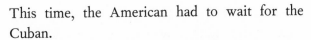This time, the American had to wait for the Cuban.

Luther was sitting in the middle of the blue three-seater bench in front of the wrought-iron gate that led to the docks, between Pier 6 and Pier 7. He was engrossed with looking out to sea and didn't notice me arriving. Knowing that parking legally at Dinner Key Marina was next to impossible, and not wanting to keep Luther waiting any longer, I steered the Escalade into an empty spot with a big official sign warning "Marina Decal Parking Only." The sign was intimidating, suggesting death or severe injury for violators, but I decided to take a chance and leave my car, without the sacrosanct decal, there.

Dinner Key was the isthmus jutting off Coconut Grove, and housed the mayor of Miami's offices. The Art Deco two-story white-washed building with sky-blue accents had become a famous image during the Elian Gonzalez fiasco. Irate Miamians had thrown bananas at the mayor's office door when he openly defied a government order demanding his cooperation in removing the six-year-old boy from his relatives before being returned to Cuba. The fruity projectiles symbolized people's anger that the mayor was making Miami look like a banana republic. It wasn't a high point in Miami history, but then nothing about the Elian Gonzalez tragedy had been a high point. Ever since then, I hadn't been able to go to Dinner Key Marina without thinking about the whole disgraceful mess.

There wasn't much I could do about my looks just then, so I settled for a quick spritz of Chanel No. 5. I decided to think like the French, and hope that perfume would mask all the ills of the world. When I got out of the car, the sound of the door closing made Luther turn around.

"Daisy!" he called out to me.

He was dressed in a khaki suit much like the one he'd worn the day before, and he looked a little out of place in such casual surroundings. It was close to a hundred degrees in the afternoon heat, but Luther looked nice and cool in his suit and tie. I had no idea how he did it. He got up and met me, taking my arm and leading me back to the bench where he had been waiting. He waited for me to choose a seat before lowering his lanky body next to mine.

"It's beautiful here, Daisy," Luther said. The wind kicked up, swirling the air around us. "Still using Chanel No. 5. It always makes me think of you."

I blushed, knowing I'd overdone it on the perfume. Then I wondered if that was all we were going to talk about, there in the sweltering heat. I could feel a hint of anxiety inside my stomach, and I was very aware of Luther's physical proximity to me.

"Are there always this many boats docked here?" Luther asked, gesturing to the docks in front of us, where every slip was occupied. I didn't remember Luther ever showing much interest in boats before. Durham, North Carolina, hadn't been a hot spot for nautical pursuits.

I didn't believe we were there to talk about my perfume, or about boats, and then a thought occurred to me: Luther was as nervous as I was, and couldn't get around to what he wanted to talk about. If that was true, then I was going to be sick. Luther had ice water in his veins. He was cool and unemotional even by American standards.

I decided to humor him. I didn't feel as if I was operating from a position of strength, not the way I looked.

"There are always lot of boats here," I said. "Some people even live on them."

Luther nodded sagely, as though this nugget of information had cleared up a lot of questions for him.

"Must be nice," he said.

"What's that?"

"You know, being able to do that."

We watched the pelicans perched on the channel markers at the edge of the marina, cackling and preening. Sometimes they would stretch in preparation for swooping down on a hapless fish that had made the mistake of swimming too close to the water's surface. It always amazed me that those ungainly beasts could actually fly, with their huge beaks and pouches underneath, and that they were actually graceful when they did, skimming the water with their wide wings extended.

I sneaked a look at my watch and saw that we had been sitting there for fifteen minutes. It looked like it was up to me. I was the mother of a three-year-old, after all, and couldn't disappear in mid-afternoon two days in a row without coming up with some kind of explanation.

"Luther, you said it was important that we meet today," I began, as gently as I could.

He turned to me with a deer-in-the-headlights stare. He suddenly acted as though he would prefer a root canal to telling me what he had to say.

"I did." He paused, took a deep breath. His eyes were bluer than ever. "I have a confession, Daisy. I didn't come to Miami because of a case."

"Then . . ."

"I'm working a case here, that's true," Luther said hastily.

"All right," I said, taking all this in. Luther took another deep breath, and I could see him steadying himself for whatever he had to say next.

"But I've come to Miami on the case more than a dozen times in the past five years. I've been coming down here for years, I just haven't contacted you before."

"You chose to call me now?" I asked. "That seems strange to me."

A sheepish expression came over his face. "Look, I don't want you to think I'm a stalker or anything."

"Luther, I didn't say that."

Apparently he was reassured. "I know," he said quietly. "But there's something else. Before, when you were working at the firm, I could see you without your spotting me."

"You were . . . watching me?"

"Look, Daisy, this is really difficult." Luther looked out over the water. He had gone this far, and it was painful for me to watch him struggling with himself.

"Just tell me," I said.

"I would watch you as you went in and out of your office building," Luther offered, wincing a little.

I didn't know whether to be insulted or flattered. I knew Luther too well to think that there was anything creepy or unsavory behind what he was saying. Still, I was really too shocked to react.

"Luther, help me out here," I said. "I don't understand this. Why . . . why did you watch me?"

I saw Luther conducting an internal monologue with himself, his lawyer's training weighing how to present his information to make his case. Displays of vulnerability were not part of Luther's character, although I had seen more in the last five minutes than I ever recalled from our dating days.

"Look, it's like this. Even after we broke up, I still kept track of you and what you were doing." Luther looked into my eyes, then away. "And I knew there were solid, practical reasons for our breaking up. Believe me, I used to repeat them to myself over and over. But it didn't matter, I couldn't get you out of my mind. I dated a lot, and I got involved with a couple of women. But I wanted you, Daisy. All this time."

Luther gently took my hand in his. I just watched him, almost feeling like my hand belonged to someone else. It was awkward, and almost uncomfortable, to be sitting there with our arms outstretched between us, our palms damp and sweaty. The oversize diamond wedding band on my finger was digging into both his and my flesh. Perhaps the ring awakened Luther to reality, because he suddenly released my hand.

"It was about a year after we split that I was assigned to a case and sent down here," Luther said. "We had agreed not to have any contact, and I had no idea how you felt about me. So I asked around about you. It broke my heart when I found out that you were engaged to marry a Cuban attorney, and so I didn't try to get in touch with you."

I sat there, stunned, pondering how all this went on without my knowledge.

"Then, the next time I came down, I found out that you had already gotten married to him."

I could hear the pain in Luther's voice. I had figured he had gotten on with his life after our breakup. Part of me didn't think that WASPs felt much of anything too deeply, and that Luther would have moved on to a whole new life without me. I looked at Luther and wondered: If I hadn't been engaged to Ariel the first time Luther came to Miami, and if he had contacted me, then how differently would our lives have been? And what if he had called me while I was engaged to Ariel, but not yet married?

Luther shook his head and laughed softly, with a look of admiration in his eyes that confused me.

"I must say, Daisy, you follow through with your intentions." Luther looked off into the distance. "You said one of the reasons you wanted to stay in Miami was that you wanted to integrate yourself into the community. That you wanted to be and feel more Cuban, after seven years away at Penn and Duke. Well, you achieved your goal. And I know you probably couldn't have gotten there with me."

It was my turn to reach for his hand, this time with the one that had no ring on it.

"Luther, I don't know what to say," I paused. "I mean, you've taken me by surprise with this. All of it."

I shifted to face him.

"But there's one thing I don't understand," I told him. "After six years, after watching me from afar, why did you contact me this time?"

The heat was starting to feel punishing, and in the harsh afternoon sunlight I saw a slight sheen of moisture come over Luther's face. I was hot enough in my cotton T-shirt, so he must have been sweltering in his suit. And, of course, this conversation couldn't have been helping matters.

"I know this is going to sound stupid," he said. "But you haven't been going to work for close to a year now. Ever since you took your leave of absence, I haven't had an opportunity to see you."

Luther took out a handkerchief and wiped his face. "Excuse me," he said. "It's so hot, I can't help it."

Americans, especially northerners, don't do well in Miami's oppressive summer climate. Even I was starting to feel a slight trickle of sweat running down my back. I was glad to be wearing a white shirt, since it wouldn't show any sweat stains. I was a firm believer in never letting them see me sweat.

We were sitting ramrod straight on either end of that royal-blue wooden bench; Luther and I probably looked like two strangers who had just happened to take a rest to admire the scene at the marina. We were the only people around, and our only company was two mangy cats napping under a red pickup truck parked across the road. Even the pelicans had retired to whatever shelter they sought during the hottest part of the day.

But Luther and I, two Ivy-League graduates and attorneys, weren't so smart as that. We chose to sweat out the largest issues of our lives in the harsh sun of a South Florida summer's day.

"I couldn't think of any way to see you, other than just calling you," Luther said. "And I was beginning to feel like a total idiot. I used to wait mornings in the coffee shop across the street from your building, just to catch a glimpse of you parking your car and going inside."

I pictured what Luther had just said. It was hard to imagine him pining away in loneliness, a forlorn character watching me from afar. But I could tell from his tone that it was the truth.

"You used to wait in the coffee shop and watch me cross the street from the parking lot?" I pictured the coffee shop, a greasy spoon owned by Cubans. I knew how clear his line of sight would be from one of the tables by the front window.

"Thank God you're so punctual," he said with a low chuckle. "Always in your office by eight thirty, otherwise I might never have been able to see you." Luther seemed to ease up a little, as though the more he talked about his actions, the more he became comfortable with them. "A couple of times I tried to see you coming out, but it was impossible. Daisy, you were sure keeping some late hours. I thought no one outside of New York worked as hard as that."

"Luther, you have to understand this is hard for me to absorb."

"I know, Daisy. I know it's a lot."

I didn't want to scare Luther off by reacting too negatively, but I also needed for him to understand that this was a bombshell. Luther had apparently been devoting so much time and energy to thinking about me, that he had forgotten he had no idea where my thoughts were going. All those days in the office, all those nights with Ariel and Marti.

"I had no idea you were even thinking about me at all in the years since we broke up," I told him. "And your watching me from the coffee shop without ever letting me know . . . do you have any idea how that sounds?"

"It sounds crazy," Luther said firmly. "I know that. But I need to be honest with you now, Daisy. I want you to know that this declaration isn't just coming out of nowhere. I've been thinking about you for years."

"Declaration?" I asked him. "What declaration?"

Luther's Adam's apple jumped. Now he was really sweating.

"Daisy, I made a huge mistake when I agreed with you that our relationship should end. When we left Duke, you were so set on coming back here that you never considered any other options. You never even talked to any of the law-firm recruiters from anyplace other than Miami. It was clear where you were going and, try as I might, I simply couldn't picture myself living here."

"You were as set on New York as I was on Miami," I pointed out.

"I know." Luther spoke slowly, measuring every word. "When I think back on that time, I know that I was in love with you from the day I met you. But the fact that you were always returning to Miami held me back."

"We never really talked about it," I said.

"What could I do? Move here with you?" he asked. "Where would that leave me? Tagging along after you? The pussy-whipped gringo?"

"Luther!" I was shocked more by his sentiment than by his choice of words. Never before had this man given me a hint about a more passionate side to his personality. The only time he had ever let go was in bed with me: Otherwise he was always calm, cool, composed. It was confusing. And a little exciting.

"Sorry, Daisy. But that's the way it felt. You come from a macho culture. Men are supposed to lead women, not the other way around. I knew I would command zero respect if I followed you to Miami. And I would have no ties of my own to anyone. I didn't speak Spanish. I knew I would just be a drag on you if I came along."

There was really nothing to say. Luther was right. Just then we heard the full, rich sound of a boat's engine starting. A few moments later a man emerged on the deck of a Hatteras that was docked just inside the gated area of Pier 7. I had noticed the boat walking up, and admired the pristine condition in which it was kept.

We watched as a woman joined him on deck; the two prepared the fifty-foot boat for a journey out into the bay. She took care of the ropes on the bow, he untied the cords on the stern and threw them onto the dock. Then he sprinted onto the bridge and carefully guided the boat out of its slip while she fended off, making sure the red and white rubber bumpers hit the wooden pilings and not the hull.

Luther and I were silent, watching the boat slowly motoring out to the channel that would take it to the bay. I wondered where the couple was heading during the hottest part of the day. They would probably be one of the only boats on Biscayne Bay in this heat and sun. Maybe they were stealing moments, enjoying the sea while they could.

"Well, we're here," I said, breaking the silence. "And you've told me all this. But what's changed, Luther?"

In perfect Spanish, Luther replied, "Everything has changed, Daisy. I'll change my entire world for you, if I have to. Anything."

 We had just finished the main course and were waiting for Jacinta to clear the plates for dessert.

"Margarita, are you all right?" Ariel asked me. "You seem so distracted."

We'd put Marti to bed and were having dinner alone. Lately Ariel had been coming home from work a little earlier, so he had time to play with Marti before putting him to bed. That day, of all days, Ariel had come home even earlier in the afternoon, excited and full of plans to play in the pool with his son. Knowing Ariel's insanely hectic work schedule, any other day I would have been pleased. But that day I'd only gotten home a half hour before him, and I hadn't had time to digest everything that had happened.

"I'm fine," I said, avoiding looking into his eyes. "Just a little tired, I guess."

Ariel cocked his head to one side—his problem-solving posture—and looked at me intently. It took all my self-control to sit there quietly while he examined me. I felt as transparent as a sheet of cellophane. I wondered how I would feel if I had actually been unfaithful to Ariel, rather than merely having listened to Luther broach the subject.

"I know what's wrong with you," Ariel said with quiet triumph. I felt my blood run cold. "You went to see your mother today, didn't you?"

As soon as his words registered, I suppressed a sigh of relief. If Ariel suspected that I had been with another man—even just to talk—I probably wouldn't have been sitting there in one piece. Ariel might have been enlightened and liberal, but beneath the surface he was still a Cuban man. And Cuban men don't react kindly to other men making suggestions to their wives of the sort that Luther had proposed that afternoon.

Thankfully, I didn't have to lie to Ariel.

"Yes," I said. "I had lunch with Mamá."

Apparently satisfied that Mamá was enough to account for my mood, Ariel went back to telling me about a personal-injury case that he was considering taking. He knew the effect Mamá had on me sometimes, and he knew better than to ask for details.

Moments later Jacinta appeared with dessert—coconut flan, my favorite, which I usually devoured. I hadn't eaten much of the main course, chicken in white wine sauce, so I dug into the flan with the gusto of a woman on death row.

It was still warm out, but it had cooled to the point at which we could have dinner outside on the terrace. I remembered the afternoon sun burning into my eyes and the back of my neck. From our table we had an unobstructed view of Miami across Biscayne Bay: The tall buildings of downtown illuminated in an array of colors, the bridges linking Miami Beach to the mainland outlined in neon light, the city lights reflected in the water. I could never tire of the view.

As soon as Ariel had tucked away his flan, he resumed telling me about a client who had come into his office. I gave every sign of listening to what he was saying, but my eyes kept darting to the lights shimmering in the distance, as if by focusing on the shore across the water I could discern what Luther was doing at that moment. It was only four miles from Miami Beach to Miami on the causeway, but just then it felt like a continent away.

Ariel was so intent on what he was saying that he didn't notice me drifting away. Or else, having thought he'd figured me out, he didn't care to make any further comment. I knew that as long as I made occasional eye contact and nodded from time to time, I could think about anything I wanted while Ariel was talking. It wasn't a strategy

I'd set out to develop, it was just something that had happened over the years. I was physically seated on the terrace, sipping after-dinner coffee and listening to Ariel's story. Mentally, I was back on that park bench with Luther. I would have given anything to be able to withdraw from my life for a few hours, just to get my thoughts together. I didn't understand how a one-hour meeting with an ex-lover could threaten my eight-year marriage. I never imagined things were so tenuous, and delicate.

But apparently they were.

I had never been unfaithful to Ariel, and I'd never even been tempted. I had thought our marriage was solid and secure, but now I wondered if my fidelity was simply a matter of the right person never coming into my life. Luther had showed up, declared his love, and made me wonder if he had been the right man for me all along. He knew I was married, with a child, and still he had contacted me. And I had listened to him.

My mind raced while I looked into Ariel's eyes. I was suddenly angry and disgusted with myself for the way I was thinking. But then, with a power beyond my control, Ariel's familiar features in the candlelight began to morph into Luther's. I shook my head to banish the image, and to concentrate on where I was.

"Ariel, *amor,* it's so nice out here," I said, standing up. "I think I'm going to pour myself a Courvoisier. Can I get you one?"

I had read somewhere that people cheating on their spouses often compensated by being extra nice. I wondered if I was already falling into that pattern. Nonsense, I thought. Jacinta had retired for the night, and it was up to us to serve ourselves. That was all.

Ariel's face lit up with delight, and he smiled so lovingly at me that I had to turn away.

As I walked into the den, I condemned myself for even considering having an affair with Luther. I reminded myself that I had rarely even thought about Luther before he contacted me. I was happily married to a man I loved, and who loved me. We had a great sex life. I had a child I adored, I lived in a beautiful house. I was a partner in a top-tier law firm.

And an ex-lover I hadn't seen in nearly ten years was making me feel like a teenager in heat.

I opened up the bar and took down two heavy, intricately cut balloon glasses. I measured out two healthy servings of brandy, watching the richness of the amber swirling in the glasses. I knew the alcohol would leave me with a little headache in the morning, but I wanted to sleep well that night. Ariel and I had split a bottle of white wine over dinner, but it had seemed to sharpen my mind rather than mellow me out. I had a lot of thinking to do, but not while the memory of seeing Luther was so fresh.

"Gracias," Ariel said when I handed him his glass.

I sat down and tipped my glass to him. *"Salud."*

It had been a while since we relaxed together on the terrace, quietly enjoying an after-dinner drink. If it weren't for Luther coming back into my life, I could have been at peace with myself and the world around me.

I sipped the brandy, feeling my throat burn and my eyes water slightly. I stared at the waves of Biscayne Bay lapping gently at the seawall just a few feet from where we sat. I wondered if Luther was out there, looking out at the same water, wondering which of the lights shone from my house. I remembered when I was a child, I used to look at the water and wonder where each drop had been in the past. I used to think about faraway places like China, but now I was thinking only of Coconut Grove.

My heart was beating faster, and it wasn't just the brandy. It was Luther. Thinking of him was making me melt. I remembered that afternoon, on the bench, when he had started talking in perfect, unaccented Spanish. It had floored me. I'd received plenty of gifts from men in my life, but no one had ever learned a language for me before. Brilliant as he was, I knew Luther had a hard time picking up languages. Learning Spanish was Luther's declaration of love for me, and his way of demonstrating that his feelings were more than just a passing fancy.

There was no point trying not to think about Luther. And there was only one way to find out what the future held. It was time to go see Violeta.

 The next morning, after Ariel had left for the office, I placed an emergency call. As usual, Violeta gave every indication that she was expecting my call at that moment.

Violeta Luz was a psychic whom I'd been consulting for the past three years. Vivian had introduced me to her—Vivian, who doubted everything she couldn't see, feel, taste, and have notarized. Tough and hard-nosed as she was, Vivian also had a firm belief in seeking out spiritual advice on the big issues in her life. Even when we were children, Vivian was the one who would keep shaking the magic eight ball until she liked what it said. When she grew up, she realized that the eight ball could be manipulated and was an unreliable adviser. That was when she moved on to the Ouija board, and she became so obsessed with it that Anabel and I ended up throwing its plastic arrow into Biscayne Bay. Within a couple of years Vivian had moved on to tarot cards and palmistry.

Before she discovered Violeta, Vivian went a few times to see a pair of middle-aged Cuban twins who operated out of their house in Hialeah. They predicted the future using seashells that they rubbed in their hands before rolling like dice. Vivian liked the twins fine, but there was always a big crowd at the house, and a long wait that turned Vivian off. She didn't think mystical advice should be dispensed like products off an assembly line. And she hated to be kept waiting for anything.

After the twins, Vivian twice visited a Santeria priest also based in Hialeah. His predictions and advice were good, but the setting in which he worked started to freak Vivian out. She could overlook the life-size statues of San Lazaro and Santa Barbara that were prominently placed in the corners of the dimly lit room, along with feathers, beads, and other odd paraphernalia. But on her first visit she had seen a goat munching grass in the backyard: The second time she went there, the goat was gone. She could only think of a recent case that had gone all the way to the Supreme Court, in which a Santeria priest sued after the State of Florida tried to prohibit him from keeping goats for ritual sacrifice. He claimed that Santeria was an established faith, and that animal sacrifice was an essential part of it.

The priest had won his case. For Vivian, it was one thing to read about it in the newspaper, and another thing entirely to see it in action. The only way Vivian wanted to deal with a dead animal was to see it wrapped in plastic in the meat section at Publix. The goat's disappearance from one visit to the next definitely dampened her enthusiasm for the priest as her spiritual adviser. That, plus the fact that he kept a store behind his house in which he sold merchandise to help the spirits do their jobs—Vivian didn't want to be tempted to whip out her American Express gold card to buy a voodoo doll representing an opposing counsel on a case.

God only knows why, but at one point Vivian decided she would give Santeria one last chance. The religion was thriving in Cuba, with hordes of practitioners both in Miami and on the island. She hoped her experience with the goat-owning priest had been an anomaly. Naturally, it turned out she had gotten off easy with the goat-sacrificing Santero.

She was talking to one of her clients—a prisoner on death row for killing and mutilating his wife's relatives because they hid his TV remote control—who highly recommended a palero, the most hardcore of the Santeria priests. Vivian later realized she should have been more discriminating about the people from whom she took advice, but the prisoner swore by the palero. The man's plight might not have looked great on the surface, but it had taken three separate trials before he was actually convicted. The judge in the first trial, a forty-year-old marathon runner, had dropped dead of a heart attack and caused a mistrial. In the second trial, two members of the jury succumbed to food poisoning after eating in the courthouse cafeteria. And he almost got another mistrial the third time around, when the lead prosecutor went down with an appendicitis attack. The lawyer was so tough, though, that he only took two days off—he was so determined to convict, he said he'd have been willing to try the case from a stretcher. Vivian's client had enjoyed two years of delay, however, time for which he thanked the palero.

Vivian was instructed to go to the palero's house during the full moon—the most auspicious time for the Santeria gods. The priest lived in a normal-looking, middle-class neighborhood in South Miami. The only clue to what the man might have been into was a pervasive smell of incense in the house—*really* strong, enough to smell from the street.

The palero was a thuggy-looking mulatto guy in his late twenties, dressed entirely in white with brightly colored beads on his neck, hands, and feet. He ordered Vivian to sit with her eyes closed in a chair in the middle of his darkened living room. Vivian wasn't comfortable with the priest or the situation, but she did as she was told. After all, coming there had been her idea, she guessed. She tried to focus, figuring that she would need to concentrate for what was coming. A moment later, she felt a thwack and a sharp pain on her head, then hot liquid spreading downward. She reached up, felt around, and grabbed something warm from her hair. With horror, she saw that it was a dove, still bleeding from its neatly severed neck. Vivian was covered in blood, and the palero was nowhere to be found.

With as much strength as she could muster, Vivian threw the dove across the room, nearly vomiting when she saw the bird's blood trace an arc in the air. Then she jumped and ran as fast as she could. Her primary regret was that she hadn't gotten a refund on the eight hundred dollars she had paid—in cash, in advance—for the experience. Years later, she still shudders whenever she remembers what happened, although even she has to laugh at the fact that in Miami someone covered in blood can drive by a police car without getting stopped.

Vivian tried a few more possibilities, such as past-life regression and channeling—swearing Anabel and me to secrecy each time, lest someone in the Miami legal community find out. Then she found Violeta, a grandmotherly woman who rocked in a wooden chair while she spoke with the spirit world. What really convinced Vivian that Violeta was on the level was the fact that the spiritualist didn't charge for her sessions. There was a glass bowl placed discreetly by the front door, and clients could pay as much or as little as they felt they should.

I know how all this sounds. I was completely skeptical at first, but Vivian started to wear me down with little details of things that Violeta had predicted for her. I still wasn't convinced entirely, and I knew that most things supernatural and psychic were bullshit designed to free fools from their money. As time went on, Vivian told me more and more things that Violeta had predicted—at work, in her family, in her love life. And, as a bonus, Violeta offered commonsense advice and insight. As Vivian pointed out, it was a hell of a lot cheaper than seeing a shrink.

Three years ago for Vivian's birthday, she surprised me by declaring that I didn't need to buy her a present—instead, she wanted me to go for a session with Violeta. If I didn't get anything out of it, Vivian insisted, then she'd never bring up the subject again. Having listened to stories of Violeta for years by then, that promise of silence appealed to me almost more than the prospect of the visit itself.

Violeta, it turned out, didn't accept just anyone as a client, and I had to be introduced to her over the telephone before she agreed to see me. While we were driving over to Violeta's house in Little Havana for the birthday session, I kept thinking that Vivian and I should both have our Florida Bar cards torn into little pieces. At the very least we should have lobbied to have our tuition money reimbursed, because obviously we hadn't learned much in law school. As practicing attorneys, we were trained in facts and logic; now, here we were consulting a psychic about our lives. Even the most practical and hard-nosed Cubans harbor a healthy amount of superstition within us, I knew, and respect anyone who claimed to be able to foretell the future. I thought I was the exception who proved the rule— until I met Violeta.

I was hooked right away. We had walked in, Vivian had told her that my first name was Margarita and that I was a friend. That was it. From there Violeta had talked about my childhood, about my family, about my career concerns, all in a totally convincing fashion. It was as though she knew me long before I came to her. I may have been put off at first by her appearance—my mental image of a psychic didn't involve a woman in her mid-sixties with a too-tight perm in a lavender leisure suit and little white sneakers. But her eyes were kind and soft, and her voice was mesmerizing. Soon I thought of her more as a spiritual adviser than a psychic, more a wise and trusted friend than a fortune-teller.

Violeta lived in a three-bedroom house in a middle-class section of Hialeah. Nothing about her or her home advertised her profession. Sessions were conducted in a sunny, tiled room in the back of the house. It was decorated with the usual smattering of Santeria saints, along with bowls filled with water, coins, apples, and lots of lit candles everywhere. There were a couple of statues of the Virgin, and a huge, impossible-to-miss oil painting of a Native American chief hung in the middle of the wall behind the spot where Violeta always sat. I hadn't yet mustered the courage to ask who he was, and why he was hanging in such a position of prominence. During sessions, Violeta sat in her rocking chair three or four feet from me, her eyes closed as she searched for visions. She would open her eyes only when she had information to impart, or to ask me a question if she needed clarification about something she was seeing.

While I drove on the causeway from Miami Beach for my latest appointment with Violeta, I was filled with gratitude for the police having raised the speed limit on that stretch of road from forty to fifty. I needed to see Violeta as soon as possible, and getting stopped by the cops for speeding would surely spoil my frame of mind. Besides, the Courvoisier from the night before hadn't done its job; instead of falling into a deep, dreamless sleep, I'd spent a fitful night and woken up with a low-grade hangover.

Ariel, thankfully, hadn't recommended his tried-and-true remedy for sleeplessness, which was to make love repeatedly until sheer exhaustion made us both fall asleep. He probably assumed that I was still upset from seeing my mother, and that she had surely voiced her opinion again that I should leave my job permanently and have another baby. He was in total agreement with Mamá, of course, but he also knew that he had nothing to gain by bringing up such a hot-button issue between a mother and her daughter. Ariel was wise and intuitive. But he was surely wrong about what was bothering me the night before.

I could hardly wait to see Violeta. I needed spiritual counsel, not to mention the sense of serenity that normally came over me after I had visited her. In the last twenty-four hours, the life I thought I was living had been thrown into turmoil. I needed to find out why.

And I hoped I could deal with the answer.

"Margarita, *mi amor*," Violeta called out to me as soon as I opened the car door. She was standing, waiting, under the portico of her house. *"Bienvenida!"* she said as she walked slowly to me. The psychic didn't drive, and didn't own a car, so there were always places to park on the easement right in front of her house. That spared me time circling the block looking for a space large enough to accommodate my huge car. I could see that Violeta had been pottering around her garden, because she was carrying a straw basket filled with pink, red, and white roses. In her other hand was a menacing pair of oversize clippers.

I locked the Escalade, pressed the button on the keychain to activate the alarm, and sprinted up the walk to kiss her. Violeta took a good, long look at me and shook her head.

"M'hija, my daughter, you are troubled. It's good that you're here." She carefully placed the clippers in the basket along with the roses and led me toward her house. "Come."

I meekly followed her inside, already feeling more peaceful. Violeta could calm me in an instant. I also knew that I could unburden myself to her without her being judgmental. There weren't too many people in my life whom I could say that about.

Violeta led me to the back room, pausing only to set down her flower basket on a table by the front door. She closed the door behind us and settled into her rocking chair, closing her eyes. I put my purse in the usual place on a stand by the door, sat down, and waited quietly for her to speak. During my first visit I had put my purse on the floor, which Violeta considered bad luck and which she swiftly corrected.

Her chair squeaked quietly as she began to rock back and forth. It might be a while before she spoke, I knew. Sometimes it took longer than others. I was bursting with impatience, though, and it felt like it was taking Violeta forever to get into the mood. I looked around the room, knowing there was nothing to do to hurry the process along. If I fidgeted too much, I would earn a lecture on patience.

Finally, Violeta stopped rocking and opened her eyes.

"You are very troubled, Margarita," she said. "But it's not the usual preoccupations that bring you here today."

We both knew what she was talking about: my job, the pressures from Ariel and my family, and the big decision that was looming over my life. She closed her eyes again, but opened them quickly this time.

"I see Ariel hovering around you," she said. Then she frowned. "But he's not the only one. Ariel is fading away. Now there is another man around you."

"That's why I'm here," I said in a miserable tone of voice. "Because of the other man."

Violeta looked puzzled. "Margarita, you've come to see me many times without ever mentioning this other man. And I have never seen him anywhere near you."

For the first time, Violeta seemed positively annoyed. She clearly didn't like being blindsided by me or by the spirits.

"That's because this man—his name is Luther—was an important part of my life years ago," I explained, somewhat apologetically. I certainly didn't want to incur the wrath of Violeta or her spirits.

I hadn't failed to notice that Violeta had immediately picked up on Luther. But, at the same time, she had failed to warn me about his reappearance in my life. I had been to see Violeta just a couple of weeks before my old lover arrived in Miami.

Once, during an early session, Violeta had warned me to avoid a black-haired Salvadoran named Melchor, who was going to bring a lot of trouble to the law firm. I was astonished when a man matching that description turned out to be a computer technician who put a virus in our computer network and deleted most of our files. I almost fainted when our office manager told me who had caused such havoc in our firm. I didn't say anything to my partners about what Violeta had told me—they might have respected my inside connection to the world of spirits, but they also would have quickly removed my name from the letterhead.

It was troubling that Violeta hadn't warned me about Luther. He had been watching me for years, he said. So why hadn't Violeta picked up on it?

My life was on the verge of unraveling. I realized how much I counted on Violeta for support, advice, and for her vision. All of a sudden I felt alone and without support. *Dios mio.* I knew that no one was infallible, but I had somehow thought Violeta came close.

She closed her eyes. "He is a good man, this Luther. He loves you very much." She opened her eyes, stared hard at me. "And you love him, too."

"But I'm married to Ariel," I said, hearing the despair in my voice. "And I love him, too."

"*Sí*, I understand, Margarita," Violeta said. "But the time will come soon when you will have to make a choice."

She rocked softly, peacefully. I remembered all the times I had held Marti in my arms, rocking him to sleep. Cubans all love rocking chairs. Maybe it reminds us of the repetitive, rocking motion of the ocean and the movement of waves as they hit the shore.

"What should I do?" I asked her. "Please, counsel me."

I knew that she wouldn't tell me what to do. She never did. But she could point out my choices, and which ones I would do well to avoid.

Violeta was silent for a moment, her eyes staring into the distance. Then she nodded, as though someone had said something to her.

"This is a decision only you can make, Margarita," she said. She tapped the sides of her chair as she rocked. "Tell me about this man. Why is he so important to you that you should be in such a state?"

How to begin to explain Luther?

I remembered the feeling that came over me when I saw him on the first day of classes at Duke. It was at the ungodly hour of eight in the morning, when all the first-year law students gathered for a presentation to mark the beginning of orientation. In order to wake myself up, I'd consumed an entire batch from the six-cup Cuban coffeemaker I brought with me from Miami. My heart was beating loudly in my ears, a sure sign that I was seriously wired. It had seemed like a great idea at the time, but when I got to school it felt as though I might have overdone it. I walked from the parking lot to the law school, trying to remember if I had ever heard of anyone overdosing on Cuban coffee.

We were all congregated in the main reception area prior to being split into two groups. The first-year class was small, only about two hundred men and women, and it wasn't hard to give the crowd a quick scan to see who I was going to be dealing with for the next three years.

I noticed Luther right away. He was standing in a corner, his body language completely at ease, his blue eyes taking everything in. His expression was quizzical, and slightly amused. He was the only person I saw who seemed to belong there.

We were all issued identification tags with our names and undergraduate schools. I maneuvered closer and learned Luther's name, along with the fact that he had gone to Dartmouth. I was disappointed when we weren't assigned to the same group, but later that day, after lunch, we landed in the same twenty-student campus tour.

I didn't want Luther to know that the very sight of him made my knees quake, so I adopted a time-honored strategy: I behaved like a complete ice queen toward him. We shared three classes, and in those first weeks I barely acknowledged his existence. All the while, my attraction to him was growing. I hadn't felt such a crush since Mariano Arango, my sophomore year at Penn. That had been understandable, since Mariano was an Argentinian polo player; the fact that he was also insufferably conceited took me a while to figure out. Luther, on the other hand, was an American, a quintessential WASP. And he seemed to be unaware that I was alive. It didn't exactly seem like a recipe for romantic success.

My friend Lola was in a study group with Luther, and she asked me to join. I refused, knowing that I would surely flunk out of school if I tried to get anything done in close proximity to him. It was getting ridiculous. As it was, I was starting to have a hard time sitting in the same classroom with him. It wasn't easy to listen to an aged professor drone on about contracts while constantly struggling not to look across the room to where Luther sat.

Another month went by and, to my complete amazement, Luther called me one day to invite me to dinner. There was no way to convey to Violeta the nervousness and apprehension I felt before that date. The day before, I got my period early. It seemed a catastrophe, and I knew my skin would break out and my body would bloat. Then I calmed myself by remembering that I was no longer in the seventh grade, and that guys couldn't tell when girls were having their period, and that they knew periods existed and weren't repulsed by the very idea. I was so anxiety-ridden that I actually took a diuretic, just to make sure my ankles didn't swell up. Mamá would have been proud of me.

We female law students were supposed to be above such trifling concerns as our appearance but, as far as I was concerned, a woman was still a woman, even if she was sitting on the Supreme Court. Even now, years later, my heart still beats faster when I remember Luther standing in the doorway of my apartment that night, his blue shirt making his blue eyes jump out at me with the color of a wintertime lake reflecting the sky above. He seemed like a man totally at peace with himself, presenting himself to the world exactly as he was. It was up to others to take him or leave him, it seemed, and he would be perfectly content either way.

In hindsight, it was probably a blessing that I had my period for our first date—otherwise, I probably would have jumped into bed with him right after dessert. I was hyperventilating in the car just from being so close to him, and by the time we arrived at the restaurant I was in need of CPR. I cursed the fact that my female condition had effectively rendered me out of commission, but I remember thinking that God works in mysterious ways. Once a Catholic, always a Catholic.

I didn't volunteer all these details to Violeta; I didn't want to change her opinion of me as a sensible, self-assured woman. But now, closing my eyes, I saw the mess I made of my bedroom that night before the date. I had pulled out and tried on everything I owned in the hour before Luther picked me up, critically examining each outfit before discarding it in an ever-growing heap. Finally I decided that nothing I owned was suitable and hopped in my car for a frenzied trip to one of the trendy boutiques in Chapel Hill. I was a woman on a mission, in search of the perfect outfit for a date with a hot guy, and nothing would get in my way. I prayed that Violeta's psychic abilities wouldn't give her a window on my behavior that day.

I forced myself to return to the present, and to my scaled-down description of the role that Luther once played in my life.

"Me quita el hipo," I said simply.

No further explanation was necessary. Any Spanish-speaking person understands the significance of something that made such a strong impression that it "scared the hiccups out of me."

Violeta nodded. "And now years have passed, and he has come back into your life. What effect does he have on you now?"

I didn't have to think before replying. "The same."

Violeta rocked with her eyes closed. "And Ariel. Tell me how you feel about him now."

Violeta knew all about Ariel, how we had met and the details of our life together. But she wasn't asking me about the past. She wanted to know how Luther's reappearance in my life was affecting my relationship with my husband. Because, obviously, it had. Nothing I said to Violeta was legally protected—even in freewheeling, loosey-goosey Florida, consultations with psychics aren't considered privileged—but I knew I could tell her anything with total confidence that she would keep it to herself.

I had been able to talk about Luther without thinking, but now I had to take a moment to consider Violeta's question. I could see by a slowing in her rocking that my hesitation hadn't gone unnoticed. Violeta saw meaning in everything, and she interpreted the slightest reaction as revealing.

"No me quita el hipo," I said sadly.

Violeta just rocked.

 After I said good-bye to Violeta I walked down the path to my car, looking at my watch. I had spent almost two hours with the psychic, a definite record. I was exhausted, and felt as though every bit of strength had been drained from my body. Normally I felt refreshed and rejuvenated after seeing Violeta, like I did after a long, restful sleep. Today, though, I felt disoriented, light-headed. It reminded me of how I used to feel sometimes at noon, during high Mass, when I had to sit for hours in a hot, stuffy, overcrowded church without anything in my stomach.

Once in my car, with the air conditioner running, I got out my cell phone and checked for messages. Although I was numb from everything I'd told Violeta, checking my phone was such a ritual that I did it without thinking. On the screen, I saw that there were three calls from Vivian. Three calls from anyone else would have panicked me, but it was perfectly in character for Vivian and her ADD personality. I was still reeling from the Violeta session, and not ready to deal with Vivian's mania. If it was a really important matter, there would have been twelve calls instead of just three.

I didn't want Violeta to see me sitting immobilized in my parked car in front of her house, so I started the motor and drove off toward the 826, the Palmetto Expressway, the first leg of my journey home. Just before I got on the ramp, though, I pulled over to the side of the road. I really didn't feel steady enough to drive and, God knows, there were enough spaced-out drivers in Miami without my adding to the number.

Even though the air-conditioning was on full-blast, I was sweating. My nerves were on edge, and I needed to relax. So I did something I hadn't done in a while: I unbuckled my seat belt, reached over to the glove compartment, and started rummaging around until I found the pack of Marlboros I stashed in there for emergencies. My current situation had reached the point at which a crisis cigarette was in order.

Before I lit up, I lowered the car window and tilted the seat as far back as it would go. I turned up the volume on the Gloria Estefan CD that had been playing softly. Then, as prepared as possible, I took out a cigarette and rolled it between my thumb and forefinger for a while. It was stale, as I feared, but it would have to do. I probably could have used a couple of tokes on a joint, but I was so unused to smoking anything that a couple of puffs on a Marlboro would be almost as satisfying.

I lay there listening to the music and trying to blow smoke rings. I wished I could stay in the car forever, never getting out, never having to make any of the decisions facing me. Up until a couple of days before, I had thought I was in a quandry about whether to stay at the firm or have another baby. Now that situation seemed perfectly manageable in comparison to Luther's appearance in my life. Now I was seriously contemplating whether to stay with Ariel, or start a new life with my old lover. My session with Violeta, if nothing else, had clarified that choice.

Looking at the cigarette, I tried to wish it into becoming weed. I never indulged in drugs in any serious fashion, but I enjoyed the feeling of a light buzz. My first year at Penn I had smoked a little too much grass, which had scared me and made me back away from it. Now I smoked sometimes with Vivian and Anabel, not enough to get wasted but enough to get giggly. In a way we were reliving our youth, when we used to get high on hot summer nights at the Venetian pool in Coral Gables. Even at thirty-five, the smell of weed makes me think of those nights—kind of like an illicit madeleine.

A song had just finished when my cell phone rang out from the passenger seat. The sound of "Jingle Bells" startled me so much that I almost dropped the lit cigarette in my lap. I picked it up and saw Vivian's office number displayed on the screen. Well, she had probably saved me from my own thoughts. I sighed and pressed the "receive" button.

"Hello, Vivian."

"*Chica!* Where the hell have you been?" Vivian shrieked. I had to move the phone a couple of inches from my ear. "I've called you three times already. Your phone was turned off."

"I went to see Violeta," I explained, dragging on the Marlboro. "That's why I turned the phone off. Right now I'm parked right by the entrance ramp on to 826."

Vivian paused. "Are you smoking?" she asked.

I chuckled nervously, which of course Violeta took for an affirmative. I could never hide anything from her.

"Oh, God, Margarita," Vivian said sadly. "If you need to see Violeta, and then smoke a cigarette afterward, that's bad enough. But the worst part is that you're sitting in a parked car by the expressway. Are you okay? Do you need me?"

Her voice raised an octave as she spoke. As close as we were, the last thing I needed was for Vivian to come and play Cuban Dr. Ruth. I knew I should change the subject from her proposed mission of mercy.

"What's going on that you needed to reach me?" I asked. I knew that getting Vivian to talk about herself was always a good offensive move.

"I can't tell you over the phone," she said, lowering her voice. "That's why I was calling. I need to set up a time and place for me, you, and Anabel to meet."

It was totally unlike Vivian to keep any kind of secret. I hoped that she didn't want to get together to deliver bad news.

"Have you talked to Anabel?" I asked.

"Yes. I reached her right away." I could tell Vivian was having a hard time keeping herself from chastising me for not being available to her twenty-four–seven. "She has a meeting all afternoon, but she's available tomorrow for lunch. Is that good for you?"

"Sure. Sounds fine." I didn't have my planner with me, so I had no idea whether I had anything planned the next day at lunchtime. But I was willing to reschedule just about anything, just to hear what Vivian needed to say only in person. I couldn't remember a time she had ever kept anything from me.

"Listen, Margarita, are you sure you're all right?" Vivian asked. "It's not exactly normal to park by an expressway. Especially the Palmetto."

I knew why she was worried. The Palmetto was an eight-lane expressway that bisected Miami east to west—the kind of highway that required nerves of steel and more than a little recklessness to drive on. It was full of speeding trucks with their overloaded rigs waving dangerously side to side, canvas tarps flapping wildly in the wind behind them. Motorists either drove so slow as to constitute a safety hazard, or else they raced thirty miles over the posted limit. There was no such thing as normal driving on the Palmetto—it was kill or be killed. The road was cracked, full of potholes and debris, but the Department of Transportation had apparently decided long ago that the situation was hopeless, and gave up on fixing it. The Palmetto made L.A.'s 405, or Boston's Storrow Drive, seem relaxing and leisurely by comparison.

"I'm okay," I said unconvincingly. "I just had an intense session with Violeta, and I need to get my head together before I drive anywhere. I'm going straight home now, really."

"Call me if you need anything," Vivian said. "Promise?"

"Yes, mother," I said before we both hung up. I was dying to know what Vivian was being so close-mouthed about, but I was also glad we were meeting tomorrow and not later that day. I had something planned that didn't involve my friends.

The night before, I had made up my mind that it was time to pass by my firm and just sort of check in. I was still officially on a leave of absence, and I wasn't expected to visit on any regular schedule. But it had been more than two weeks since I'd gone into the halls of Weber, Miranda, Blanco, et al., and I knew that I should show my face.

I also needed distraction from the Luther situation, to ground myself in something familiar. I reminded myself that I *did* have a life before he called me up: a husband, a son, a fulfilling career. I couldn't figure out why Luther was threatening all that. I supposed it was possible that I wasn't as happy as I thought. I couldn't tell whether what I felt for Luther was real, feelings long buried by circumstances, or just some kind of bizarre early midlife crisis. The more I thought about it, the less I knew. It was flattering to hear everything that Luther said to me, but Ariel had said all the same things many times before. And I knew that it was impossible to keep the same level of intensity in a marriage that had existed in the beginning.

I knew a lot of things. I also knew that Luther and I had unfinished business between us. Our relationship hadn't run its course, I understood that now. Our lives had kept us apart, not our feelings for each other. He had gone back to his WASP life, and I had immersed myself in the life of a Miami Cuban exile. We had each sought our roots. It might have been what we both really wanted, but it might have just been the easiest road to take.

Luther and I had never really fought to stay together and make our relationship a success. It had been too easy to say that the differences in our backgrounds would keep it from working. Looking back on how things ended for us, I saw that we were both scared to be the one who tried hardest.

I married Ariel, a fellow Cuban American who didn't share my social class or background—it might sound shallow, but it was the truth—in part because of our shared ethnicity. I couldn't deny that Ariel's being Cuban was a major factor in my picking him as a mate. After seven years of living in the north away from my roots, I was looking for a man who saw the world as I did, who understood the tragedy of the exile experience and who would know what Cuba meant to me. The fact that he was intelligent, attractive, and ambitious hadn't hurt his chances, either. He was everything I wanted. And he openly cherished me.

So why was I considering getting involved with Luther? I was taught in law school to think a certain way, to analyze every situation from different angles. Luther had been back in my life for less than a week, and I had devoted an inordinate amount of time to thinking about him. The lawyer inside me couldn't help but think about how many billable hours I'd racked up.

I was, if anything, more amazed now by Luther's declaration than I had been when he made it. I thought I knew him pretty well, and I never thought he was capable of such passionate feeling, and that he'd had the patience to wait for the right opportunity to speak with me. And as for his learning Spanish, I still remembered how he would struggle in French restaurants ordering dinner, so I knew how much time and effort he must have spent learning a new language. He had proved to me that he had meticulously planned his proposal, and that he wasn't treating my feelings lightly.

Apart from holding hands at the Dinner Key Marina, we hadn't had any physical contact. I knew I might have been unfaithful to Ariel in my thoughts, but so far I hadn't broken anything that couldn't be fixed. But it wouldn't be long before Ariel realized that something deeper than a spat with my mother was making me distant and preoccupied. He was too perceptive not to figure out that something seriously wrong was between us.

Even with all the years that had passed, thinking of the sex life I had once enjoyed with Luther was enough to make me blush. I don't think there was a centimeter of his body that I hadn't explored, and vice versa.

I got on the expressway, shaking my head. What a mess.

 Ashley Gutierrez, my firm's receptionist, spotted me and shrieked out my name in her earsplitting, high-pitched little girl's voice. I took a quick, instinctive look around as I stepped out of the elevator, hoping there were no clients around to hear her very unprofessional greeting. Mercifully, we were alone, which was a blessing because a moment later she enveloped me in an aggressive bear hug.

One might think from her first name that Ashley was an American, but the truth was that she was a Cuban from Hialeah. It wasn't uncommon for first-generation Cubans to give their children American names, hoping it would help their offspring assimilate into their new country as easily and quickly as possible. Really, though, those names rarely went well with Spanish surnames. I knew a Samantha Perez, a Tiffany Gonzalez, a Sean Gomez, and a Zack Ramirez. Sometimes intermarriage resulted in Anglo first names paired with Spanish last names. The results, to my mind at least, were often hilarious.

Pamela Anderson was Ashley's role model in life, and it showed. She resembled nothing more than a Cuban version of the former *Baywatch* temptress. Her hair was died a shocking blond, and she liked to wear it gathered on top of her head and accented with multicolored glass barrettes. Long tight curls cascaded down to the middle of her back. It was a hairstyle not often seen since the seventies. Someone seemed to have told Ashley that her black eyes looked best with smoky-colored eye shadow, so to accentuate them she applied makeup from her eyelashes up to her eyebrows. She ringed her eyes in midnight black liner and, to make sure everyone got the point, heavily coated her lashes with mascara. To balance out her eyes, Ashley wore crimson lipstick applied so heavily that her teeth almost always sported traces of red.

A firm believer in manicures and pedicures, Ashley often sneaked out to the nail salon in the basement of our building for frequent touch-ups of her two-inch-long fingernails. It was hard to type, operate the switchboard, or accomplish any of the tasks associated with being a receptionist with those beauties on the ends of her hands, and as a result she was a pretty haphazard worker. But as time passed we all got used to her ways, and by and large we saw nothing unusual in employing a receptionist who couldn't type, answer the phone, or even effectively sign for packages. She had taught the FedEx, UPS, and DHL couriers to forge her signature so she wouldn't have to risk chipping her nails on such a mundane task.

Ashley was tiny in stature, but her breast implants were so big it was rumored that she'd had to pay extra to her plastic surgeon, who balked at their size and grumbled about losing his license. She was so proud of her breasts that she made sure everyone could see them in all their glory. Her outfits seemed strategically designed to show as much cleavage and nipple-through-fabric as possible. Her breasts were so big that she was always tipped forward by their weight, making total exposure a constant possibility. Her miniskirts were so small that I wondered whether she was on a crusade to conserve the world's supply of fabric. And, as everyone in the office knew from watching her bend over, she wore Victoria's Secret panties exclusively.

But she was a good young woman. Personally, I had liked her from the moment we met, and I took her appearance and drama-queen tendencies in stride. Her peculiar ways never seemed to adversely affect the firm in any way. I think outsiders viewed Ashley with curiosity, as though our firm was flaunting its success by showing it could even employ someone like Ashley and still thrive. One of my favorite thrills upon arriving at work each morning was seeing what Ashley was wearing.

Ashley had been our receptionist for three years. She hadn't exactly applied for the job: In fact, she was working off her husband's legal bills. One of my partners, Miguel Blanco, represented Ashley's husband Freddy, the owner of a chain of stores called Saints-R-Us, on an arson case. Miguel lost the case, which was no surprise to anyone. His real job was to minimize the punishment Freddy Gutierrez would receive for his actions. It was no secret that Freddy wasn't the brightest bulb on the marquee, and it was obvious that he had torched six of his stores because they were hemorrhaging money. He had never been much of a businessman, but even Freddy should have known better than to open up stores selling Santeria relics and objects of voodoo worship in white, upper-middle-class neighborhoods. As if the fact that all six stores were torched by the same method within a two-hour period wasn't enough to raise suspicion, Freddy had applied for the insurance money while firefighters were still trying to douse the flames in six separate locations. The partners had agreed that Miguel had an uphill climb, and that the case was a surefire loser. Still, as long as Freddy footed the hefty bills, no one minded.

At the conclusion of the case, Freddy revealed a particularly unpleasant surprise: He'd had to liquidate the last of his possessions to pay off gambling debts, and he had no money to pay the final installment of his massive legal fees. Freddy figured he'd rather deal with us than his bookie, who apparently said that it would be no problem exacting revenge even if Freddy was in jail. To mollify us, Freddy offered the good-faith gesture of the services of his wife. We had no choice. Anyway, as someone pointed out, her breast implants alone were worth thousands. Freddy was going to be a guest of the State of Florida for the foreseeable future, so we had no choice but to accept his offer of a discount receptionist. We at the firm are nothing if not realistic.

Mauricio, our accountant, projected that, based on what a receptionist in our office earned, it would take Ashley about seventy-five years working in our firm to pay off the debt. When Miguel told Freddy, Freddy replied: "Well, she can start tomorrow. Time's a wasting."

Our only other option was to eat the bill, so we took on Ashley Gutierrez as our receptionist. We arranged to pay her a nominal salary—I mean, we weren't completely heartless—and she had health insurance and benefits. Still, I had no idea how she got by. Her husband was incarcerated and, unless he was pardoned by the president, he was going to stay that way for many years. Still, Ashley maintained a consistently cheery disposition. As far as I knew, she hadn't been involved with any other men since Freddy was sent to prison, although I'm sure there was no shortage of potential suitors. There was something about those astonishing breasts that invited curiosity.

Ashley called out my name a second time and hugged me so tight her rock-hard breasts nearly knocked the wind out of me. My instinct for self-preservation made me jump back. Ashley must have been in a *Beverly Hillbillies* mood that day—she looked like a Latina interpretation of Ellie Mae in her denim hot pants topped by scraps of lace dangerously masquerading as a blouse. We were standing a couple of feet apart, but I was still smothered in her perfume. I hated to be catty, but it smelled like Eau de Swamp.

"Ashley, how are you?" I asked. It was hard to be put off for long by someone so genuine and friendly. "Great outfit. Very Appalachian."

"Thanks, Margarita," Ashley frowned. "But it's not a designer outfit. I put it together myself."

I felt a little ashamed of myself for being so thoughtless. Being witty with Ashley always went over her head, and anything I said could be misinterpreted. I had been away from the office for ten months, and it showed. Already I felt out of sync.

Next to Ashley I felt positively matronly in my khaki skirt, white T-shirt, and black cotton blazer. I used to wear conservative suits before I made partner, or dresses with jackets or sweaters, but after I felt secure I relaxed a little and experimented with different looks. I still remembered the liberating day in August a few years before when I decided to stop wearing stockings altogether. The firm didn't have a dress code, but there were unwritten rules that everyone was expected to follow. The men wore dark suits, both in summer and winter, but they took off their jackets and loosened their ties as the day wore on. Nonattorney men dressed more casually, in pants, button-down shirts, and ties. As for the women, there was a marked difference in how the attorneys and support staff dressed. The lawyers were expected to wear suits or dresses with jackets, stockings, and heels. The staff had a lot more latitude. In the years that I'd been with the firm, no female attorney had ever showed up for work in pants, or simply a skirt and blouse, but the staff could do so. The rules were bent out of shape for Ashley, of course. She could wear whatever she wanted, as long as she wasn't naked.

I was the only female partner at Weber, Miranda, and I set the precedent for what was sartorially acceptable—although I knew enough to tread lightly about making any major alterations in what was conventionally acceptable. I tested the waters by chucking my stockings, and experienced no major repercussions. I was biding my time before the next step—going without a jacket on the days when I wasn't meeting with a client. I didn't want to show up in a sweat suit, but I liked to be comfortable.

No matter what anyone said about sexual equality, the playing field wasn't level in the legal community, and I had to watch my step carefully in everything I did. I always worried about my actions backfiring, and doors closing without explanation. I was a full partner in my firm, but I was a woman who practiced immigration law. I was a low-priority player, and not in a position of real power. I wasn't a high-visibility rainmaker. My position might have seemed secure, but I was always aware of its limits.

Weber, Miranda still adhered to the principles of the old boys' network—all it took was one look at the office layout to know that was true. Our offices occupied the top three floors of the First Dade Corporation building, with the twelve partners and their personal secretaries on the penthouse floor. The offices of the other attorneys and their secretaries—which they shared—were on the floor beneath. Support staff, clerks, bookkeepers, and paralegals were on the lowest floor. All three stories were connected by spiral staircases, but no one visited the other floors much unless they had specific business. No one went up to the penthouse floor unless specifically invited by one of the partners. Until I was made partner, my office was on the middle floor. I had been a lot more at home there, and felt a lot more camaraderie than I did with the partners. But there was no choice—when you're made partner, you come upstairs.

I moved past the cloud of Ashley's perfume in the reception area with a smile and a wave. My worries about my professional life were a welcome distraction from thinking about Luther every waking moment. Even the feel of my shoes on the padded carpet transported me to a major part of my life that I had recently forgotten. Now that I was back, I needed to think about whether I was going to stay there. Working part time wasn't an option. My choice was plain: quit, or resume working the same grueling hours as everyone else at the firm. Weber, Miranda didn't believe in of counsel positions, or any halfhearted solutions. In the life of the firm, five partners had either died or retired; as soon as they did, their names were removed from the letterhead. Sentiment didn't carry much weight at a powerful law firm. If you didn't heap up billable hours, then you weren't a player. Death was no excuse for failing to generate revenue. It was a tough philosophy, but one that I knew about and accepted before I joined the firm as an associate after law school.

I knew that I was living under a microscope. Once there were other female partners in the firm—whenever that happened—the old male partners would get used to them, and the climate would change. But for now, I was the only one. I had to be purer than Caesar's wife. And, although partners were ostensibly permitted a year's leave of absence from the firm, no one had ever used the time before for personal reasons—those who had taken leave had gone into some government post, or taught at a university somewhere for a year. I was the first to take leave to be with my family, and I had held out as long as I possibly could before filling out the paperwork for the year off.

Now, after about ten months, I saw that I was no longer as much a force in the firm as I had once been. Everyone knew that I was a mother and, partner or not, they suspected that at some point I would be derailed from becoming managing partner. I was on the mommy track, the road to powerlessness and oblivion. Taking leave had done nothing but solidify this impression.

If I left the firm, I knew, the chances of another woman being made partner would be set back for years. The firm had been around for sixty years, and no male partner had ever left his job for personal reasons. The excuse sounded wimpy even to me—it was as though I couldn't deal with my life outside the office, and needed to drop my responsibilities in order to cope. It was called real time, and everyone knew what it meant: billable hours, the bottom-line reality that affected everyone in the firm.

I really did feel a sense of responsibility about the sort of legacy I would leave at the firm if I did, in fact, resign. I knew that my partners viewed me as a living example of their keeping up with the times, and ostensibly abolishing the glass ceiling that had traditionally kept women from climbing to the top in law firms and other high-powered businesses. If I quit, they would feel less pressure to make another woman partner. They would be off the hook, able to point to me as an example of how they had tried to cultivate a female partner only to see her resign to stay home with her kids.

The phone rang, and Ashley scampered back to her desk. I knew I had unnerved her a little bit by trying to walk across the reception area without saying a word. I had a lot on my mind, but Ashley wasn't used to being ignored; she gave me a little wave as she pressed the speaker-phone button with a pencil, her usual means of answering calls. I heard the pencil clacking on the phone and hoped she was successful in patching the call through—her usual success rate was about fifty percent.

The reception area was truly beautiful, with floor-to-ceiling glass walls and a view of Biscayne Bay and Key Biscayne to the east, and Coconut Grove and Coral Gables to the south. The only furniture were two dark brown leather couches separated by a simple square-cut glass table bearing an always-fresh arrangement of tropical flowers. The lighting came from hidden, strategically placed high hats in the ceiling. It had taken a lot of billable hours to make such a room.

But it was for guests, not me. I took a deep breath.

I walked to the big wooden door that led to the partners' offices, then punched in my four-digit access code on the pad next to the door. I heard a soft click, and realized that I was relieved my code still worked.

I was in my office in seconds. I closed the door behind me. I was in my second home—although sometimes in the past it had felt like my first, with all the time I spent there. The thing was, I had liked it. And I had missed it.

 There was a big pile of papers and mail on my desk, but I paused in the middle of the room. I had to reacquaint myself with the place. After a couple of weeks away, it was almost as though I had never seen my office before.

It wasn't an overwhelmingly feminine space, but any astute observer would figure out quickly that it was a woman's office. Instead of hanging pictures or prints on the walls, I had opted for framed charts of Cuba and the waters around it. On the west wall was a big square map of Havana, my favorite. I had learned the hard way that trees didn't flourish in my office—either because of sharing breathing space with a lawyer, or because I had drowned them with too much water and fertilizer. So I had wrangled funds from a friend in the accounting department and invested in four tall, artificial royal palm trees to place in each corner of the room. The trees looked pretty real in the soft light—so much that more than one visitor had asked how I managed to keep them looking so healthy indoors. So many palms had died on me in the past that I didn't even go near them in garden stores. I was convinced that my very presence caused them to wither and die.

Accounting had granted me a budget to furnish the office, and I had bought an antique wooden desk, a credenza, and a dark-green-leather chair. For a while I haunted auction houses on the weekends, and I found two sleek, tall polished-silver lamps with sea-foam-green linen shades for my desk. I also spotted a silver upright lamp, then found a shade that matched the others, so all three seemed like a set. Across from my desk I placed two oversize, too-comfortable arm-chairs I'd had upholstered in a green-and-white checked pattern. It took a while, but I had gotten the office where I wanted it—comfortable, but formal and professional, the kind of place where I could get work done and feel at home. It might have seemed excessive to spend so much energy and money furnishing an office, but it wasn't when I considered how much time I spent there. I also had to make sure the room projected the image of a serious player—in the testosterone-drenched environment of the partners' floor, little signals meant a lot.

My eyes finally landed on the huge pile of documents awaiting me. I had put my purse down on my chair when my cell phone rang. I looked at its screen and saw that it was Luther. What timing. I let it ring twice more before answering.

"Daisy, it's so good to hear your voice," Luther said. "I hope I'm not interrupting anything. I just needed to know how you're doing."

"You're not interrupting anything," I said. Then, without even thinking, I added, "I wanted to hear your voice, too."

"Really?" Luther asked, every bit the eager schoolboy. I felt a smile cross my lips and my heart beating fast. I might as well have been back in junior high.

"I'm at the office, I just got here," I said, starting to unconsciously sort through the mail and files on my desk. "I've got a truly frightening pile of work to catch up on."

"So you're downtown," Luther said. "I'm at the office, too. You know, I'm only a couple of blocks away. Want to get together?"

I looked at my watch. Two o'clock. I had planned to spend at least two hours in the office, opening mail, visiting with the staff, checking in with my partners.

That was what I had planned to do.

"Sure," I said, grabbing my purse.

We agreed to meet for a late lunch at Bice, an Italian restaurant in the Grand Bay Hotel, in a half hour. I knew it was a place that Ariel would never patronize—he seldom went out for lunch, unless one of his clients insisted, and then he only went to the Cuban place across the street from his office. To him, spending an hour or two on lunch was a waste of time, an indulgence eating up billable hours. Unless, of course, he could add the time to the client's bill.

I walked to the door, thinking that I was just going out for an hour or so, and that I could come back after lunch. I knew, though, that this was probably an unlikely scenario. In Cuban Miami, there was no such thing as a one-hour lunch—Ariel excepted.

I had just started to turn the knob when there was a familiar soft knocking on the door. I sighed, realizing that this wasn't going to be a quick, clean getaway. The door opened, and I knew I was going to be late to lunch with Luther.

"Maria," I said with a smile, thinking up some story to tell my secretary about why I had to leave.

Maria and I got along very well and, perhaps most important, we really liked each other—which wasn't always the case in the pressure-filled atmosphere of a high-powered law firm. We worked well together and respected one another, and under normal circumstances I would have been happy to spend time with her. But this wasn't an ordinary day, as I knew that Maria would be perplexed by my leaving right after I arrived.

She called me at home every couple of days, asking when I was next planning to come to the office. There were a lot of matters that needed my attention, she said. I knew that Maria was perfectly capable of taking care of some of my business on her own, or by consulting with one of the other attorneys or paralegals. The majority of my case work, though, required my personal attention. Judging from the pile on my desk, she had made sure she was ready for me.

Maria was a wife and a mother herself, so she outwardly understood and supported my leave of absence. We had never really talked about it, but she knew that I took the leave because the number of hours I had been working had stretched me close to the breaking point. She also knew that, as a Latina woman, I had to work longer and harder than my partners. I had the added pressure of being a wife and mother, though, while the male partners all had stay-at-home wives who organized their lives and took care of their children. I didn't resent this disparity—it was the price of admission for playing in the big leagues—but it took a toll on me. I knew that pioneers always paid a price for their accomplishments, and as a woman and a Latina I had double pressure to be a model minority. The inescapable reality, though, was that in order to preserve my marriage and health—and to see Marti during the daylight hours—I had needed time away.

Maria was a mother hen, always cautioning me to take care of myself and worrying about me. As much as she supported my decision to take a leave, though, I knew she was inwardly worried about her standing in the firm. Because I was a woman, and because I practiced immigration law, I was perceived as lowest in the hierarchy of partners. Now there was a possibility that she could become a lame duck because of my actions. She knew she wouldn't be fired, but if I left the firm she would probably be sent back down to the second-floor secretarial pool. Maria was in her late fifties, a few years from retirement, and after spending the last twenty years at the firm she wanted to go out on top—as personal secretary to a partner, and not just one of the dozen or so secretaries on the floor below.

We had never talked about it, but it was clear that Maria's future at Weber, Miranda was in my hands, therefore that she had a big stake in what I decided to do. Although I had no obligation to come into the office, she prodded me to do so. We had worked together long enough for me to know exactly how her mind worked.

Needless to say, Maria was Cuban.

Maria had figured that she should find a way to produce billable hours despite the fact that her boss was on official leave—if she continued to generate income for the firm, then the partners might recognize her value. Whenever I had showed up at the office during my leave, she'd had work all laid out for me, so I could zip through case files in record time. Then, after I left, she cleaned up the mess, billing out cases and writing up invoices until the next time I returned. I had to approve the bills she sent out and, although I would never admit it, I wasn't really sure that the hours she billed correctly reflected the amount of time I had worked. As long as the quality of work was high, my partners never asked questions. And, since the clients never complained, I wasn't about to bring up the subject.

"I heard you were here!" Maria said with true zeal, kissing me quickly on the cheek then pushing past me to get to the desk. She had a foot-high stack of files pressed against her chest.

"Thank God you came in today," she panted. "There's so much work we need to do!"

Maria knew of my arrival at the firm within moments. Word traveled fast. Ashley was the only person I had encountered on the way in, but I was sure she had risked her acrylics sending out an e-mail alerting everyone to my presence. I groaned inwardly when I saw Maria busily opening several files and efficiently arranging them on my desk.

"You're looking great, Maria," I said, trying to soften her up for the coming blow with an innocent fib. Maria looked the same as ever, in a dark blue shirtwaist dress, black pumps, and her chin-length salt-and-pepper hair pulled back off her face in a severe style. Maria always wore two pairs of glasses, both hanging from gold chains that inevitably got tangled—one pair was for reading, the other for distance. I figured that wearing bifocals was a white flag to the aging process that she wasn't willing to wave.

Her back to me, Maria waved off my compliment. She was busy with the files, which had spread out to cover all the space on my desk.

"Okay, Margarita, I've arranged the files in a certain order," she announced. "This way you can get through them as quickly and efficiently as possible."

She waved her hand from left to right. "These are urgent, these are important, these are necessary but no rush." She indicated the last, highest pile. "These you can take home with you. I've marked the relevant pages with Post-its, which should make it easier for you."

Maria had never before prepared files for me to take home, but I decided not to point it out.

I was still standing close to the door, my purse over my shoulder. Maria must have figured that, having just arrived, I hadn't had time to put it down yet. This made what I had to tell her even more difficult.

"Maria, thanks for doing all this," I said. "You've done a terrific job. It's really amazing."

I looked over the neatly stacked documents on my desk with open admiration. Maria's organizational skills were legendary, but this time she had outdone herself. If she kept it up, I wouldn't even be needed—an alarming thought.

"Here." Maria took out a document from the top of the urgent file. She started to explain what it was when I stopped her. Still standing by the door, I spoke as gently as I could.

"I can't look at that right now," I said. "I have to go out for a couple of hours."

A stricken look came over her face. "You're leaving now?" she said, sputtering. "But there's so much that needs to be done!"

"I'm sorry," I said, reaching for the door. "I'll try to come back as soon as I can."

Maria pointed at the clock on the wall. "It's just after two now," she pointed out. "So you'll be back by four o'clock?"

God, being around lawyers had certainly rubbed off on her.

"Yes," I confirmed. "I'll be back by then."

I left an openly angry and disappointed Maria standing in my office, and guiltily walked out to the reception area. Maria knew that I wasn't leaving for a family crisis—I would have explained that to her. Now she would speculate, and none of her explanations for my rapid disappearance would prove very flattering to me.

Ashley wasn't at her desk, so I was spared having to say anything to her as I headed for the elevator. No doubt a second e-mail would get out, alerting everyone to the fact that I had gone already. I pressed the button for the elevator and realized that my involvement with Luther was screwing up my professional as well as my personal life. Two weeks ago, nothing short of a calamity could have pulled me away from working on the files that Maria had meticulously laid out on my desk.

I didn't know what the hell was happening to me.

 I sat in my car in the driveway of the Grand Bay
Hotel, waiting my turn with the valet, and ner-
vously checked my watch—about ten times in just
a few minutes. I felt the muscles in my jaw tight-
ening as I watched the seconds tick by on the watch face. I was already fifteen minutes late for lunch with Luther, and I counted three
cars ahead of me. It looked like I was going to be even later.

Usually there were several valets on duty at the Grand Bay, but
on this day naturally there was only one young man tending to the
entire line of cars. I tapped away on the steering wheel and cursed
under my breath about his leisurely pace. Everything he did—handing out tickets, moving the cars—seemed to be taking much longer
than it needed to. Finally, after an eternity, it was my turn to hand
over the Escalade. I sprang out of the car so fast that the valet's eyes
popped in wonder. He probably thought I was a sprinter in the
Senior Olympics.

Inside the lobby I rushed past the arrangement of beautiful flowers in an enormous Chinese vase, past the front desk. I decided not
to wait for one of the four elevators, and instead rushed up the stairs
two at a time to the mezzanine level where Bice was located.

Luther was waiting at the bar, just outside the restaurant, but instead of fuming over being kept waiting he was comfortable perched on a bar stool. I had been desperately worried about making him angry with me, I realized, but he was calmly talking on his cell phone and writing something down on a pad of paper. It was clear that Luther was completely immersed in his conversation—but even as he nodded and jotted down notes, his body and manner remained relaxed and at ease. Luther was a year older than me, but still at thirty-six he retained an athlete's natural grace; even though he was wearing a suit he seemed obviously fit, toned, ready for any challenge. He was more physically attractive now than when he was in law school. Back then, he always wore baggy clothes and seemed rangy, lanky almost. Now he seemed to have fully grown into his body.

All his life, Luther had loved playing squash, and he was even captain of his team at Dartmouth. I remembered how, at Duke, his opponents would invariably underestimate his abilities when they challenged him to games. They may have heard how good he was, and they may have even seen him play before, but few believed he was capable of being a fierce competitor. He gave off such a relaxed and laid-back impression that, when he won, it seemed a fluke rather than the consequence of his talent and abilities. Still, many times we had gone out to dinner with the money he won off one of the suckers who thought they could beat him.

I could tell that Luther was about to conclude his conversation when I approached him. I admired the way he was dressed, in his navy-blue suit, white shirt with French cuffs and gold cuff links discreetly peeking out from under the sleeves of his suit, and a wine-red tie. He gave off an aura of power and self-assurance. I timed my arrival perfectly, because he clicked off his call just as I slid onto the bar stool next to him.

"Daisy," Luther kissed my cheek. "You look wonderful."

In one graceful move, he stood up to look me over. My slight embarrassment over my casual outfit vanished, and I felt as though I was decked out in Chanel. Luther's blue eyes ran over my face and my body, giving me such a feeling of intimacy that I felt a rush of blood to my cheeks.

"Thanks," I said, reduced to monosyllables. "You, too."

And, God help me, he really did. I was glad I was sitting down, because otherwise my knees might have started knocking. He was making me feel like a moderately popular schoolgirl who couldn't get over the fact that the quarterback of the football team had invited her to the senior prom.

"Shall we?" And, without waiting for an answer, he took my elbow, guided me off the bar stool, and led me to the dining room. I was very aware of how close he was to me; if I were wearing high heels, I probably would have tottered on them.

Even at this late afternoon hour the restaurant was still quite full, with only a couple of empty tables. Luther and I waited at the maître d's podium to be seated, and I scanned the place to see if anyone I knew was at a table. Mercifully, I didn't recognize any of the other patrons, so I might be spared a potentially uncomfortable encounter. We were led to a row of booths in the center of the dining room, and seated at one of the most coveted tables—at the corner, by the terrace. With great ceremony, the maître d' pulled out the table; I slid onto the light-yellow leather banquette. Luther took the seat directly across from me.

The maître d' handed us each a menu, then the wine list to Luther. He glanced at it and immediately ordered. The man knew his way around a wine list, I thought, when I saw the self-assured way he told the waiter his selection. It was certainly a development since the Gallo jug-wine days in law school.

We were brought bread while we waited for the wine to arrive. The decor at Bice was sleek and sophisticated, yet managed to somehow be warm and welcoming—kind of an upscale trattoria. I had been there half a dozen times, and enjoyed it more with each visit. It reminded me of Italian ambience with faintly Japanese undertones. My favorite part of the design was the floor—alternating planks of smooth, highly polished two-toned ash and dark woods. The lighting was soft, and the cream-colored tablecloths were soothing. On the center of each table was placed a single, perfectly formed, aromatic rose in a vase.

A bottle of Banfi Chianti Classico was brought to our table and, just like at Nemo's, Luther waved the waiter away after he had opened it. The waiter's expression as he listed the specials broadcast the fact that he didn't like being summarily dismissed before he completed the wine ritual. To make amends I ordered two specials: the appetizer—mussels—and red snapper with roasted fennel as a main course. The waiter's spirits lifted visibly. Luther chose a goat-cheese salad, followed by the veal chop Milanese.

Just before he hurried off with our orders, the waiter paused.

"I must inform you," he said with great gravity. "The chocolate soufflé takes more than fifteen minutes to prepare. Please take this into consideration if you wish to order it."

"Thank you," Luther and I said, nodding with such solemnity that anyone watching would have thought we were listening to a decision being handed down by the Supreme Court.

Finally we were alone. Other than a few words at the bar, we hadn't spoken to each other. During our years together, Luther and I had never lacked for conversation. But things were different now.

Luther obviously sensed the awkwardness between us and, like me, he didn't know how to break the suddenly heavy silence. He busied himself pouring a little more wine into each of our glasses, offering a shy smile. I picked up the basket of bread and offered it to him. Nodding, Luther accepted one of the thickly cut slices. I looked around for something else to do and, without asking, poured a healthy dollop of olive oil onto his butter plate. Then I helped myself to a packet of Grissini and placed it on my bread plate. I made opening it up much more difficult than it really was, carefully taking out the thin bread sticks one by one and aligning them side by side. I was tempted to dip the ends of the sticks into the pad of butter on my plate, but thought better of it. Awkwardness or not, I didn't want to add more calories to my meal than absolutely necessary.

I looked up. Luther was staring at me.

"Daisy, this is ridiculous," he said. "We've always been able to talk. I'm still me, you're still you."

I was so relieved that I began to laugh out loud. Cubans don't generally do very well with silence.

"You're right," I agreed. "Let's start over."

We got into a discussion of the case that had brought Luther down to Miami. We never stopped talking, even when the waiter brought us the food. And we ordered the chocolate soufflé, which brought a smile to our waiter's lips. I was glad not to have dipped my Grissini in butter.

Then, during the espresso, we finally got personal. My blood chilled.

"I meant what I said about wanting you to be with me," Luther said, folding his napkin. "I love you. I know how hard this is, but I love you. I always have and I always will."

He reached across and took my hand, pressing it gently. I was surprised by how warm it was. I looked around nervously, half afraid to see Ariel emerge from some hiding place.

"I believe you, Luther. But I have a life now." Then I uttered the words that I knew would jolt us both back to hard reality. "A husband. A child."

My words hit their mark; Luther jerked back a few inches, as if he had been slapped by an invisible hand. It took him about ten full seconds to compose himself.

"I know I'm running the risk of completely alienating you forever," he said. "But I am going to point out a fact of life to you. Obvious as it may be, it might have escaped your notice."

My heart beat faster. Somehow I knew what he was going to say, and I didn't want to hear it. I sipped my espresso as if nothing was happening.

"If you were absolutely happy and fulfilled with your life, you never would have met me at Nemo's."

I started to talk, but he held up his hand to silence my protestations. He knew my counter-argument in advance.

"You can tell me you met me out of sheer curiosity," he said. "Because you wanted to see how I was, how I turned out, if I had lost my hair or gotten fat. You wanted to see if I'd gotten married—all the things that normal people wonder about their former lovers."

I felt trepidation about where this was going, but I allowed myself a small smile.

"I was wondering about all those things," I said. "And you passed with flying colors."

"Thanks," Luther said, but he was obviously not going to be side-tracked by my compliment. "But one time was enough to satisfy your curiosity. Then you met me again. I know you, Daisy. You don't take anything lightly, you don't make any move without considering the consequences. In your whole life, you've never gone into a situation without knowing what you were doing."

Until now, I thought.

"All right," I said. "But this is more than a legal argument, Luther. I'm confused. I can't make a decision yet."

The strange thing was that everything felt right when I was with Luther: I had no overriding guilt, or feelings that I was betraying everything I held dear. It was like stepping into another dimension. My instincts told me to propose we get a room upstairs at the Grand Bay Hotel, but I held back from crossing that line. I could attribute some of my lustful urge to the wine I'd just drunk, but not all of it.

Luther dug into his pocket and produced a small manila envelope. He slid it across the table to me.

"It's for you," he said. "There's a key ring inside with two keys—one is to get into the building, the other is for my apartment door. There's a slip of paper with the address and the security code. There's underground parking. All you have to do is come see me. It's as simple as that."

Simple. That's the last word I would have used to describe the implications of Luther's little parcel. I looked down at the envelope as though it was going to rise up and bite me.

"Luther, I don't know."

"No pressure," Luther said calmly. "I just want you to have these in case you decide you want to be with me."

I still hadn't picked up the envelope. "I can't promise you anything," I told him.

"I know that, Daisy," Luther said. "I can't deny that I want to make love to you, but I know I have to wait for you. I had that in mind when I made these keys for you, but I figured that, if nothing else, they would allow us to meet in less public places."

I picked up the envelope slowly, feeling my life change, then put it in the zipper compartment of my purse. I couldn't shake off the sensation that some kind of bargain had just been sealed.

"No pressure, huh?" I said, lamely trying to joke.

I closed my purse. Now we both knew there was no going back. It was just a matter of when.

 I wasn't a genius at introspection. In fact, I thought it was a waste of time. If I couldn't understand something about myself or others quickly, then I just left the matter alone until an answer revealed itself. It was Vivian and Anabel, in a moment of high insight, who pointed out to me my greatest fear: That I would become as self-absorbed as my mother. Maybe that was why I shied away from contemplating my life, and why I prided myself on being a doer rather than a thinker.

I didn't make it back to the office after lunch with Luther. There was no point, I was too preoccupied by what had happened at Bice. Dealing with Maria and pressing matters at the office was too much to contemplate. I would have to return to Weber, Miranda another day. Still, I remembered wincing at Maria's tone of righteous indignation when I called her from my cell phone and confirmed her worst fear—that I wasn't coming back as promised.

Instead, I went straight home after leaving Luther and played with Marti for the balance of the afternoon. I needed to get grounded in my real life and real responsibilities. Marti had been gleefully surprised when, upon arriving home, I invited him for a romp in the pool. We didn't actually get into the water until late afternoon and the sun had started to weaken. There wasn't a sunblock strong enough to fend off the afternoon summertime Miami sunshine.

I was tempted to tan a bit, to add some color to my skin, but I didn't give in to the idea. Only the tourists are tanned in Miami; the residents know how harmful the sun is, and avoid it as much as possible. I have olive coloring and probably could withstand some sun without turning into a withered old lady, but my mother had for decades instilled the fear of God in me about spending a single moment unprotected in the sun. My gynecologist once startled me during an examination by observing that I was his only patient with no discernible tan lines whatsoever. Mamá would have been proud.

Splashing around in the pool, I realized that too much time had passed since I'd last played with Marti. I knew that I took care of his needs, and I made play dates with his little friends. I made sure he ate right, got enough sleep, and saw the pediatrician when he was supposed to. But I had neglected to spend time with him one-on-one, playing the games that he liked to play.

I turned my head to keep from being splashed in the face: For about the fiftieth time, I caught Marti as he dove from the side of the pool into my arms. It had been just over ten months since I'd worked, and gradually in that time I had filled my days until I spent a couple of hours at most with my son. If I wasn't with Vivian and Anabel I was with a family member, or checking out antique stores or art galleries, or going in to the office. It was amazing how busy I could be without working. The time away from the firm had gone by in a flash, and now I was feeling like I had little to show for it. I had taken a leave to spend more time with my family, but lately it had felt as though I was simply developing a new lifestyle. I was no closer to figuring out whether or not to go back to work, and Luther had come into my life and made me face some pretty unpalatable truths.

It wasn't easy to make big life decisions while playing Marco Polo with a three-year-old boy, so I decided to put them off. Thankfully, Marti was beginning to slow down, and his splashes and thrashes grew a little less maniacal. I figured it was time for a break, so I swam over to one of the brightly colored plastic floats we kept by the side of the pool. I put it in the water, and heaved Marti on top of it. He must have been exhausted, because he just lay there with his eyes closed, not putting up a fight as he usually did. Looking at his face, I was struck again by his resemblance to Ariel. If anyone ever doubted Marti's paternity, they could just place father and son side by side—that would be enough to make anyone throw out the DNA test.

Ariel came home and found us lying on chaise longues, wrapped up in huge beach towels and staring up at the sky, laughing as we identified the clouds as different animal shapes. The game was going to end soon, because the sun was beginning to set; soon it would be dusk, and the clouds would disappear.

As soon as he saw us, Ariel dropped his briefcase and, apparently not too worried that his fancy British suit would get wet, slid onto Marti's chaise and joined in the game. A few tigers and several elephants later, it was clear that Ariel was even better than Marti and me at spotting the animals in the sky. I must have still had some Chianti from lunch in my system because I couldn't stop giggling.

Lying there, happy with my husband and son, I asked myself why I was even contemplating starting an affair with Luther. It was strange. When I was with Luther, it seemed that everything was right with him. Now that I was with Ariel and Marti, I couldn't imagine risking my happy family life.

After a while it was too dark to see much of anything, so Ariel and I took Marti inside. Ariel retreated to the den to watch the news, and I carried Marti to the bathroom for his bath. After a long soak in a tub filled with Mr. Bubble—the only way I could get him to bathe without protesting—Marti was so relaxed that he was about to fall asleep from sheer exhaustion. I dried him by rubbing him with a towel until his skin turned pink, then sprinkled some baby powder on him and dressed him in pajamas that Jacinta had laid out on his bed.

There was a short window of opportunity left for feeding Marti something before he fell completely asleep, and it was rapidly closing. I carried him into the kitchen and put him in his booster seat. Before he passed out, I managed to get him to eat some of the spaghetti that Jacinta had made for him. Then I put him to bed and said his prayers over him—he was too sleepy to join in—then leaned over and kissed him good night. My eyes welled with tears as I held his soft, sweet-smelling, warm body close to mine.

I went to my bedroom and took a quick shower to wash off the chlorine from the pool, then dressed in a pair of chinos and a black T-shirt. I found Ariel happy in his favorite leather armchair, sipping scotch and watching the evening news. There were splotches of pool water on his shirt from when he laid on the chaise longue next to Marti. He looked tired, but he also looked like a man at peace with himself and his world.

Before guilt consumed and paralyzed me, I perched on his armchair. Ariel pressed the mute button on the remote control.

"A glass of wine?" he asked, getting up, confident that I would accept his offer. On his way to the bar he hugged me and kissed my lips.

"Great," I said.

"God, Margarita, you look like a teenager," Ariel said in an admiring tone. He stepped back to admire me more closely. "Look at you. No makeup, wet hair, pants, and a T-shirt. And you look like a young girl."

"Thanks." I laughed. "I like it when you don't wear your glasses."

Ariel walked over to the wet bar and opened the small Sub-Zero refrigerator under the counter. He peered inside and reached for the Morgan, a California chardonnay.

"This okay?" he asked, holding up the bottle. He knew it was my favorite.

"Perfect." And it was. Ariel always knew what I was in the mood for. *"Gracias,"* I said as he handed me the glass.

He refreshed his scotch, and we went back to the chairs positioned in front of the TV. By then the news was over, so we switched over to *Law and Order,* our favorite show. We decided to have dinner on trays while watching it, so during a commercial I told Jacinta then settled back in my chair.

"This is nice," I said, almost purring.

Ariel smiled. "You know, not working agrees with you. Playing with Marti, staying home, all that," he said, keeping his voice casual and his eyes on the TV screen. "You look so relaxed and carefree. It makes you seem years younger."

"Does it?" I asked.

I guess he sensed me stiffening. "No, *querida,* don't take it wrong, *por favor.* It's a compliment. I don't mean to pressure you. The decision about going back to work is yours to make, really."

I took a sip of my wine. Why was it, I thought, that both the men in my life pressured me about the biggest decisions, then said that they hadn't? First Luther at Bice, then Ariel at home.

No pressure. Right.

The next morning I set off for the office, making good on a promise to Maria. I had mentioned to Ariel the night before that I would be going in to clear up some paperwork, but I don't think the information had sunk in. He looked completely surprised when I came out to the terrace for breakfast in a cotton dress and high-heeled sandals, holding a jacket over my arm. I was wearing makeup, and had washed and blow-dried my hair. I definitely didn't look as though I was planning to spend the day at home playing with Marti.

To his credit, Ariel refrained from commenting. He kissed me as I sat down at the table. He had already finished, and he read the *Herald* while I sipped my café con leche and buttered my toast. Marti was busy flicking Cheerios at the seagulls milling around our feet. It was the picture of a normal, relaxed family about to start a busy day.

Before I went to sleep last night, lying in the dark, I had made up my mind never to see Luther again. I was taking too much of a risk by having contact with him, and it had to stop.

It wasn't a decision I made lightly, but last night had convinced me that I belonged with my husband and my son. Ariel and I had had dinner, and afterward made love for hours, tenderly and inventively, in a way that we hadn't in a long time. Afterward I lay in bed listening to Ariel breathing quietly next to me.

I still loved him deeply, but I had to be brutally honest with myself: He was not the love of my life. Luther was. And I hadn't realized it until he showed up in Miami.

I've always believed in the romantic idea of one person being the greatest love in an individual's life. And if that person is lucky, and the timing and circumstances work out, then they end up together. But it doesn't always work out, and that doesn't mean fulfillment and happiness can't be found elsewhere. Sometimes getting together with one's true love isn't meant to happen, I don't know why. The same idea probably applies to friends, houses, cars, all the big-ticket items in life. Sometimes things don't work out. That doesn't mean that a woman can't be content.

It was hard to get to sleep that night. I should have been tired, after swimming with Marti and energetically frolicking with his father in bed. It was reassuring to know that, even at thirty-five, Ariel and I could still romp around like a couple of randy teenagers.

After tossing and turning for a while, I had given up on falling asleep and got up, careful not to wake Ariel. I went to the den in my nightgown, opened up the refrigerator, and poured myself a healthy glass of the Morgan that Ariel had opened earlier in the evening. I switched off the alarm, walked out to the terrace, and stretched out on one of the chaise longues where I had played with Marti hours ago.

I felt the night breeze and watched the waves lapping up against the dock, sipping wine until I dozed off without realizing it. The sky was beginning to lighten when I woke up. I gathered up my wineglass and went inside with hopes of taking a brief nap before starting the day. Ariel was sleeping so deeply that he never noticed I was missing.

Although I had only gotten a couple hours of sleep, I felt wide awake at breakfast. Ariel and I left the house together just before eight, headed for Miami. Fifteen minutes later I was pulling into my assigned parking space downtown.

I arrived so early that Ashley wasn't yet at her post in the reception area. I was disappointed to miss her outfit, but I knew I could see it on the way out. At least I had something to look forward to.

Maria arrived just after nine; by then, I had gone through a quarter of the documents she had left on my desk to review. Her look of disbelief when she found me in my office, sitting at my desk hard at work, was something to behold. I knew she doubted I would keep my word and show up in the morning. Years working with her had taught me that Maria was a glass-half-empty kind of thinker. She never gave anyone the benefit of the doubt. I didn't know any of the details, but I suspected that life hadn't been kind to Maria.

By leaving yesterday a few minutes after arriving, I knew I had shaken Maria's faith in me. I was going to have to work hard to get her to trust me again. With that goal in mind, I worked through documents that represented billable hours that Maria could send off to the firm's clients for collection. I knew that would make Maria happy, keep up our visibility in the firm, and maintain a perception that we were valuable and productive.

Maria and I worked without a break for the next two hours, going through about half the stack of work, when my cell phone rang. I held my breath until I saw Vivian's number appear on the screen.

"I called your house, and Jacinta said you'd gone to work," Vivian announced. "You're not back there permanently, are you?" she asked, sounding suspicious.

"*Hola*, Vivian," I said, vaguely remembering that I'd promised to do something with her. "No, I'm not back full time. You know I'd tell you if I was. I'm just here clearing my desk. What's up?"

"You didn't forget about meeting with me and Anabel, did you?" she asked, peeved. "Remember, we talked about it yesterday?"

"No, of course not," I lied. Yesterday seemed like years ago. "Give me the when and where, and I'll be there."

I sensed Maria stiffening with thinly disguised displeasure as she listened to me making plans, realizing that the workday was most likely going to be cut short. She had been in a frenzy deciding which files were most important, and even as I spoke on the phone she was rearranging them and placing them in front of me.

"Anabel said she can meet us at noon at Greenstreets," Vivian informed me. "She's in the Grove this morning, checking up on that project at Cocovillas."

"Fine." I looked at the clock. It was just past eleven. Forty-five minutes until I would have to leave. "Noon at Greensteets."

Having heard my plans and calculated a timetable, Maria started shoving papers in front of me. During the next hour I signed off on so many documents that my hand started hurting, but we finished going through the pile. It was almost noon when I grabbed my jacket from the back of the chair and sprinted out the door with a wave. This time, I didn't make any promises about returning.

 I drove as fast as a teenage boy on the way to a Friday-night date, but I was still almost half an hour late for meeting Vivian and Anabel. I called on the way and placed an order for tuna fish on whole wheat and an iced tea, so my tardiness didn't really delay our lunch. I would have liked a glass of wine instead of tea, but I knew that my drinking had really picked up ever since Luther came to town. Besides, I had drained that glass of Morgan in the middle of the night, so technically I'd already had a drink that day.

Greenstreets was one of the outdoor restaurants—a café, really—in the heart of Coconut Grove, on the corner of Main Highway and Commodore Plaza. Its menu was pretty basic: salads, sandwiches, and omelets. But it was centrally located, and there was parking nearby. Vivian and Anabel were waiting for me inside, because it was far too hot even to contemplate eating in the sun. Outdoor dining in the Miami summertime was strictly for tourists. After a quick glance once I was inside, I saw that my friends had already started their lunches. My tuna fish sandwich and iced tea were waiting in front of an empty chair.

"*Hola,* sorry I'm late," I apologized as I kissed them. "I had a hard time getting out of the office."

"Busy working? Just like old times," Vivian said, rather dryly. For some reason, she was annoyed with me.

Instead of replying, I shrugged and started my sandwich. Vivian wasn't usually so crabby. I hated to invoke her time of the month, but maybe that was what was going on. The three of us concentrated on our lunch; whatever Vivian wanted to talk about would have to wait until we were finished.

Anabel was off in her own world, making serious headway on her omelet; that was a good thing, considering the effect her clothes were having on Vivian and me. I wished Anabel had consulted with someone at home before venturing out that day because her outfit screamed to the world that she was color-blind. She was dressed in a grungy green, like a female Peter Pan on St. Patrick's Day. But none of the shades of green matched, so her pants, T-shirt, and jacket made her look like an urchin who had put together an outfit at Goodwill. The greens clashed violently with her flaming red hair and brilliant blue eyes. I was used to Anabel's sartorial felonies, but I would remember this one for a long time.

Vivian saw me glancing at Anabel and knew exactly what I was thinking.

"I know, Margarita. I already talked to Anabel about her outfit. She's promised never to wear it again," Vivian said, delivering this devastating pronouncement in an icy-cold voice. She could be ruthless about a fashion faux pas, and Anabel's color blindness didn't earn her an exemption.

Vivian was dressed in her latest Armani, a form-fitting, tailored slate-gray suit with color-coordinated purse and shoes. Her blond hair, although real, was streaked through with lighter tones. It was impossible to tell whether it was natural or not. Of course, I knew the truth.

The contrast between the three of us was normally stark, but that day it was even starker. As usual, I was somewhere in the middle, between my two friends. My dress and jacket were nondesigner, but at least they matched. Anabel made me feel like a fashion plate, while I was a frump next to Vivian.

The waiter cleared away our plates, took our coffee orders—three double espressos—and then left us alone. It was time for Vivian to talk.

"You two are my best friends in the world," she said in a halting voice. "That's why I'm telling you this first."

Anabel and I looked at each other. This was a new Vivian, hesitant and unsure of herself. I began to think that she had been so short with us because she was worried and preoccupied with the news she needed to deliver. Was she getting married? Coming out of the closet? Pregnant?

No, not Vivian. She would never stand for pregnancy, losing her figure and suffering stretch marks.

The waiter appeared with our espressos. I could have strangled him because the interruption made Vivian lose her nerve. The three of us sipped our coffees until she was ready.

Suddenly, she blurted out, "I'm adopting a child."

That was a good one. It certainly proved that Vivian never did anything half-assed.

"She's a little girl," Vivian added.

Anabel and I clinked our coffee cups down onto our saucers at the same instant, as though we had rehearsed it. Nothing had prepared us for this news, no warning or premonition.

"Maybe I'm wrong," I said to Vivian. "But I think you just said that you're adopting a baby."

"Not a baby," Vivian corrected me. "A child. A two-year-old little girl."

Vivian reached into her purse and produced a photograph.

"Look," she said, suddenly beaming.

Anabel and I pulled our chairs together and huddled over the picture. Anabel, being nearly blind, had to hold the picture up to her face, which made it hard for me to see. I made out the form of a small child.

"I don't understand." Anabel looked up. "You've never seemed interested in kids, Vivian. I mean, you're great with your nieces and nephews. But adopting a child?"

"You've never talked about this with us!" I cried out, hurt that my friend had gone out and done such a monumental thing without telling me first.

"Okay. I should explain." Vivian held out her hands to calm us down.

Anabel and I nodded, our heads going up and down as though we were bobbing for apples. Vivian was exactly my age, we were born just two months apart. I wondered if she was going through a midlife crisis. First I had thought it was her period, now I suspected early menopause. Maybe that explained why I was going crazy, too.

Of course, I was also sick and tired of having every aspect of a woman's behavior attributed to hormones.

"All three of us are thirty-five," Vivian explained. "Both of you are happily married, with children. Anabel, you have the triplets. Margarita, you have Marti. But my situation is totally different from yours. There's no man on the horizon that I would even consider marrying, much less having children with. And my biological clock isn't ticking anymore—the alarm's gone off."

She took a deep breath. I was amazed by how hard this was for her.

"I've had to do a lot of thinking," Vivian continued. "I decided I don't believe in having a child out of wedlock just to satisfy my own maternal feelings. It just seems selfish to place that kind of burden on a child."

Vivian looked imploringly from me to Anabel. "You know what I mean. No matter how liberated we think we are, none of us could deal with having a child outside of marriage."

I had to agree with her. Regardless of how far we'd come, we were still the product of our shared background. In the Cuban social circles in which we were brought up, unwed motherhood was a huge taboo. Many a Cuban girl had entered into a loveless marriage because her belly was expanding. I knew lots of brides who had to get their wedding dresses let out before they walked down the aisle.

Thinking about it, I couldn't recall any girl or woman in my social circle who decided to have a child on her own. Somehow a husband and father always magically materialized at the critical moment to ensure the child's legitimacy. In some cases, the name on the birth certificate might not have been the biological father's, but the important thing was that the child *had* a father. No one commented if a child had no resemblance to its father, as long as the child had a last name that wasn't its mother's.

I finally got to look at the photograph that Anabel left on the table between us. It was fuzzy, out of focus. All I could make out was a barefoot little girl dressed in a too-big cotton dress, her dark hair chopped unevenly around her face. She was standing in the middle of an unpaved road.

"Here." Vivian took a little magnifying glass out of her purse and handed it to me.

I wondered how many times my friend had looked at this photo. Most women didn't carry a magnifying lens close at hand. I peered closer until I could make out the little girl's features. Her face was delicate, almost doll-like, but her eyes immediately captured me. They were huge, black, and round; even in this poor photograph, they shone with intensity.

"This is her?" I asked, feeling stupid for asking the question. "Your daughter?" I added, as though speaking the word could make the reality settle into my mind.

I thought I saw tears glisten in her eyes, but this was Vivian. Apart from the scene at Caballero Funeral Home a few days past, when she bumped into her married lover and his wife, she hadn't cried since the sixth grade, after her archenemy, Maria de la Concepcion Immaculada, won a prize for best student that Vivian had thought she had in the bag. I wondered if this was a new Vivian, with some of her barriers of protection dropped.

Anabel still seemed shell-shocked, but she was always practical and wanted to know the details.

"So it's official and legal?" she asked.

I knew exactly what Anabel was getting at. We needed to know if this was a done deal before we went any further. If the adoption had already gone through, there was no point bringing up the obvious arguments about Vivian adopting a child on her own.

"The paperwork is finished," Vivian said. "All the little girl needs is a visa from the U.S. Consulate. I've been told it's just going to be a couple of days before she comes to Miami, a week at the most. One of the nuns from the orphanage is bringing her here."

I had to admit, Vivian had a glow about her that I'd never seen before.

"Do you know this child?" I asked. "I mean, you've met her, haven't you?"

I knew about bait-and-switch tricks, when a prospective adoptive parent was shown a picture of a cute, healthy child, only to end up with another one entirely. I had heard horror stories about children adopted from Third World countries, with problems that didn't surface until they reached America, so I was skeptical.

"I've met her twice," Vivian said. Then she told us about the adoption and how it took place. Vivian had heard about the agency that arranged the adoption through her church. She was close to her priest, Father Tomas, and he had been telling the congregation about an orphanage in Honduras and the sad plight of the children living there. Sermon after sermon, he mentioned the poverty, hopelessness, and despair there. He brought pictures to Mass and described the conditions. The little girl Vivian was adopting had lived in the orphanage since her birth—her parents were dead, and she had no known relatives. It was a tragic story. Along with Father Tomas and three other members of the congregation, Vivian had flown to the Honduran capital of Tegucigalpa. When Vivian met the child, she fell in love with her instantly.

Anabel and I listened spellbound. Vivian, who talked over everything with us, my friend who could not keep a secret, had gone to Honduras and back without ever mentioning a word. And, hell, I never knew she had a maternal bone in her body. I don't know how Anabel felt, but I was a little hurt that Vivian hadn't confided in us. I suspected Anabel felt the same. I wondered if Vivian feared we would have disapproved and tried to talk her out of it. We both knew how stubborn Vivian was; how if she wanted to do something, no one and nothing in the world could discourage her from her goal. Throughout her life, that had been both her greatest strength and weakness.

Vivian must have sensed we were not wholeheartedly enthusiastic about her plan. She held up the little girl's picture like a magic totem.

"Look, *chicas*, I know you think I'm nuts to do this," she said. "But I've thought it all out carefully. I'm financially secure enough to be able to take care of a child. I love my house, but I know it's too small, so I talked to my neighbor with the house on El Prado and made an offer to buy the place. I know he's taking advantage of me, and I'm paying too much, but I can't help myself."

Vivian shrugged, as though resigned to the injustices of life.

"I need the space to expand," she added, "because I need to put in an extra room for a live-in nanny. I'm going to need one because, obviously, I'm not going to put her in day care while I'm at work. I'm not bringing her all the way here to do that."

She caught her breath. "The architect is drawing up the plans right now," she added. "Once the city of Miami approves the drawings and the permits, then we'll begin construction. I wish everything could be ready when my daughter arrives, but it can't be helped. I'm making everything happen as fast as I can."

"You've already done all that?" I asked. I was flabbergasted on two fronts: hearing how little I really knew about the intimate details of my friend's life, and hearing her use two words, "my daughter," in a sentence. I couldn't understand how she would casually discuss with us the most intimate details of her affairs with married men, but kept mum about wanting to adopt a child.

"It's a good thing I won the Carrillo case," she said breezily. "Otherwise I wouldn't be able to afford all this. I hope I keep on a roll because I'm going to need the income. I mean, think about it: I'm going to have two extra mouths to feed—and a salary to pay."

Vivian laughed, seemingly carefree about the difficulties she had ahead of her. All I could think about were the layers of secrets in people's lives. Vivian had gone to Honduras, adopted a child out of a Third World orphanage, bought the property behind her house, and drawn up plans to build an addition on it. And I had known nothing about any of this.

But, of course, I was in no position at all to pass judgment on Vivian. I hadn't told my friends anything about the situation with Luther since the first lunch at Nemo's. Probably I didn't want to hear them tell me I was crazy for jeopardizing my life with Ariel and Marti for an old lover from law school. And I feared them judging me, and losing respect.

Vivian and Anabel, I'm sure, would have sworn that they knew everything about my life, but the envelope of keys in the zipper pocket of my purse proved that not to be the case. I looked over at Anabel, wondering what secrets she was keeping.

"What's that look for?" she asked, blinking.

"Nothing," I said. Anabel went back to trying to see the photo of the little girl, holding the magnifying glass right up to her eye, struggling to see what she could.

For all I knew, we were all keeping secrets. Everyone I knew might be keeping secrets.

Anabel put the picture back on the table. I picked it up again.

"Does your daughter have a name yet?" I asked.

Vivian blushed and looked down at the table. "Margarita Anabel. I've decided to name her Margarita Anabel Mendoza."

Now it was our turn to tear up.

[21]

 As soon as lunch was over I left Vivian and Anabel, returning to my car, which I'd parked by one of the meters on Commodore Plaza. I felt drained by what Vivian had told us and the reality of how well she'd hidden her secret from us. I couldn't decide what I thought about her decision to adopt, and I was looking forward to the inevitable debriefing with Anabel. I reminded myself not to judge my friend's actions. It was her life, to live as she wished. And that little Honduran girl was surely going to be better off with Vivian.

I hadn't known about it in advance, but Vivian's decision to become a mother must have been crucial and fundamental; she had decided to share her life with a little girl who had few opportunities otherwise. For that, Vivian deserved praise—not skepticism or criticism. I needed to be respectful and supportive, especially in the beginning. Vivian had been around kids before, but she didn't know what it was like to be a mother. She was in for a rough time. Adjusting one's life to the presence of a child is one of the most difficult things that life offers. At least I had gone through the wars with Marti, and I would be in a position to offer support.

I walked slowly whenever I was thinking of something, almost at a snail's pace, and by the time I reached my car I was sweating in the hot noonday sun. I felt droplets of perspiration rolling down my back. It was so hot and steamy that I could smell the street asphalt melting as I rummaged in my purse for my car keys. The sidewalk under my feet felt sticky, a sensation I remembered from visiting New York in the summertime. My outfit was doing nothing to help me cool off—my jacket and dress stuck to my skin. The air felt alive with heat, and even the slight breeze carried more warmth. It was a feeling that everyone in Miami knew well.

Once I was inside the car I turned the air conditioner on full-blast and aimed all the vents directly at me. I sat back and waited for the car to cool off, and for my internal temperature to return to tolerable levels. I looked back at the restaurant, and realized that the entire journey to my car had been about twenty yards. I had no idea how anyone survived South Florida summers before the advent of air-conditioning.

I closed my eyes for about twenty seconds, then opened them again. The air-conditioning was starting to do its job. It sounded like a jet airplane taking off, but I didn't mind. Now that I was feeling fairly human, I reached for my purse. Without really thinking about what I was doing, I unzipped the side compartment and found the envelope Luther had given me. I upended it and gently shook it until the key ring and folded piece of paper fell into my lap. I unfolded the paper, realizing that I hadn't seen Luther's handwriting in years. I immediately recognized the pointed, stark lines of his script. He hadn't changed at all.

In this age of e-mail and electronic greeting cards, I've often found that I wouldn't recognize close friends' handwriting if my life depended on it. I've gotten so used to typing everything out that my own handwriting had deteriorated to the point of illegibility. Luther was obviously the exception to this trend—his pen was still crisp, clear, and unmistakable.

One style of handwriting that never changes is the script taught by the nuns of the Order of the Sacred Heart. A girl who attended that school is forever identifiable by her even, sloping letters. You can graduate from Catholic school, but part of you never gets out.

I was holding the piece of paper in my hand. With the other, I took the cell phone out of my purse and punched in a now familiar number. It was almost as though I was watching myself perform in a play, acting out a script that had already been written. My flesh was weak, as far as Luther was concerned. My resolve of the night before to stay away from him had dissipated like the early morning mist over Biscayne Bay. And once the mist burns away, I thought, there was nothing left but light and heat.

There was also more to my actions than lust. Listening to Vivian talk about adopting a child, I realized I needed to resolve the situation with Luther. Maybe I was rationalizing, but I admired Vivian for taking a risk. I had never risked anything in my life, no matter what I'd accomplished. When had I ever been true to myself, and damned the consequences? I knew I was going to have to live with myself, but that future was somehow pushed into another category of experience. The future was the future. Now was now.

I felt a lurching sensation. What was I thinking? I was going to have to go home and spend the evening with Ariel.

I shook my head. No, I had to do it.

I had never been unfaithful to Ariel, I'd never even come close. For me, fidelity was a reality of marriage and not a great sacrifice. I never felt as though I had given up anything by marrying Ariel; it had simply been the logical progression of our relationship. I had gained, not lost, by joining my life to his. I had done it happily and willingly, with no hidden agenda or feelings of regret or recrimination.

Ariel's proposal, years ago, had made me think long and hard. Once I decided to accept, I took my vows seriously. I had never once succumbed to the temptation of a passing fling with anyone. I'd seen the pain and damage that infidelity inflicts on a family. I didn't want to be like my father, with an Ofelia in my life, or even a one-night stand. I knew there was no way Luther would agree to being kept a secret for a decade, like my father's mistress. If Papa hadn't had his heart attack, he and Ofelia would probably still be secret lovers, and might have remained that way until one of them died with their secret.

My beliefs and convictions had been clear-cut and straightforward. Now I was listening to the phone ring. Luther picked up. I imagined him recognizing my number on his caller ID screen.

"Daisy," he said. "I was hoping you'd call."

His voice sounded hearty, and he was obviously delighted to hear from me. After our lunch at Bice yesterday, there was no need to pretend I had called just to chat.

"Are you busy right now?" I asked him.

"I'm in the office going through depositions," Luther said. He paused for a moment, thinking. Like any good lawyer, he was pondering the options. "Look, it's nothing I can't take a break from. Why do you ask?"

"I'm . . . I'm taking you up on your offer." I took a labored breath. My heart pounded as though I was running up a steep hill. "That is, if you can meet me soon."

"I'll be there in twenty minutes," Luther said quickly, not giving me time to back off. "Maybe less. I'm leaving the office right now."

I heard noises in the background, papers being shuffled, then a drawer opening and slamming shut.

"I'm already in the Grove, so I'll be there first," I told him. "I'll wait for you." I had the keys to his place, but there was no way I was going into the apartment by myself.

"That's fine," Luther said. He sounded as though he would have agreed to anything I suggested. "We can meet in the parking lot, if that would make you more comfortable."

"See you there." And, without giving him a chance to say anything else, I hung up.

Although I knew perfectly well where his building was, I looked at the paper in my hand again. It seemed to communicate more than an address. I had crossed a bridge the moment I accepted the envelope from Luther. Now I realize we had both known it would only be a matter of time before I acted on the unspoken promise between us.

My soul-searching on the terrace the night before had represented my last vestige of inner resistance.

I didn't need to leave for fifteen minutes—the blink of an eye in the grand scheme of things, but an eternity if spent contemplating adultery for the first time. I started to think of Ariel, then stopped myself. I had made a decision, and I couldn't take Ariel into consideration. I was going to meet Luther, and these errant thoughts weren't going to stop me.

Instead of getting lost in the enormity of what I had decided, I would focus on practical things. I wondered whether I was too sweaty, and tried to remember which underwear I'd put on that morning. It had been close to ten years since I went to bed with Luther. I had gained a few pounds, and had a baby. I knew how sharp Luther's memory was. I hated to think how much I might suffer in comparison to my younger self. And I was on the Pill, so I wouldn't get pregnant, but I hadn't thought about diseases. I knew I was clean, but I knew nothing about Luther's recent sex life. I would need to protect myself, but I didn't want to kill the spark between us.

Going to bed with Luther opened up a dizzying range of questions. In the decade since college and law school, sex had lost its simplicity. We had more money, we had more experience, but our complications and problems had risen in direct proportion to our gains. I started to laugh out loud, alone in my car, at my situation. I was about to go to bed with a lover I hadn't been with in ten years, who might or might not be turned off by my post-childbirth body. I was worried that I might catch a disease and pass it on to my husband. I was sweaty, I might even smell bad, and I was wearing a totally sexless dress and jacket that made me look like a junior executive at a third-tier credit union.

My worst problem, it turned out, was something I could do nothing about, given my time constraints. A quick check of my bra strap reminded me that I was wearing white cotton underwear, a time-honored lust killer. I had a drawer full of beautiful underwear from Wacoal and La Perla, but that morning I had worn underwear that my mother would have sent with me to sleepaway camp. I wondered if, subconsciously, I had been trying to sabotage my lustful feelings for Luther. Maybe so, but it hadn't worked.

All this worrying had actually eaten up a lot of time; as a result, I was in danger of being late to meet Luther. I pulled out of the parking space and wondered if I was even going to enjoy the experience, with all of these thoughts and worries swirling in my head. I had always associated adultery with pain, betrayal, and hurt. It wasn't supposed to be fun.

My heart was beating wildly with anticipation.

 Luther and I arrived at the parking lot of his building at precisely the same moment. I followed him into the drive, where he parked his car in the spot reserved for Apartment 31 East, then I continued on to the visitors' parking spaces and slid the Escalade into a spot closest to the wall.

I got out of the car, locked it, and looked up to see Luther approaching.

"It's good to see you, Daisy," he said as he placed a discreet peck on my cheek.

I nodded in response, incapable of saying anything. Luther was wearing a charcoal suit, a blue shirt, and tasteful striped tie. The parking lot was sweltering and my summertime misery index was rising just from standing there for fifteen awkward seconds. But he looked great, even in the harsh sunshine. He had never looked better.

"Let's go," Luther said, gently taking my arm and leading me toward the building. I followed, relieved to be led, and relaxed a fraction when we entered the air-conditioned comfort of the lobby.

"The elevators are this way, at the end of the hall," he said.

We crossed the minimally furnished lobby and reached the elevator doors, where Luther pushed the button. I looked up at the numbers displayed over each of the doors. They were both in service. We would have to wait.

Luther's building was in the heart of Coconut Grove, a block away from Biscayne Bay near Kennedy Park. I had driven by it countless times but never noticed it, much less been inside. It was relatively small, only six stories high, narrow, and painted green to blend in with its immediate surroundings. I hated to think this way, but Luther's building was ideal for an illicit rendezvous. Though it was set on a small hill it escaped immediate notice because it was set back from the street and hidden by a row of tall and densely planted ficus trees. The building was in central Miami but it gave off a sense of reassuring privacy. It wasn't even possible to enter the property without knowing an access code, and it seemed clear that unwanted visitors weren't at all welcome. Which was just fine with me.

It was hard to tell how old the building was, but it was actually really handsome, with lots of wood and huge windows everywhere that let in lots of light. Everywhere in sight were leaves, branches, and sunshine, as though we were in a treehouse. The only furniture in the lobby was a pair of rattan chairs, a three-seater sofa opposite them, and a low wooden coffee table. It wasn't exactly warm and welcoming, but neither was it austere and unfriendly. No one was around, and I felt a sense that no one would be.

Luther stood by me quietly. Every pore of my body was conscious of his physical presence a couple of feet away. I felt such nervous anticipation that I was transported back to Duke, the night of our first date more than a dozen years before. I hadn't known that an anxious girl still lived inside the grown-up woman.

Finally one of the elevator doors opened. Mercifully, there was no one inside it whose presence we might have to acknowledge. I felt painfully aware of the two of us together, how we would be perceived as a couple. Once inside, Luther pressed the button for the third floor. During the short trip up, we each managed to move to an opposite corner of the elevator, putting as much space as possible between us. We said nothing, and avoided eye contact.

Luther opened his door and stepped aside to let me go in first. I gasped when I walked inside. Nothing had prepared me for what I saw.

It felt as if I was standing in the top of a tall tree. The apartment was in the corner of the building, and the outer walls were all glass and unadorned by curtains. I stared out into heavy green, broken only by golden sun. The windows were all open as far as they could go, which was incredibly rare in Miami. I realized that the apartment faced east, and was cooled by sea breezes coming directly from the bay. I could hear the leaves rustling gently just outside. The air in the apartment was kept circulating by palm-tree ceiling fans that twirled gracefully above.

Whoever the designers of the place had been, they were brilliant. Wall-to-wall sisal carpet covered the floor. Yards and yards of white muslin cloth was generously arranged throughout, draping door-ways, covering rattan couches, tables, and chairs, and suspended from light fixtures. Even the tall palm trees in the corners were par-tially camouflaged with white fabric. It was all remarkable. Luther must have known the first-time impact the place would have on me, because he stayed a few feet behind and let me take it all in. My eyes moved back and forth, finding new details; but I had to admit that all the white gauze made me feel as though I were in the center of a very large merengue. If I didn't dissect things too much, then there was a definite otherworldliness about the place.

"Wow," I said, my voice unintentionally hushed.

"I know," Luther said with a quiet laugh. "Even after years of renting this place, I still haven't gotten used to it. Sometimes I wake up during the night, smell the breeze, and see all this white, and for a second I think I might have died and landed in heaven."

Luther took my hand and led me to one of the sofas. He pushed some muslin aside, and invited me to sit down.

"Something to drink?" he asked.

"Yes. Thanks." I accepted his offer more to buy time than because of thirst. I took off my jacket and put my purse on the floor, stopping to reach inside and turn off my cell phone. I watched Luther walk away to the kitchen and tried taking a few deep breaths to relax myself.

Soon I heard the sound of cupboards being opened and closed. A few moments later Luther returned with a silver tray; on it was an ice bucket with a bottle sticking out of it, along with two flute glasses. He set the tray down carefully on the table in front of the sofa where I was sitting.

"Veuve Clicquot still your favorite?" he asked in perfect Spanish as he sat on the other side of the sofa and got to work. "I took a chance that it still would be."

"*Sí. Gracias,*" I said, touched by his memory. He carefully twisted the cork off the top of the bottle, poured two glasses, and handed one to me.

We touched the tops of our glasses lightly and took a few sips, avoiding looking directly at each other. Noticing that I had discarded my jacket, Luther seemed to realize that he was still wearing his. He stood up and took it off, draping it over the nearest chair.

"Luther, I'm really nervous about this," I blurted out, putting my glass on the table. I felt like I couldn't keep it together much longer.

"Me too, Daisy, me too," Luther confessed. Then his face took on a mischievous look. "And, *querida,* in my case that could be problematic."

It took me about ten seconds to replay what Luther had said, then to figure it out. I started laughing, more from nervousness than anything else, but it was the right thing to do. Luther and I moved together and began kissing, softly first, in an exploratory manner, but then with increased urgency. Luther tasted like Binaca and champagne, a Proustian moment that made me feel as though the years since law school had never happened.

We moved to the bedroom, which was furnished in the same style as the rest of the apartment. Breezes made the white fabric sway and undulate everywhere, billowing and tangling. The bed was huge, an extra-size four-poster, canopied with tons of fabric. Apart from a rattan dresser in the middle of one wall and matching dressers on either side of the bed, the only other item of furniture in the room was a big-screen TV in the corner, situated to face the bed.

Luther had started to unzip my dress when he looked hard into my eyes. "I'm going to put your mind at rest, because I don't want you to feel uncomfortable or embarrassed," he said softly. "I've been tested, and I'm clean. I have no diseases, I'm not going to give you anything. I promise you that. But if it'll make you feel better. I'll still use protection."

"Thanks," I said, filled with relief over the information and not having to ask about it. "And no, I trust you."

Luther finished unzipping my dress, holding my hand so I wouldn't lose my balance as I stepped out of it. I cringed at the sight of my white underwear—one step up from Sparky pants and a training bra, but Luther seemed not to notice. He carefully put my dress on a dresser, then returned and reverently laid me down in bed. He made me feel so special that I almost forgot to suck in my stomach.

There was lots of natural light coming in through the wide windows, but it was indirect and diffused by gauzy fabric, so I began to relax about my body. As though sensing my modesty, Luther turned down the white sheets and slipped me between them. The fabric was so soft, I thought, that the thread count must have been in four figures. Softly, gently, but with the assurance of a practiced hand, Luther turned me over slightly and unhooked my brassiere and slipped off my panties. He covered me up with the top sheet and started to take off his own clothes. This took less time because he let his shirt and pants slip unceremoniously to the floor.

Suddenly we were back at Duke. The awkwardness between us was forgotten, and we made love with no reservation, the way we always had, holding nothing back. But, as much as it was the same, it was also different. I felt a sweetness and affection between us, almost a protectiveness, that had never been there before. It infused our mutual lust and passion with a sense of trust and comfort.

In the beginning, I sensed we were both trying not to show our extensive experience and expertise in lovemaking. It was as though we were trying to appear innocent in each other's eyes, as if we hadn't learned anything from anyone else in the years we'd been apart. But soon we became more open and adventuresome, and our reluctance to show it dropped away. Then the obvious fact that we'd had other lovers in the intervening years added to the sexual energy between us, and made us more sensual than I could ever recall.

Finally, after what seemed like hours, we separated, so hot and sweaty that our bodies made a smacking sound as we broke away. I lay on my back, exhausted, feeling the sweat rolling off my body. It was a sensation I would normally have found unpleasant, but it felt like a just consequence of the past few hours. The breeze from the ceiling fan started to cool me, and I began to dry myself off with the bed sheets. Unfortunately, Luther and I had pretty much soaked through them, and it was hard work trying to find anything dry on the bed.

I faced the window and looked outside, seeing that the sun was no longer shining brightly. I spoke for the first time since we entered the room.

"Luther, I have to go now." I saw his disappointed expression. "It's getting late. I'm sorry."

"You know I don't want you to go, but I understand," Luther replied. "I'm not going to make things difficult for you."

Luther propped himself up on one elbow and gently kissed me. Then he swung his legs over the side of the bed and went to the dresser, where he found my clothes.

"Do you want to take a shower before you go?" he asked.

"No, I think I'll wait until I get home." Despite what we had just done, taking a shower in his place felt like a line that I didn't want to cross. It was more than a little crazy of me. "Thank you, though."

Despite having spent hours exploring each other's body, Luther hadn't yet seen me standing up naked. Although what we had just done could have probably gotten us arrested in some southern states, I wasn't about to walk across the room without my clothes on. Luther might have known every inch of my body lying down, but not standing up. Every woman thirty-five or older who's had children knows about the difference between the two. For now, I was going to make sure Luther saw only the best view of me. I would rather go home smelly, sweaty, and sticky than have Luther watch me parade across his bedroom naked.

I took the clothes from him and, quickly as possible, got dressed. Luther lay in bed, naked and uncovered by sheets. When I was finished, he got up and hugged me tight.

"I love you, Daisy," he said into my ear. "With every breath and every second of the day."

"I know," I told him. "I love you, too."

And I did. God help me. *Ay.*

 As I sprinted out of Luther's apartment toward the elevator, I realized that we had exchanged barely more than a dozen words during the course of the afternoon; for some reason, it hadn't seemed necessary. I waited for the elevator to come, and waited, pressing on the call button again and again as though that was going to make it come faster.

To avoid cracking the plastic button, and to keep myself from going crazy until the elevator came, I took my cell phone out of my purse and checked my voice mail. I was alarmed to see that I'd had four calls, but I relaxed when I played them back. There was one each from Vivian and Anabel, both asking me to call ASAP. I knew what they wanted—they were bursting to talk about the adoption. There was one from Maria at the office, telling me I had to return at once because a new batch of documents had come in that afternoon which required my immediate attention. I knew nothing was that urgent, and that Maria just wanted to send out some more bills. I hoped the call didn't mean that my secretary was insecure about our position in the firm. I knew I was going to have to perform some serious handholding. The final message was from my mother, asking me to call her back, saying she urgently needed to talk. I didn't worry about Mamá using the word "urgent," because if it had really been an emergency I would have had ten calls from her, not to mention from all the relatives she had panicked when she wasn't able to get hold of me right away.

In other words, there was nothing I needed to deal with immediately. In my circle of family, friends, and colleagues, everything was an emergency and all matters required immediate attention. I was so used to such messages that I was able to filter out the true emergencies from routine calls. No one ever said to call back when I had a chance anymore.

I had to laugh as I deleted Mamá's message. As usual, she had prefaced it by saying that she wasn't sure if I would get it because she "didn't know how to use the machine." I've had a cell phone for years, and I've gotten every single message that anyone has ever left me. True, Mamá had reason to doubt the reliability of our messaging system—but that was because sometimes I didn't consider it an emergency to call back to gossip about how my tia Norma's dermatologist had botched her latest round of Botox injections.

The elevator arrived just as I switched off the messages, and I hopped on board and pressed the button for the ground floor. I don't know what explanation or excuse for my presence I would have offered had I run into someone I knew just then. Now that I was leading a double life. I realized I was going to have to be prepared for such eventualities. It didn't matter how big it seemed to an outsider; for me, Miami could be claustrophobically small.

I walked to the visitor's parking area as quickly as I could without drawing attention to myself, got in, started up the car, and drove away. As I headed for the Beach, I concluded that I couldn't go home in this physical and emotional state. I needed to regroup.

A few blocks after exiting the MacArthur Causeway, I stopped off at my regular gas station at Alton Road and Fifteenth Street. I pulled over to the full-service pump and asked the attendant, who recognized me and raced over to help, to fill up the car. The Escalade's tank is so huge it takes forever to fill, so I knew I would have ample time to use the rest room and pull myself together.

I'd used that service station at least a hundred times, but I'd never been inside the ladies' room. From my initial inspection of the place, I hadn't missed much. My bladder felt like it was exploding, though, and I didn't have the luxury of shopping around for better facilities. The bathroom was awkwardly laid out but blessedly ill-lit, so I didn't have to confront myself too closely in the mirror when I was done peeing. I didn't know what I was searching for in the mirror, maybe some kind of instant transformation from wife and mother to adulteress. The days of Hester Prynne were long gone, I reminded myself, and there was no scarlet letter to be sewn on.

The face that stared back at me was the same face I'd worn that morning. Only my eyes darting for clues gave away any sign that something had changed within me. I hoped I would be able to hide my inner agitation, and not show it at home. Standing there in front of the chipped and broken mirror, in a bathroom overrun with cardboard cutout pine trees that were old and smelly, I asked myself what had really changed about me.

In high school, people said that everyone was able to tell when a girl was no longer a virgin. I wondered, superstitiously, if that kind of thing applied to adulteresses. I looked straight into my eyes and told myself to stop thinking idiotic, paranoid thoughts. I was going to drive myself crazy. I was Catholic, but I wasn't about to flog myself for what I'd done, or shave my head, or wear sackcloth and ashes. I had to snap out of this and get on with my life—and, in the process, figure out what my life was. This smelly bathroom wasn't the place to do it.

Now I had to fix myself up as best I could. I splashed some water on my face, then wet one of the brown paper towels that were stacked on top of the toilet. I ran it over my neck, arms, and legs, cringing as the rough paper scraped against my skin. I threw that one away and wet another. I unzipped my dress and wiped my breasts, my belly, between my legs. I cupped some water from the faucet in my hand and rinsed out my mouth, spitting into the sink. Just before I left, I opened my purse and took out the bottle of Chanel No. 5, which I sprayed all over myself and my clothes. It served to mask the putrid pine-cleanser smell that permeated the place, so the next woman to use the bathroom would be spared the Christmas-in-July effect that was slightly nauseating me. There was nothing else I could do with the materials at hand, so I went back outside to retrieve my car.

My timing was perfect; the attendant was screwing on the gas cap. I waited as he cleaned the back window, then I signed the credit card receipt, tipped my usual five dollars, and was on my way.

It was close to six, but the sun was still bright and blinding, forcing me to squint as I drove north on Alton Road. I had to be careful because at that time of day the street was full of pedestrians, bikers, Rollerbladers, skateboarders, dog walkers, and kids on scooters. No one ever paid attention to traffic signs or signals on South Beach, and the last thing I needed was to hit someone. The worst, most dangerous corner was at the intersection of Alton and Lincoln Roads. The new multiplex movie theater built there had sparked a renaissance in the western leg of Lincoln Road, the eight-block South Beach walking mall, and hordes of people flocked the place, particularly on the weekends. For some reason, visitors to South Beach invariably leave their law-abiding ways on the causeway, and jump right into the lawless fray.

That day, I made it through the danger zone without incident. Soon I turned from Alton onto North Bay Road. To my profound relief, I saw that Ariel's car wasn't parked in his slot in the garage. I needed some time before I could be around him—or anyone, for that matter.

I quickly parked the Escalade next to Ariel's empty space, then hurried into the house. Instead of calling out that I was home, which I always did, I rushed straight up to the bedroom, stripped off my clothes, and ran a hot bath with a capful of gardenia oil. While I waited for the bath to fill up, I threw my underwear into the dirty clothes hamper, and my dress and jacket into the shopping bag reserved for clothes bound for the dry cleaner. There was one more preparation I needed to make. Wrapped in a white terry-cloth bathrobe, I went to the den and found a split of champagne chilling in the refrigerator, along with a flute glass.

Walking back to the bathroom, I heard peals of laughter coming from Marti's room; from the sound of it, they were playing hide-and-seek, his favorite. I was tempted to stick my head in and announce my presence, but I decided that I needed to cleanse myself before touching my son. I resolved not to take a long time doing it, because I felt a strong need to be with him. In the bathroom, I opened the champagne and poured myself a glass. I had a flashback to Luther's apartment, and the Veuve Clicquot he had poured for us but which we had pretty much left untouched. I drank one glass and quickly poured another. This glass I placed carefully on the side of the bathtub.

The moment of truth had come. I couldn't avoid it any longer.

Our bathroom walls were all mirrored, and the overhead lights were so bright and focused they could have served an operating room. I could see myself from all angles. One more sip of champagne, and off came the bathrobe.

I looked over every centimeter of my body, as closely as a homicide detective searching a corpse for clues. I found no marks, which was surprising. Luther and I had made love with so much fervor that at times it had verged on roughness. Taking apart my body with a ruthlessness that sort of surprised me, turning this way and that in the mirrors, I decided that my extreme modesty earlier in the day hadn't really been necessary. In spite of my age, and having had a baby, I honestly didn't think this was a body that I needed to hide under sheets. I looked over my skin, saw no telltale marks, and moved on to my face. I looked at myself the way a stranger would.

I rolled my shoulder-length hair into a French twist and secured it with a tortoiseshell comb. My normally light blue eyes seemed a few shades darker, even under the bright light of the bathroom.

Strange. Try as I might, I couldn't find anything outward about myself that had changed. What was inside me was a different story.

Soon I would have to go face the outside world. I wasn't getting any answers from the mirrors, and I knew that whatever I was looking for couldn't be seen. I was going to have to look inside myself, figuring out what I was feeling. *What next,* I thought. *Self-help book, yoga, and vegetarianism?* The very idea was enough to make me shudder.

I finished off the last of the champagne and stepped into the tub. *At least I could cleanse my body,* I thought, as I lowered myself into the steaming, heavily perfumed water. I watched my skin turn from its normal olive tone to a rose color. I immediately felt my muscles relaxing.

I was a Cuban in water, in my element. But water could destroy as well as give life, I reminded myself. What felt the best could also be the most dangerous.

 The telephone ringing woke me up. I groped for it in the dark, groggy, one eye open to look at the clock's lighted dial on my bedside table. Four in the morning. I felt the taste of bile in my mouth. No one ever called with good news at four in the morning.

"Margarita!" I heard Vivian's voice loud in my ear when I picked up. "She's here, Margarita! They just called me!"

I heard Ariel stir next to me and grumble. The only news he wanted at that time of the night was a call notifying him that Fidel Castro had died.

"What the hell's going on?" Ariel mumbled.

"Wait a sec," I said to Vivian as I put the call on hold. I quietly threw off the covers and went into the bathroom. I didn't want to wake up all the way, so I left the lights off. I picked up the extension from the wall and asked, "Vivian, are you all right?"

"Margarita, come on and wake up!" Vivian said, sounding excited and frustrated with me. "I'm talking about the baby, your namesake!"

"The baby . . . the baby arrived?" I asked, having trouble focusing. "At four in the morning?"

Vivian paused for a second. "Look, I don't know the exact time she got here, but I just got a call from Father Tomas telling me I could pick her up now at the parish office."

"Well, what are you going to do?" I asked, part of me dreading the answer I knew I was going to hear. I really didn't want to get involved in this situation, but Vivian was my closest friend, and the fact that she was calling at the ungodly hour of four in the morning meant she really needed my help. I couldn't desert her now.

"Margarita, would you—" Vivian stopped, tentative. "I mean, *could* you—"

"I'll be right over," I sighed. "Just give me a couple of minutes to get dressed."

I hung up the phone, said a few choice curse words in Spanish, and went to the sink to wash my face and brush my teeth. I decided to dispense with a shower because I'd soaked for a half hour in the bathtub yesterday afternoon, and hadn't done anything since to get sweaty or dirty. I headed for the closet to pick out some clothes— blue jeans, a white cotton tailored shirt, and espadrilles. I pulled my hair back into a ponytail, and didn't bother with makeup. It was the middle of the night, for God's sake. Vivian and the little Honduran girl couldn't expect a beauty queen to show up.

Before leaving, I went back into the bedroom to speak with Ariel. "I have to go meet Vivian," I whispered into his ear. "It's an emergency."

"What's the matter?" he asked. "Is she sick?"

"No, nothing like that," I told him. "Her baby arrived."

"Her what?" Ariel asked, beginning to wake up. "I didn't even know that Vivian was pregnant."

I hadn't told Ariel yet about Vivian adopting the child, since I thought it was up to her to set a timetable for making the announcement. She had just told Anabel and me at lunch the day before and, as far as I knew, she hadn't even informed her own family yet. And, knowing Vivian's folks, the *mierda* was going to hit the fan when they found out.

I needn't have worried about Ariel losing sleep, because he was back in slumberland by the time I reached the bedroom door. Even though there was little chance I would wake anyone, I still tiptoed through the house as I headed for the garage. I yawned loudly as I unlocked the car and got in. No wonder I was so tired, I thought, this was the second night in a row that I failed to get a decent night's sleep. I pressed the button for the automatic gate opener and fiddled with the radio dials as I waited for the iron doors to swing out and allow me to head out onto North Bay Road.

I drove toward the mainland, thinking about this strange situation Vivian had allowed herself to get into. I didn't know much about adoption laws, but it seemed strange that a young child would miraculously appear in Miami without the adoptive parent having more notice. I thought that adoptive parents would travel to the child's homeland and travel out of the country with the child. Vivian had said that all the paperwork was completed. I didn't know about family law, but I worked in immigration law—and I knew that visas to the United States were extremely hard to get for Central Americans and, for Hondurans, next to impossible. Maybe it was a special case because the Catholic Church was involved. I tried to calm my fears and hope that Vivian had some idea of what she was getting into.

I had never dealt with a situation in which an American was adopting a child who was simultaneously applying for a visa to enter the country. But then, I thought, the child would become an American citizen as soon as Vivian became her mother. I didn't know the details, and I was a business immigration attorney—my specialty was helping clients with their immigration status in civil matters. I never dealt with children, and this entire situation was out of the scope of my expertise. I tried to force myself to stop worrying.

But I couldn't because Vivian's behavior was so out of character, and because I worried about the strain she was about to put herself under.

Stop it, I told myself. *You can't run Vivian's life.* The way things had been going lately, I could barely run my own.

At that early hour in the morning, there was almost no traffic on the road, so I made good time from the Beach to Coconut Grove. I called Vivian from my cell phone when I was about a minute away from her house. I needn't have worried about her being ready.

"I'm standing outside, waiting for you," she told me.

"I'll be right there," I told her, refraining from pointing out that standing outside alone in the Grove in the middle of the night wasn't the most intelligent thing she could be doing.

Vivian's street was typical of her part of the Grove: The houses were set back from the street, the roads were winding with heavy foliage and limited visibility. In other words, it was perfect for muggings and break-ins, and there were many of each. Vivian's house was in the southern part of the Grove, at the end of a tiny cul-de-sac off El Prado Boulevard. It was minutes from downtown, but it felt so secluded and out of the way that Vivian claimed she felt like she lived in a small town.

True to her word, as soon as I pulled into Vivian's driveway, she emerged from the shadows and jogged over to my car. She had a pink diaper bag slung over her shoulder, and carried a gigantic black and white stuffed panda bear.

"Thank God you're here!" Vivian exclaimed as she threw open the passenger door. "I'm a nervous wreck."

I looked over at her and, although I didn't say anything, I had to agree. For the first time, Vivian looked every one of her thirty-five years. She wore blue jeans, a T-shirt, her hair pulled back and fastened with a barrette, and no makeup. I couldn't remember Vivian ever looking so unkempt and disheveled. I couldn't help but wonder if motherhood had already done that to her. Usually it took a while before the stress and strain of caring for a child affected a woman, but I supposed the nervousness and anticipation of the adoption could have had the same effect.

Thinking about Vivian's appearance, I shook off the unsettling notion that I might have also changed a lot since Marti was born. I remembered the afternoon with Luther the day before, hours of sweet delight that felt as though they had elapsed years ago. What had consumed me hours before had slipped into the past. This was Vivian's moment, after all, and not mine.

I forced myself to concentrate on the moment. "So, what happens now?" I asked as I made a U-turn in her driveway before heading out onto Douglas Road. "Where are we going?"

"Father Tomas called and told me I could pick her up at the rectory," Vivian said. She was so agitated that her words came out in harsh, clipped bursts. "You know where St. Aloysius is, right, Margarita?"

"Uh, yes, I know where it is," I said, holding back my sarcasm. Vivian had enough to deal with.

I felt her fumbling around in the dark, then the crackle of paper followed by a lighter flicking on. "I know, I know, I gave cigarettes up years ago," Vivian explained defensively, inhaling deeply. "But right now I need something to calm me down."

The sweet smell of a Marlboro wafted over me, and I felt an intense craving. Vivian read my mind, and lit one and handed it over.

"Here," she said. "You need one, too."

Did I ever. We drove in silence, each lost in our own thoughts; within minutes we had crossed U.S. 1 and reached the church parking lot. I slowly pulled round to the back, to Father Tomas's rectory residence, and parked directly in front of the door. All the lights were turned on inside the house, and I saw the shapes of people moving around. I felt Vivian tense up next to me as she took the final puffs off her cigarette.

"Do you need me to go inside with you?" I asked her.

Her eyes fixed straight ahead, Vivian didn't answer. She clutched the diaper bag like someone holding on to a life preserver in high seas. I felt for her, but it was also close to dawn. I fantasized about going home for an hour or two of sleep before starting the day.

"Vivian, they know we're here." I saw a woman part the curtains and wave at us. "Really, *chica*, It's time."

"I know." She nodded, but still didn't move.

Vivian's cigarette had burned down to the filter and gave off a sour chemical smell. I took it from her fingers and crushed it in the ashtray, next to mine. Then I put my hand on hers.

"Do you want to change your mind?" I asked quietly. "Do you not want to go through with the adoption?"

I thought it would be helpful to remind Vivian that she could still back out. I could have handled the situation with more tact, but it occurred to me that Vivian had rushed into this.

My words must have had an effect on her. She frowned, shook her head, and flung open the car door. With the diaper bag in hand, Vivian stepped out into the quiet, muggy morning.

"I'll be right back," she said.

She left the panda bear in the car to keep me company.

I listened to the radio for nearly an hour. Dawn had started to break when I saw the rectory door open and Vivian emerge, awkwardly carrying a bundle. I saw that she needed help, so I got out of the car and stepped out to meet my friend.

Vivian moved slowly to the passenger-side door. I opened it and helped her in, placing the diaper bag at her feet. Vivian had arranged a pink blanket around the child, making it impossible to see her face. I made sure they were both comfortable, pulled the seat belt around them, and closed the door. I wished she'd placed the child in Marti's car seat, but at least it was a short drive in light traffic. I came around to my side, got in, and started the motor.

"She's sleeping," Vivian whispered, as though explaining something very important as I put the car in gear. "I don't want to wake her up."

I thought it was a little strange that Vivian didn't want to show me the child, but I kept it to myself. Vivian was as nervous and unsure of herself as I'd ever seen her, and I wanted to give her space during this incredible life-changing moment.

So much for space. Vivian's voice sounded too strange to me. I stopped the car just before pulling out onto the street, and turned to look at her.

Vivian had an odd expression, almost as though she was in shock. She was staring straight ahead, not looking at me. She had claimed to want this child more than anything, and now she acted as though she had received shattering news. It was starting to frighten me.

"What's wrong?" I demanded.

Vivian didn't reply.

I felt a rush of cold fear. Looking around the parking lot, I spotted a secluded corner, away from sight of the rectory, and drove the car there. I stopped, turned off the motor, and turned again to look at Vivian. Something was wrong. Vivian wasn't acting like a woman overjoyed to be reunited with her newly adopted child.

"Vivian, let me look at her," I said. "Now."

Vivian didn't reply, and still stared ahead. I opened up the car door and stepped outside. I began to sweat instantly as I moved around to her side and threw the door open. I reached over my inert friend and unbuckled her seat belt. I turned Vivian around, so she was facing out, and gently unfolded the blanket that was covering the child's face.

It was light enough for me to see clearly. And what I saw threw me into shock as well.

No wonder Vivian had reacted that way. The child sleeping in her arms was not the one in the photograph that Vivian had showed Anabel and me. This girl was very dark-skinned, almost black. She had beautiful, delicate features and very curly jet-black hair cut close to the scalp.

"This is Margarita Anabel?" I asked.

Somehow this explained why the circumstances of the adoption had been so weird. This was why Vivian had been summoned in the middle of the night. Somehow, at some point, another child had been sent.

The sound of my voice jolted Vivian back to reality. She looked down at the innocent child sleeping in her arms, then back up at me.

"Yes," she said, her voice loud. "This is my daughter, Margarita Anabel."

She leaned down and kissed the little girl's forehead.

My fears went away. There was no question that Vivian was already feeling protective, and I instinctively knew that Vivian would never mention or admit the fact that they had switched children on her.

I buckled them back in, closed the door, and went around to my side of the car. We reached her house in minutes, and I helped her inside.

"Should I stay?" I asked her.

"No," Vivian said, her voice a little shaky. "We should . . . I think the two of us should be alone for a while. I'll give you a call."

I put my hand lightly on Vivian's daughter.

"She's beautiful, you know," I said.

"I know she is," Vivian said, turning to go inside. I knew she was too proud to let me see her cry.

I headed toward U.S. 1 and went north, joining the morning commuters on the road. Unlike those who were heading for work or school, I had a very different destination in mind: my bed.

 Ariel had left the door between the bedroom and the bathroom open, and I could see him through a cloud of steam emerging from the shower when I arrived at home.

"I'm back," I called out as I went into the bedroom. I threw my purse on the love seat by the window and collapsed into bed. My body was crying out for sleep, and I intended to listen.

Ariel dried himself a bit and wrapped a towel around his waist; he came to bed and laid down, making himself comfortable next to me. He smelled so nice and clean that I felt a twinge of desire. I wondered what it meant, that I now had a husband and a lover, and that I felt lust for both. It wasn't that I was starved for sex—the day before with Luther had taken care of my appetites until the next leap year. I somehow managed to feel strongly attracted to both the men in my life.

Ariel and I hadn't made love in a couple of days, which was pretty close to a record for us. The night before, I had dreaded the idea that Ariel might want to have sex. Sleeping with both men the same day was too much for me. But Ariel had telephoned from the office and said that he was stuck in a deposition that was going to take a couple more hours. He had called during a break, and didn't have much time to chat. That had been a blessing, as far as I was concerned.

After my bath, I had put on a nightgown, played with Marti, watched a little television, and read a couple of chapters in a detective novel I'd just started. Then I turned off the lights, exhausted physically and mentally. I remembered Ariel trying to wake me up when he got home, and giving up after finding me deeply asleep. I remembered that I could probably have woken up, but chose not to. The next thing I remembered was Vivian calling at four.

This morning was the first time we'd been alone together in a couple of days and, from Ariel's behavior, I could tell he missed me in the carnal sense. He began kissing me, nibbling at my ear, which he knew always worked. We were so experienced with each other that we could skip the preliminaries and move straight to what most turned us on.

"Tell me again what emergency got you out of bed in the middle of the night," Ariel said, pausing between kisses. "What was it, something about Vivian and a baby?"

For a moment, I thought about telling Ariel about the baby switch, but I thought that would be betraying Vivian. I simply relayed what Vivian had told Anabel and me at lunch the day before, then told him about picking up the child at the rectory. Ariel was so intrigued that he stopped trying to get me worked up. He knew Vivian well, and he was astonished that she had decided to become a mother, and in this fashion.

"Vivian really kept this a secret from you and Anabel?" Ariel said, a puzzled expression on his face. "I wonder why."

"I don't know," I told him. "I was a little hurt."

Apparently Ariel decided he'd devoted enough time to trying to figure out Vivian, and he began to stroke me again. When he saw me respond he jumped out of bed.

"Just a second," he said. He went to the bedroom door and locked it. "Just in case."

I nodded in agreement. Now that he was ambulatory. Marti had gotten into the habit of walking into our room first thing in the morning. "Good planning," I said.

It was probably too early for Marti to be up and around, but the last thing we wanted was for him to come into the bedroom and catch his parents in a compromising position. He had almost caught us in the act a few weeks before, which had taught us to be vigilant. Jacinta knew by now that if she heard him struggling with our bedroom door, she should scoop him up and take him elsewhere until his parents emerged.

After he locked the door, Ariel dropped the towel from around his waist and lay on the bed next to me. He took off my shirt and began fumbling with the clasp of my brassiere. No matter how often he tried, or however many different models I wore, he always had problems with bra clasps. I used to tease him about his lack of coordination, and tell him he needed to go back to high school and learn that particular skill.

Ariel then moved on to relieving me of my jeans and panties. Then, lying on top of the sheets, we made love slowly and sweetly. It was reassuring and comforting, feeling the familiar contours of Ariel's body, and afterward we dozed off for a little while in each other's arms.

I lay there, completely satiated, drifting in and out of sleep until my eyes opened wide. I couldn't help comparing what had just happened to my experience with Luther the afternoon before. Then, and now, I had been able to give and receive pleasure with a man I knew and loved. I knew I should be feeling crushing guilt.

But I didn't.

I looked over at Ariel sleeping peacefully next to me, his strong features relaxed in a sexual afterglow. If he had even suspected there was anything amiss between us, he surely would have said something. Ariel was sensitive to me, and he knew whenever I was troubled. But he had said nothing.

If he did see anything clouding my mind, he would think it was the looming decision I had to make soon about returning to work.

It was a subject that he hadn't brought up in a couple of days. But he would. And I knew that I wasn't a good enough actress to maintain my passion and enthusiasm with him without eventually revealing my confusion. I wondered, though, if my passion that morning had somehow been inspired by my experience with Luther. It didn't feel at all strange to make love to two men in a twenty-four-hour period.

I wondered if I was becoming like a Cuban man, compartmentalizing my life and staying one step ahead of guilt feelings. I had been worried about being with Ariel, how I would act and feel, but it melted away.

Before Luther, I could never even conceive of having a lover while married to Ariel. And, at first, I had been deeply uncomfortable even listening to Luther's declarations of love for me. I had felt more guilty before having sex with him than afterward. Maybe I felt that physical fidelity was less important than emotional. I remembered reading about prostitutes who would do anything a client wanted, except for kissing them on the mouth. That they reserved for their boyfriends.

Now, why had *that* come into my mind?

I was becoming too introspective, which I'd always dreaded. I always thought introspection was an indulgence for people with too much time on their hands. Cubans are not, as a general rule, introspective people. We're too busy getting ahead and making money. And having affairs.

Just then, Ariel rolled over, turned to me, and opened his eyes.

"I forgot," he said. "Your mother called early this morning, while you were still out with Vivian."

"Oh, God." I sat straight up. "She left a message on my voice mail yesterday, and I forgot to call her back!"

Ariel chuckled. "Well, I think she suspects something weird is going on. You weren't home at seven A.M., and I left it pretty vague about where you were."

A feeling of dread came over me. My own mother was going to expose me. My own husband didn't suspect that I had been unfaithful to him with an old lover, and yet my mother had immediately picked up something. Cuban mothers!

But before I judged her too harshly, I reminded myself that I was a Cuban mother as well.

"What's so funny?" Ariel asked.

"Oh, nothing," I replied. "What did Mamá want, anyway?"

Ariel sighed deeply, like a diver taking one last breath before diving into the depths.

"She wanted to remind us about the family dinner at your parents' house tonight," he said.

I had completely forgotten. A family dinner. *Mierda.*

I planned to sleep for a few hours after Ariel got out of bed, but that proved to be impossible—I immediately heard him and Marti laughing and joking in the hallway outside. Yawning, I put my clothes back on and went to join them on the terrace, where Jacinta was serving breakfast. I was just going to have to accept my state of sleep deprivation.

Ariel was intently reading the *Miami Herald* and looking particularly handsome in a dark-green linen suit I'd bought him about a month before and which he was wearing for the first time. He wore neither a tie nor socks, and his feet were in black leather loafers. He hadn't shaved that morning, and between his Italian clothes and his two-day beard, he had a bit of a *Miami Vice* look going on—rough, ready, and casual. It really suited him.

I sat down at my usual place and poured a café con leche from a silver pot on the table. I served myself twice the usual amount of coffee I drank. I was so tired I had to hold the cup with both hands as I raised it to my lips. After a few careful sips, I sat back and waited for the inevitable jolt from the caffeine. Cuban coffee was like mother's milk for Cubans—we could be weaned off it, but the craving never quite went away. The aroma alone was nearly orgasmic. I drank some more, and felt life begin to flow through me.

I looked over at Marti, wondering why he was so quiet all of a sudden. He was dressed in his favorite zebra-patterned pajamas and was completely engrossed in his project, which was to make as big a mess as possible of his breakfast in the shortest amount of time. I knew I should say something to him, but I simply wasn't up to it. Instead, I looked away from the sight of Marti pouring orange juice over the Cheerios he'd plucked from his bowl and piled in a mound on the table.

Ariel looked at his watch, oblivious, and gulped down the last of his coffee. "I'd better get going," he said, then kissed me and Marti good-bye. "I don't know if I'll have time to come home first, or if I'll have to meet you at your parents'. I'll give you a call and let you know how it's going."

With that, he waved good-bye and was gone. I poured myself another cup of café con leche, ignoring the pounding in my heart, and looked out over the bay. Even though it was still early, heat from the sun was making the air over the water shimmer in waves. It was going to be a scorcher, which shouldn't have surprised anyone. In Miami, we have two seasons—hot and too hot. I didn't know why the meteorologists announced the barometric pressure on TV every night. We can all measure the humidity by the degree of frizz in our hair.

I heard a squishy sound from Marti's place at the table, and looked over to see him moving around his orange-juice-soaked Cheerios. I probably should have stopped him, but I hated to do anything to inhibit his creative side. No one in our family is even remotely artistic—the sad truth is that we're all too busy making money, so I encouraged Marti whenever he showed the slightest interest in anything creative.

Finally, he tired of smearing the mess around. He looked up at me expectantly, wondering what we were going to do next. It was barely nine in the morning, and I groaned at the thought of enduring the day ahead in my state of exhaustion—culminating with, horror of horrors, dinner with my family at my parents' house.

It was all too much to contemplate. In a burst of maternal spirit, I turned to Marti.

"Hey, kiddo," I said. "How'd you like to play in the swimming pool with me?"

His face lit up as though I'd told him Santa was on the way and I could hear the reindeers' hooves on the roof of the house. He sprinted out of his chair and headed for the water.

"No, wait! Not in your pajamas," I said, laughing. "You have to change into your swimsuit."

I got up and stopped Marti just before he jumped in. "Come on, I have to put on my suit, too."

Jacinta appeared, and I asked her to take Marti to his room and change him into his bathing suit. I could see from her expression that she thought we were crazy, but she didn't say anything.

I hurried into my bedroom to change. Even as I took off my clothes, I wondered why on earth I'd decided to go swimming at that hour of the morning. I was probably feeling guilty, I realized. I was inviting him to his favorite activity because of how I'd spent the afternoon before. I pulled on my demure one-piece black suit, and decided that I was simply going to enjoy the time with Marti. I was on leave from work, I reminded myself, and I didn't have to be a slave to the clock. That would probably change in the near future. For now, I wanted to splash around mindlessly in the pool, and not think about all the other things that might change as well.

Marti and I played in the water so long that our skin started to wrinkle. I decided that we'd been in the pool long enough, even though he clearly wasn't ready to get out. I ordered him out of the water, wrapped him in a thick towel, and carried him to his room. He had grown so much that I was surprised to find myself having trouble walking steadily with his weight by the time I reached his bed and lay him down softly.

I couldn't remember ever having difficulty carrying him before. My baby was growing into a real little boy, and I had barely noticed. I guessed the clichés were true, that children really did grow up without their parents noticing. And then, one day, they left. I wondered if the same was true of adults.

I changed him out of his bathing suit and into dry clothes just as exhaustion hit him; he was having trouble keeping his eyes open, so I covered him with a blanket and kissed him. I knew that he would be down for at least a couple of hours.

Softly, I closed the door to Marti's room and went down the hall to mine. I slowed down to look at the many photographs on the wall, stopping before a picture of Mamá and Papa taken just after they arrived in exile in Miami. They looked so young and—in spite of having been forced out of their homeland—full of hope. Their arms were wrapped around each other, and they were looking into one another's eyes, seemingly confident of their future together in a new country.

I moved on to a picture of Ariel and me taken on our wedding day. We were standing close together, but we were neither touching nor looking at each other. Although we were in our mid-twenties, to me we looked painfully young. Instead of getting married, we might as well have been dressed up for our First Communion. I remembered the day like yesterday. Ariel had very little family in this country, so the wedding guests were overwhelmingly from my side of the family. I knew with confidence that bets were being placed, even while we were at the altar taking our vows, that the marriage wouldn't last. We were simply too different and, although the fact that we were both Cuban was the basis of a strong bond between us, the general consensus was that the disparity in our backgrounds doomed our lives together.

Standing in my wet bathing suit in the air-conditioned hallway was giving me a chill. I shivered, hurrying into my bedroom, where I took off my suit and got into a hot shower. I luxuriated in the water caressing my body.

I turned off the water and wrapped a towel around my wet hair, then put on my white terry-cloth bathrobe and lay down on the bed. Between the time in the pool with Marti and the shower, I felt completely waterlogged. I looked over at the clock on the bedside table and blinked several times with astonishment to see that it was only a little after ten.

It was going to be a long day. I meant to nap only a few minutes, but the next thing I knew the phone was ringing. I opened my eyes and saw that it was noon already.

I had told myself a few hours earlier that I no longer needed to be a slave to the clock; still, I didn't want to be caught napping in the middle of the day, so I cleared my throat before answering.

It was Maria from the office on the line. I cursed under my breath when I remembered her call that I hadn't returned. I hadn't called Mamá, either.

"Margarita," Maria's voice sounded even more agitated than usual. "You have to come into the office today!"

Maria was normally never so direct with me, and I was immediately concerned.

"I got your message yesterday, and I'm sorry I haven't called you back yet." A little groveling always helped with Maria. "Please forgive me. I'll be in as soon as I can to sign those papers."

"Margarita, this isn't about any papers," Maria announced. "It's getting far more serious than that."

I sat straight up in bed. More serious than signing off on work so we could bill accounts? Now I was *really* worried.

"What is it?" I could barely bring myself to ask.

Maria took a deep breath and exhaled loudly into the phone. "A huge case has come in, one that has lots of immigration law points that are going to take a lot of work. It's a really big one."

"What's going on, Maria?" I demanded. "Give it to me straight. I need to know."

"The partners are talking to an attorney from another firm," Maria said, speaking in a tentative, quiet voice. "He's been here about five times, and he's met everyone here."

"So?" I didn't see the problem. "They talk to attorneys from other firms all the time. You know that."

"It's not so simple." Maria took another deep breath. "He's an immigration attorney. From what I've been able to piece together, they're talking about bringing him in as a partner."

"A partner!" I almost screamed. "I'm the partner who specializes in immigration law!"

Silence.

"What time can I expect you this afternoon?" Maria asked sweetly. "Because you know what this means."

"I'm on my way." I hung up the phone.

I flung off the bathrobe and headed for the closet to pick out the best power outfit I could find. This situation called for nothing less than Armani.

 Less than an hour later, I stepped out of the elevator and into the reception area at Weber, Miranda, et al. I knew that office gossip traveled fast, but it was measured in nanoseconds that day, because Ashley was already up and waiting to greet me when I arrived.

Ashley had chosen to come to work dressed as her own version of Carmen Miranda, the "Brazilian Bombshell." Her body was poured into a tight-fitting, long green-sequined dress adorned with flourishes and ruffles that accentuated her curvaceous figure—especially her breasts, which were struggling to break free from her bodice with every breath of her healthy lungs. I tried to hide my disbelief as I took in her costume—and that was the only possible word to describe it. I actually found myself feeling a bit nostalgic for her microminidresses. The only thing she needed was a basket of fruit on her head, and a toucan sitting on her shoulder. I felt positively dowdy in my two-piece, light gray gabardine suit.

"*Hola,* Margarita," Ashley called out in a bright, but slightly nervous tone as I crossed the reception area. Something sounded false in her greeting. No question, she had heard that the partners were interviewing.

"Hi, Ashley," I replied evenly. "How are you?"

Asking in such a disinterested manner was my way of trying to avoid a prolonged conversation. I wanted to say something about her outfit, but I couldn't think of anything sufficiently neutral. In the years since she started at the firm, I could never remember her wearing anything that outrageous. If I hadn't been so infuriated about what my partners were trying to do, I'd have been more in the mood to stop for a chat.

Looking at Ashley, I was reminded of how speechless I felt when, a couple of years ago, I went to visit a friend and her newborn baby. It wasn't just any baby, I realized when he was shown to me, it was actually the ugliest baby in the history of the world. He had slitty eyes, a scrunched-up face, sallow skin, and a blotchy bald head. I was left stumped for what to say. All I could muster was "What a baby!" In Ashley's case, I couldn't trust myself to get away with "What an outfit!" so I knew I should move on quickly.

I hustled to the door leading to the partners' offices, and punched in my security code. I heard a familiar click, which meant they hadn't gotten rid of me yet. The door opened. I took a deep breath, squared my shoulders, and began my campaign.

Instead of going straight to my office, I made a point of slow-walking the entire corridor, greeting each and every secretary, clerk, and paralegal by name. I even chatted with the repairman in the copy room. I felt like a politician courting voters. After this performance, it would be impossible for anyone not to know I was in the office.

Maria had watched me silently, following as I made the rounds. Once we were back in my office, the door closed, she gave me a sly smile.

"Going for the Oscar?" she asked. Her eagle eyes had already taken in my new Armani suit, my black stilettos, and my flesh-colored stockings—all clear signs that I was dead serious about my mission that afternoon.

"Hey, this is war," I told her. Then I added, "You know what this means as much as I do. I'm pretty sure you don't want to return to the secretarial pool."

Maria blanched, then composed herself. "No," she said. "No, I don't."

I sat down heavily at my desk. "I'm sorry, Maria. I shouldn't have said that," I smiled wanly. "I guess the stress is getting to me. I shouldn't take it out on you."

"It's okay." She sat down on one of the green and white chairs in front of my desk. "I'm worried, too."

"So. What's the latest?" I asked, dreading the answer.

Maria reached into the pocket of her severe navy-blue shirtwaist dress and pulled out a pack of Kools. She held it out to me with a questioning look, and I nodded and reached over the desk to accept one.

Our office was a smoke-free environment, and each office was equipped with a detector. But we had been in crisis mode before, and I knew what to do. I dragged a footstool until it was just under the detector, climbed up to it, and covered the electronic device with a black pashmina shawl I kept for whenever the air-conditioning was turned up too high. Then I went back to my desk and cracked open the window. These two precautions, I knew, would spare us the humiliation of being busted for smoking at work. I took the ashtray out from the bottom drawer of my desk and put in on the windowsill. Maria and I took position on either side of the ledge.

Maria lit both our cigarettes with the gold lighter she always carried. We both took drags, inhaling deeply. I felt better instantly, and the thought crossed my mind that I might be turning into a closet smoker. Dying of cancer was, for the moment, a secondary preoccupation. For the moment, the most important concern was making sure that my position in the firm wasn't being sabotaged by my own partners.

"I wanted to tell you about all this yesterday, but you weren't here," Maria said. "You said you were coming back, but then you didn't."

"I know, I got held up," I told her. "I'm sorry about that."

Maria always softened in the face of groveling. It was part of our dynamic, and she required a certain degree of subservience from me. I wondered what she would think if she knew what I had really been doing the afternoon before.

Which reminded me. Luther.

Maria took another drag. "I'm friends with Susanna, Luis Miranda's secretary," said Maria. Miranda was the senior managing partner at the firm. I knew Susanna, a serious fiftyish woman who always seemed to be carrying the weight of the world on her shoulders. I had heard a vague rumor once about her being engaged, then left at the altar.

"Well, she asked me to take a break with her yesterday after you left—only not in the office," Maria said. "She wanted to meet outside, in the plaza, at two. And in this heat!"

I was hanging on Maria's every utterance. No one, and I mean no one, ever sat at the four cement picnic tables on the plaza behind our building unless they were absolutely forced to. The tables were aesthetically striking and modern, inlaid with chips of colored glass, but in reality they were so uncomfortable that no one ever used them. The tables were out in the open air, with no shade for protection from the sun—not to mention the frequent contributions from the pigeon population out there, which made the place a disgusting mess more often than not. Most everyone at the firm took breaks and ate lunch in the office, especially during the hot summer months. There were two conference rooms: one formal, used by the attorneys for meetings, and another just off the kitchen that attorneys and staff used as a lunchroom. The kitchen was also fully equipped, and a lot of people used it.

"What did Susanna want?" I asked Maria. I pictured the two middle-aged women sitting at the picnic tables in the sweltering July heat, trying to avoid the pigeons as they ate their lunch and traded information.

"First she swore me to secrecy. She said she could get fired for talking to me." Maria puffed on her cigarette, waving the smoke away with her free hand. "I agreed to keep things private, but I told her that if it concerned you, then I was going to have to use my judgment about what to tell you."

"What did Susanna say to that?" I asked.

"She thought about it, and she agreed," Maria told me. "She understands there are some things that I wouldn't keep from you."

"I appreciate that," I told Maria.

"Just remember," Maria warned, "we have to keep Susanna out of this."

"I promise."

"Well, a couple of weeks ago three of the partners met in Luis's office," Maria told me. "They didn't close the door all the way, and Susanna was able to overhear what was going on. She listened to pretty much the whole meeting."

I suppressed a smile. Any attorney who thinks her support staff doesn't know what's going on is deluding herself.

"The partners were talking about whether or not you're going to come back to the firm after your leave of absence," Maria explained. "They were asking each other what they thought, and whether any of them had talked to you about it."

I frowned as I listened. "Maria, you know the terms and conditions for a partner's leave of absence," I said. "I don't have to notify the firm about my intentions until the day before the leave is up."

"I know," Maria replied. "And I also know you're the only partner ever to actually use the leave this way. It shouldn't be like that, but it's the truth."

"You're right," I admitted.

"Susanna told me the partners met again a couple of days later," Maria said. "This time it was in the conference room, with all the partners. Susanna had overheard that one of the main items on the agenda was to discuss your status at the firm."

"My status at the firm!" I repeated, outraged. "Just what the fuck is that supposed to mean? I'm a partner!"

Maria ignored my outburst; she obviously was prepared for a strong reaction from me.

"Apparently, they don't think you're coming back," she explained. "And they don't want to be left high and dry when you get around to making your decision."

"But I don't have to—"

"Margarita, listen, I'm on your side," Maria said. "Susanna told me that they talked about the new case that's coming in, and how it needed an immigration law expert. They didn't want to have to tell the client that the firm can't handle the case because they don't have a qualified partner to deal with it. I asked Susanna for more information, but that's all she would tell me. And, believe me, I owe her one for what she did tell me."

"Do you think Susanna was holding out on you?" I asked. "I mean, has some kind of decision been made?"

"I'm not sure." Maria stubbed out her cigarette. "Susanna and I have been friends for a long time. I think she just wanted to make sure we had fair warning. She knows what bringing a new immigration attorney into the office could mean for me. She doesn't want to see me go back downstairs. I mean, it isn't a given that I'd be reassigned to the new attorney."

I nodded. Maria's thought process made sense, and I appreciated the candor with which she described her own interests. It was best to get everything out on the table.

"So that's why they interviewed the other attorney," I said, calming down. I put out my own cigarette. "But, Maria, they could have just called me to come in and work the case for them. They know I would have done that."

I was angry about being screwed over by my partners, but I also had to admit I understood their motivation. Their concerns were always, above all, practical. If they thought I was going to resign, it made sense to have a replacement ready to start. They wouldn't want me to take a case in an ad hoc manner, start working on it, and then resign. The next attorney would practically have to start all over again. This was a big case, from the sound of it, one that the firm couldn't turn down. And in my lame-duck condition, I represented the most ghastly specter a law firm could ever contemplate: down time, with no hours being billed to a major client.

I had been able to manage my leave so far. In fact, I thought I had done pretty well given my indecision. But now this case had forced the issue. The firm needed an immigration attorney, and it needed one right away.

What I wondered was when the partners planned to tell me about all this. They were, after all, actually considering bringing in an immigration lawyer as a partner. If they hired him and I stayed, there would be two partners specializing in a kind of law that was normally not vital to the firm. There simply wasn't enough work to keep two full-time attorneys busy.

I was going to have to read my partnership agreement very closely, and figure out what my rights were. I knew I was going to have to walk a thin line between exercising my rights and alienating my partners. I certainly didn't want to have an antagonistic relationship with my partners. But I also wasn't about to become a doormat.

News traveled fast at a firm, and even though Susanna had sworn Maria to secrecy, I wouldn't be surprised if word had already spread that there were changes in store. Each partner had a secretary, and they all talked to each other. I didn't want to jump to conclusions, but I remembered Ashley's reaction when she saw me that morning. Maybe I had imagined it, maybe I was being paranoid. One thing I knew: No one was going to force me out of the firm. If I left, it would be on my own terms.

Maria, apparently feeling there was nothing more to discuss, stood up slowly. "Sorry to give you bad news," she said. She walked toward the door. "You know where I am if you need me."

I sat there and lit another cigarette from the pack Maria had left on the window ledge. I realized I no longer had the balance of my leave in which to decide what to do. I had to figure out what to do and tell my partners right away, for their sakes as well as my own. And I had to be careful not to reveal how I found out what I knew, because Susanna would be in deep trouble if the leak was traced back to her.

I smoked the cigarette down to the filter, then waited for the butts in the ashtray to cool before I poured them onto a sheet of typing paper and rolled the ashy mess into a ball. I climbed back onto the stool and took the pashmina shawl off the smoke detector. I sprayed some air freshener, then waved the shawl around to circulate the air in the direction of the open window. Soon there was no noticeable trace of the cigarettes Maria and I had smoked.

After I was satisfied that I would not be busted for smoking, like a girl in a high school rest room, I sat down at my desk and took my cell phone out of my purse. I punched in a now-familiar number and waited for Luther to answer. I wondered how he was doing, and what he thought about the events of the afternoon before. And I wanted to hear his voice.

I listened to the phone ring, and slumped with disappointment when his voice mail picked up.

"It's Margarita," I said. "I was . . . calling to say hello."

Then I hung up.

I said a brief prayer to the Virgin de la Caridad del Cobre, the patron saint of Cuba. Then I got up, deciding to pay each of my partners a nice long visit. Until I decided what to do, I would kill them with kindness.

As I stepped out, I had a brief thought. What kind of psychic was Violeta, anyhow? She hadn't seen Luther coming back into my life, and she hadn't foreseen my partners going behind my back.

Going behind my back. Like a married spouse scouting the options before sleeping around. I had to smile ruefully at the irony.

 Making sure my presence was felt at the firm took longer than I had anticipated, so I didn't have time to return home to Miami Beach before I went to my parents' house for dinner. I wished I could have had time to visit with Marti and change my clothes, but schmoozing with my partners had been more critical. When I realized how late I was running, I called Ariel. His first response was a stony silence that spoke volumes—I knew he was having a flashback to a time when a call like that was an everyday occurrence.

None of the partners I spoke with even hinted that they had discussed my status at the firm behind my back. They might have been avoiding a confrontation until it was absolutely necessary, or they might have actually believed the office grapevine wouldn't divulge their secret to me. Whatever the reason, they couldn't have been more cordial and welcoming, asking about my family and gossiping about what was going on at the other major Miami firms. If I didn't trust Maria so much, I would have thought she was delusional and had imagined the whole thing in her paranoia about being banished back down to the secretarial pool.

I had certainly taken full advantage of my visit to the office, and made sure the partners knew I was alive and still wanted to be a player. I hadn't ceased to be a lawyer with a taste for the jugular just because I'd become a mother. My hips might be wider, but giving birth hadn't caused a complete personality change in me.

I hadn't really asked myself why I was fighting so hard to make certain my position at the firm was secure, given the fact that I really hadn't made up my mind what I was going to do when my leave was over. I guess it was a knee-jerk reaction to Maria's news of my possible replacement. I had jumped into full battle mode without really thinking about the long-term consequences. From my partners' reactions that afternoon, I knew I had put out the fire for the time being. But I didn't buy much time, and the fact that none of them mentioned the big new case wasn't lost on me.

My cell phone rang just as I was turning out the lights in my office. The number on the display was Luther's. My heart thumped in my chest, both from relief that he had called and apprehension about what he might say. For the second time that day I felt like a silly high school girl; this time, it was as though my eyes were glued to the pink princess phone in my room, waiting for the captain of the football team to ask me to the prom.

"Daisy, how are you?" Luther spoke quickly and softly. "I'm sorry I couldn't get back to you before now. I've been stuck all afternoon in a deposition. I kind of manufactured a break so I'd have a minute to call you."

"I wasn't calling about anything important," I said.

"Everything you have to say is important," Luther replied.

I smiled in the dark of my office.

"You know, I was just calling to see how you're doing," I said.

I tried to sound casual, not demanding. I knew how much men hated that in women. Although I might have sounded relaxed, I was anything but. Suddenly I wasn't in high school anymore. This was a lot more serious. It was vital that I found out how he felt about yesterday. I was loathe to admit it, but I needed for Luther to assure me that making love meant as much to him as it did to me. All his declarations of love were touching to remember, but our relationship had moved to a deeper level and I needed to know how he felt. I didn't consider myself insecure, but I needed reassurance from Luther that this was real, important, meaningful. Because I had betrayed Ariel, and nothing was going to change that.

"Listen, Daisy, they're heading back into the conference room," Luther said, hurried. "I can't talk anymore. Are you free on Monday? I really need to see you. Can we get together?"

Maybe that was all the reassurance I needed, right there in the longing in his voice. Visions of Ariel, and Marti, came into my mind. But that wasn't enough to stop me.

"Yes, Monday would be great."

We made plans to meet at noon at his apartment, then hung up. I stood there for a second, listening to silence.

When I looked at my watch, I was alarmed to see that it was almost seven o'clock. I was expected at my parents' in thirty minutes. Unlike most Cubans, the Santoses were punctual to a fault when it came to family gatherings—if someone wasn't early, they would become the object of unspoken condemnation, usually from my mother. My brothers and I used to joke that one of our ancestors must have had an affair with an Anglo, leaving us with a punctuality gene in a vestige of WASP blood in our veins.

I had hoped to have a chance to check in with Vivian, to see how she was doing with Margarita Anabel, but I didn't have time for the long conversation that would inevitably ensue, so the call would have to wait. Between fighting for my life at the firm and trysts with my lover, I didn't have much time left over for family and friends. It looked as though I was going to have to become a better schedule keeper.

Even though it was seven, the office was humming along with as much activity as regular office hours. Several of the attorneys would probably not even go home that night. They would shower and change clothes in the twenty-four hour gym in the building's basement. It wasn't unusual to see an attorney down there at four in the morning, working out to relieve stress from the intensity of the office. Then they would go back upstairs, hair wet from the shower, face shiny from just having shaved, and wearing a fresh shirt to begin another workday.

I missed the adrenaline-laced atmosphere in the office during the days before a big trial, but I could do without the stomach-churning stress of fearing I might somehow drop the ball and lose the case for the firm. I'd had Maalox for breakfast plenty of times, washing the taste away with Cuban coffee. It was a miracle I didn't have a hole in my stomach the size of the Florida Straits.

Sometimes the stress at the office, though, was positively enjoyable compared to the stress of a Santos family dinner. We got along well enough otherwise, but at some point—usually after consuming a prodigious amount of alcohol, the only way to get through the evening—the shit would hit the fan. During our periodic family gatherings, Mamá could have made Mother Teresa snarl with anger.

I punched the button to summon the elevator. All I had to do was get through it. Then I could see Luther again.

 I made myself as presentable as I could, using the resources available to me from my purse. Most of the traffic lights were red on the way over, so I could apply my makeup without steering with my knees at the same time—the custom in Miami. I did a pretty credible job, I thought, looking in the rearview mirror to check out the results.

I wondered how Ariel was going to act toward me. He hadn't sounded happy at all when I told him I was working late at the office. Normally I wouldn't have been apprehensive about his reaction, knowing that I could humor him without too much trouble, but that was before Luther. Now I had to be careful. I didn't want Ariel to notice any changes in my behavior that might make him suspicious.

A Santos family dinner was not the ideal environment in which to ease Ariel's unhappiness about my working late. It would have been better to see him at home, where I could control the situation. Ariel might have even worked later than me, and never known how much time I had spent at the office. Instead, we were going to see each other in the Santos family pressure cooker.

I probably wasn't in the best frame of mind. I was preoccupied as hell, both about the politics at the firm and about Luther. Mamá's invitation couldn't have come at a worse time. I knew what lay ahead that night for me, and none of it was good. I reminded myself not to take Mamá's bait and argue with her, although I knew I would.

We were a close-knit family, like most Latinos. We all lived in Miami, save for my cousin Magdalena—Tia Norma and Tio Roman's daughter, an actress who waited tables in New York while auditioning in parts for plays that were so Off-Broadway they were actually staged in New Jersey. Papa was every bit the Cuban patriarch, and Mamá loved to show off, so our regular get-togethers were almost always held at my parents' house.

All together, there were sixteen of us in attendance. There were my parents and my two older brothers Mickey and Sergio. Mickey was still unmarried but Sergio was newly married to Victoria. There was Ariel and Marti and me—although my son was spared enduring the family dinners. Mamá was the only one on her side of the family still alive; her parents and older sister had passed away many years before, so long ago that my brothers and I never knew them. Apart from a few distant relatives we didn't hear from very often, our family consisted of Papa's siblings, along with their spouses and offspring.

Papa had three brothers. Roman was married to Norma, and they were the parents of Magdalena and Francisco, whom we called Frank. Felix was married to Veronica, with no children. Ricardo was married to Maureen but recently separated—the rumor was that he got caught having an affair. Their three daughters were my cousins Bridgette, Moira, and Shannon.

When we were younger, it was funny to watch the grown-ups making fools of themselves as the alcohol kicked in, but when we got older we realized that the drinks were acting as truth serum, and that long-hidden sentiments were coming out at the dinner table. *In vino veritas* was never truer than at a Santos family gathering.

I turned onto North Greenway Drive, hoping that this night would be different, and that I wouldn't get embroiled in some conflict. I couldn't deal with it. Maybe, just maybe, we could coexist for an evening without arguing about politics, religion, and who had disappointed whom.

I hadn't spoken with Mamá yet, and I didn't know which of my relatives would be in attendance that night, but judging from the number of cars parked on the street, it seemed dinner was going to be well attended. Cars filled the driveway and spilled out onto both sides of the street—my family doesn't carpool. I saw there was no place to park the Escalade, so I swung around the driveway back out onto the street, where I eased into a spot between my cousin Bridgette's black VW Beetle and Moira's dark-green Cabriolet. Parked between those two small vehicles, my car looked like a huge, shiny, gas-guzzling set of wheels straight out of the 'hood. As I maneuvered into the tight spot, I tried and failed to conjure up some guilt about how much gas it consumed and how much air it polluted. I was simply too pleased with it.

I was relieved not to have seen Ariel's Lexus when I pulled up, assuming that he hadn't arrived yet, but then I saw it partially hidden from view under the giant oak tree by the driveway. I had hoped to get there before Ariel, knowing it was the best way to fend off gratuitous remarks from my family about how I worked harder than my husband.

Just outside the giant mahogany front door, I adjusted my clothes, pinched my cheeks to give them color so I wouldn't be told I looked pale from working too hard, and knocked on the door. Mamá had gone overboard on the Spanish theme for the house's exterior as well—the door knocker was made of solid iron, and must have weighed close to twenty pounds. My wrist always gave a little twinge of discomfort after I used it.

The house's front door was about six inches thick—Mamá must have feared an assault from the Moors when she bought it—but I swore I could still hear the rustle of Yolanda's crisp, overstarched uniform as she approached to open it for me. It took both her arms and a great deal of effort to open the slablike door. When I stepped in, one look at the poor maid's face spoke volumes about her misery. It didn't take a psychic to see that Yolanda hated these family gatherings. Mamá, difficult under the best of circumstances, would invariably become ballistic with the stress of trying to impress all of Papa's relatives.

"Señora Margarita," Yolanda greeted me. "Señora Mercedes was asking Señor Ariel about you, because you're the last to arrive. Señor Ariel told her that you were working late at the office."

My stomach sank as I absorbed this unwanted bit of information. It wouldn't be the first time that Mamá and Ariel ganged up against me. I knew that Yolanda telling me this was her way of putting me on notice that my mother was on the warpath and that I'd better be careful if I didn't want to get chewed up. Yolanda and I got along pretty well, and we found solidarity in the fact that we both had to deal with Mamá's moods. We tried to help each other out when the shit hit the fan, but so far I hadn't been able to do anything about Mamá's insistence that Yolanda wear stockings year-round. I was working on it, though.

It wasn't unprecedented for Yolanda to phone me at home and report an instance of Mamá's impossible behavior, so that I could put out the fires she had lit as a consequence. We both knew that Mamá didn't behave the way she did from any innate meanness of character, but rather because she was unhappy with her life. She may have had all the material things that she ever needed or desired, but I suspected that emotionally her life was empty.

I had to apologize to the pool-cleaning service almost on a monthly basis because Mamá insulted one of their employees. She continually berated them about not knowing how to clean a swimming pool, and once tried to make them agree with her that an entire colony of frogs was living in the drain system. Mamá would point to some minuscule bits of dirt in the water and claim they were tadpoles. It was no use when the owner of the pool service came out in person to politely inform her that tadpoles couldn't survive in chlorinated water.

"*Gracias,* Yolanda," I said. In a lower voice, I added, "Thanks for the warning."

With a sigh, I left the safety of the foyer and headed for the living room, where the family had broken off and clustered into small groups. In the gothic, dimly lit pseudo-Spanish decor, they looked as though they were plotting and planning conspiracies against each other. Order reigned for the moment, but I knew how quickly that could change. One look around told me all I needed to know about how the evening would go. Nino, the octagenarian butler whom Mamá hired when she was entertaining, held a silver tray and worked the crowd with brimming glasses of mojitos, a Cuban specialty. A mojito was a delicious but deadly combination of rum, lime juice, sugar, and crushed mint leaves. The consequences of drinking several were comparable to having injected pure alcohol into one's bloodstream.

I said hello to my brothers and two of my uncles, Roman and Felix, who were seated opposite each other, hunched over a square table. They were so engrossed in their game of dominoes that they barely acknowledged my greeting. Dominoes is a passion for Caribbean men, and my family was no exception. Because the game was all-consuming and provided the men with an excuse not to socialize, Mamá had forbidden anyone to play during family dinner nights. This was one decree of hers that no one had ever paid much attention to.

Seeing as how I wasn't going to get much interaction from my uncles or my brothers—who were concentrating on watching Roman and Felix, and offering heckling and advice in equal measure—I kept going. The next person I saw was my Tia Norma, the plastic surgery addict. She was talking in an excited tone of voice to my other aunt, Veronica, the liposuction queen. They both stopped to greet me, and I almost reeled from shock when I leaned over to kiss Tia Norma.

I thought Mamá was exaggerating when she told me about Tia Norma's latest face-lift, but for once Mamá's observations hadn't been malicious gossip. My poor aunt's face was stretched so tight that it was reflecting beams from the overhead lights, like a skin-colored mirror. I was almost tempted to get closer, just to check how my hair looked, but I was frightened by the fact that I might actually be able to. I turned away so I wouldn't have to get a better view of my aunt's latest foray into plastic-surgery hell.

Instead I turned my attention to Aunt Veronica who, according to Mamá, had just undergone yet another round of liposuction. I had no idea where the plastic surgeon had found any fat on her; my aunt was already so thin that her veins were visible through her skin. Surely all of her procedures were putting her surgeon's children through private school. I was very fond of both my aunts, although I knew for a fact that they were both confused and basically unhappy women. It would probably take years of therapy to begin to straighten them out.

I moved on to my cousins. Bridgette, Moira, and Shannon were all dressed in total hootchie-mama outfits, and I could see that they were doing their best to establish a world record for mojito consumption in the shortest possible period of time. I caught a glance of Nino's long-suffering expression, and could tell that he didn't appreciate slaving in the kitchen squeezing all those limes just so these teenage girls could get buzzed. Their Irish-American mother, Maureen, would never have allowed them to dress or act that way, but Maureen wasn't there.

"Margarita!" Bridgette, the oldest, said with transparent mojito cheerfulness. "Come sit with us! Have a drink."

"In a little while," I said. "I have to find Ariel."

"Oh, that's nice," Moira gushed. "They're still in love even though they're . . . they're . . ."

"Old and married?" I laughed.

"No!" Moira said, mortified. She nearly spilled her drink on Mamá's sofa cushions. "I meant—"

"I know, Moira," I said, putting my hand on her shoulder. "I'll come back and have that drink with you, I promise."

Papa and Tio Ricardo—and my good-for-nothing cousin Francisco—were standing together over by the French doors. There were several empty mojito glasses on the table beside them, and they were smoking cigars and telling jokes. From their loud laughs and exaggerated joviality, I could see they were competing with my young cousins for the mojito-drinking record. It felt as though the general volume level in the room had risen in the short time I'd been there, with the deep voices of the men competing with the women's laughter. I put all the men's glasses on a small empty tray on the table, knowing that Nino and Yolanda would probably receive a dressing down from Mamá for failing to clear away the empty glasses fast enough. I broke through the thick cloud of cigar smoke, kissed all three of the men briefly, and moved on. I could sense their relief when my unwelcome female presence was lifted, and they could return to their innuendos and stories.

Then I saw them: Mamá and Ariel, huddled together just inside the dining room, so engrossed in conversation that I was apprehensive about going over there. From their guilty looks when I approached, I could tell that they had been talking about me.

"Margarita!" Ariel came to me with such enthusiasm, anyone would have thought he hadn't seen me in months. "How are you, *querida?*"

He kissed me and escorted me and Mamá to an open set of armchairs. I leaned down to kiss Mamá, who was impeccably turned out in her favorite Valentino. I could see that she'd spent the day at the hairdresser and stylist, and her coiffure framed her professionally made-up face. Mamá had gone all-out for this dinner—she had opened up the safe, and was wearing the set of diamond earrings, necklace, and bracelet that had belonged to my maternal grandmother and which had been smuggled out of Cuba.

"Margarita, dear, you look lovely," Mamá said, taking me in. "I really like that suit. Armani. Last season, right?"

I smiled in agreement, but inwardly I was gripped by anxiety. I knew from experience that Mamá was never so gracious about my clothes and appearance unless she felt guilty about something she had done to me or said about me.

Ariel let his hand rest on the back of Mamá's chair, as though they were the best of friends. I couldn't help but remember the first time they met, when Ariel came to the house to pick me up for our first date. Mamá had totally disapproved of this penniless young liberal Cuban lawyer—from the wrong side of the tracks, no less. As time went on and our relationship got more serious, Mamá softened and got to know Ariel better. The Matos settlement, of course, had cemented my parents' approval of Ariel, and from that day on Mamá became one of his most enthusiastic backers.

Mamá knew she always had an ally in Ariel as far as I was concerned—they may have been on opposing ends of the spectrum politically, but they thought alike in regard to me. Mamá could even tolerate the fact that Ariel had voted for Bill Clinton because he agreed with her that I had proved the point that I could succeed in the cutthroat Miami legal world. Having made partner in a major firm in my early thirties, they both felt it was now time to dedicate myself wholeheartedly to my family.

I knew they spoke often and that I was the primary topic of their discussions. Mamá and Ariel didn't feel they were being malicious or in any way conspiring behind my back—they thought they were trying to do what was best for me, and looking out for my best interests. They both thought I was too involved with my career to know what was best for me. My head had been turned by success and women's rights, and it was up to them to lend a hand and show me what was important. Sometimes I was insulted that they thought of me in such a patronizing manner, but I knew their attitude came from love and not condescension. It was simply part of being a Cuban woman with a strong mother and a husband who felt protective toward me.

Still, it pissed me off sometimes.

That night they had probably been talking about the possibility— no, the probability—of my return to the firm after my leave of absence concluded in a few weeks. Neither of them would come right out and say anything to me, but I knew how they both felt about the decision. I should stay home with Marti, and have another child with Ariel right away. They were as close to me as anyone could be, but I couldn't trust their clouded judgment or come to either for an unbiased opinion. They each had an agenda, and I was at the top of it.

Ariel was ostensibly a liberated Cuban man. He voted a straight Democratic ticket and even admitted to doing so—an amazing feat for a Miami Cuban. But at heart he was still traditional. He wanted his wife at home waiting for him, and at the end of the workday he wanted to be greeted by his numerous children and smell food cooking in the kitchen. He was proud of me and my accomplishments but, to his mind, it was time for our family to get back to basics. Scratch the surface of any Cuban man—Democrat or Republican, liberal or conservative—and he wants his woman barefoot and pregnant, cooking up some arroz con pollo in the kitchen while her children all play around her.

Mamá's reasons for wanting me not to work were more complex. She wanted more grandchildren, first of all—Mickey was a bachelor, and Sergio was newly married and couldn't be counted on to produce children with his wife anytime soon—so I was the best candidate to fill that need. Mamá's competitive side kicked in when it came to family size. All of her close friends had many grandchildren, and she had only one. I could see in her face that she felt she was losing ground.

There was another, unspoken reason. Because I worked and had a career, she felt she suffered in comparison, as though her value was lessened because she stayed at home, and because her greatest achievements were radical home redecorations. The truth was, women of her generation and class weren't expected to work outside the home or have careers. I'm sure that, if she had really wanted to, Mamá could have worked outside the home. She hadn't chosen to, and she still believed that wives should only work if it was an economic necessity. The reality was that Mamá lacked the education and skills necessary to find work that was on a level with her social standing. Her reasoning on this topic was pretty much bullshit, and I had gently hinted as much, but she didn't take my opinion into account. I knew it was harsh for me to think this way, but I knew part of Mamá wanted me to quit working because then I would be on her level.

There was a third reason Mamá didn't want me to work—if I didn't, I would be available to meet with her more often, and spend days together with her at Bal Harbour, the very upscale mall in North Miami Beach. What she didn't realize was that, if I started to live my life like that, pretty soon I would start adding vodka to my orange juice at breakfast.

For all the frenzied activity and fuss that filled her days, the bottom line was that Mamá was lonely with a big void to fill—and she had decided I was the perfect candidate to do so. I had encouraged her to take up a hobby—apart from spending Papa's money redecorating—but she had never been the slightest bit interested.

Mamá got up, stood between Ariel and me, and slipped her hands through the crooks of our elbows. She guided us toward the living room.

"Shall we join the rest of the family?" she asked regally.

With a wink at Ariel she must have thought I wouldn't notice, she led us to the din and smoke in the living room. Nino was busy dispensing yet another round of mojitos, which were being thrown back with alarming speed. My relatives' voices were getting higher pitched, the laughter was becoming more shrill, and the clink of dominoes was getting louder. Another family dinner was underway. With any luck, this one wouldn't turn out like the others in the past. But from the speed with which everyone was drinking, I knew I couldn't count on it.

"Señora Margarita," Nino said, nodding to me with a smile that I returned, a gesture of silent commiseration.

"We're keeping you busy," I said to him.

"Many limes," he rasped. "Many limes used up in the kitchen."

I noticed there were still a few mojitos on his tray that hadn't been pounded back by my cousins.

"Go ahead," Nino said. "Take one. I don't think it's possible for you to catch up with everyone else, though."

I finished off my mojito while he was standing there, then took another before they were all gone.

"I can try, Nino," I told the old man. "I can always try."

 My prayers for peace and civility were, for once, answered. There was no blowout during the family dinner. All the mojitos consumed during cocktail hour had actually put everyone into a pacific mood. Mamá, in particular, was gracious to everyone and to me in particular. She never once mentioned my going back to work, and she took my hand in a touching gesture when the family decamped for the patio after coffee. I was so relieved, I didn't even think to question her behavior.

Later that night, at home, Ariel didn't mention my working late at the office. He talked a little about the difficult personal-injury case he was working on, and how he was convinced his client was lying to him but he didn't know how or why. The client was a driver for a water-delivery company who claimed to have hurt his back while making his rounds on his route. According to the client, the trolley he used to carry the water into the homes broke apart while fully loaded, causing several bottles to fall on him and ultimately to incapacitate him. He claimed that not only couldn't he work, his injuries had also deprived him of the ability to conduct a sex life with his wife. Ariel was suing the water company—as well as the manufacturers of the trolley—for millions of dollars.

Listening to Ariel describe the case, I pointed out that it was no surprise he thought the client was lying somehow. Most of our clients routinely lied to us; those were the facts of life for attorneys.

"Hire a private investigator," I advised. "Have the client followed around for a few days, just to see what he's up to."

"I'm definitely going to do that," Ariel replied. "I'll get in touch with Paul Street on Monday."

Paul Street was a former federal agent Ariel had used several times in the past and whom I'd met a few times. I was glad to hear that Ariel was going to use a private eye, but I wished it were someone other than Paul. I neither liked nor trusted the man, and I never would have recommended him to my firm. Maybe Ariel's liking him was just a matter of personal chemistry, but I always thought there was something sleazy about Paul, and I was always interested in finding out why he no longer worked for the Feds. It wasn't my case, so I kept my opinions to myself.

"It seems strange, spying on my own client, but I'm going to do it," Ariel said. "I wonder how I'm going to account for it in the client's bill."

Ariel was semi-joking, and I laughed along with him until a strange thought struck me: Would Ariel ever resort to hiring Paul if he suspected something was going on with me?

"What's the matter?" Ariel asked.

"Oh, nothing," I lied. "I'm just exhausted. You know how family dinners always take it out of me."

"You don't have to tell me," Ariel said, smiling. "But it was nice to see you and your mother getting along so well tonight."

"Almost too well," I said quietly.

Ariel let my comment pass, and, since we were both spent, we wished each other pleasant dreams and turned out the lights. I was so tired I slept like the dead, and didn't even run through my day before falling asleep, as I liked to do. My last thought before passing out was that each of my days was turning out to be stranger than the one before it.

On Monday morning Ariel was still clearly preoccupied by his case, and eager to speak with Paul Street, so he left for the office early, while I was still in bed. That was fine with me; if we'd had breakfast together, Ariel would have asked me about my plans for the day. I wouldn't have outright lied to him, but I would have committed the sin of omission—and, for a Catholic, that amounted to the same thing. I was happy to avoid breaking any more sacraments and commandments than I already had.

It was going to be a busy day. I had plans to meet Luther at noon, and I wanted to stop by and see how Vivian was doing with Margarita Anabel. Chances were, I wouldn't have much time to play with Marti later on, so I knew I had to go to him soon if I wanted to spend time with him.

Groaning, I got up and headed for the shower. It took about ten minutes standing under steaming hot water before I felt human again. I would follow that with about a gallon of Cuban coffee to revive me. After I showered, I lathered myself with Chanel No. 5 lotion, which I knew would be both subtle and long lasting.

The first time I went to Luther's apartment I had gone ill-prepared; this time, I was able to choose my outfit with more care. After a thorough search of my underwear drawer, I settled on a light gray satin bra and matching panties. I thought black lace would be making too much of a statement, and I had already worn white, so gray would strike just the right note—sexy, but not verging on femme fatale.

The rest of my outfit was easier to pick. I chose a black, narrow-cut gabardine skirt, an olive-green cotton twin sweater set, and black leather slides. Casual and comfortable, but I looked good. And easy to get in and out of. I was always thinking practical.

I thought about blow-drying my hair to straighten it, but there was no point, not with the Miami humidity. Mother Nature had defeated me once again before I could even put up a fight. No wonder I always resisted going to summer camp when I was a child. I never did well with the elements.

Instead of blow-drying, I opened up a bathroom drawer and pulled out one of the half-dozen tubes of Alberto VO5 conditioner that I kept there. I squeezed a dollop on my palm, rubbed my hands together, and ran them through my hair until I was sure the conditioner had coated every strand. That conditioner had changed my life. I used to think it was old-fashioned, used only by balding men, but it was a worthy opponent to frizzy hair. I braided my hair back and tied it off with a bit of rope threaded through with gold filigree. I put on sunblock under my makeup, then put two sets of diamond studs—one larger, one smaller, in my ears. I wasn't working that day, and so I didn't have to be mindful of clients' opinions and could wear double-pierced earrings without offending anyone. After a few squirts of perfume, I was on my way.

I glanced at the clock in the hall on the way to Marti's room to check if he was awake, and saw with alarm that it wasn't even eight yet. I immediately felt exhausted. I couldn't believe that I'd been so active already, at such an early hour—and without a drop of Cuban coffee in my system. If I wasn't careful, I was going to become Americanized.

Marti was still sound asleep, looking so angelic that I didn't have the heart to wake him. Instead, I stopped by the kitchen to wish Jacinta a *buenos dias,* and to ask her for breakfast on the terrace. I picked up a mug from the counter and filled it from the pots of coffee and hot milk that were simmering on the stovetop, slowly sipping the hot fragrant liquid as I went outside. I sat in my usual chair, skimming the newspaper. It was hot already. I wondered how bad it was going to be by afternoon.

At around nine, after I'd finished the paper, Marti came out and got in my lap. He smelled sweet, and was still warm from his bed. I felt a wave of tears and tenderness wash over me as he nestled close.

We heard a splash from the nearby waters of the bay that startled us. Marti and I looked up at the same time and spotted three dolphins jumping several feet out of the water, their gray skin shimmering like sparkling diamonds in the morning sun. They hit the water, one after the other, and swam off with speed. Marti and I said nothing, preferring to share the perfect moment.

Marti and I stayed awhile longer, looking out over the bay. We speculated about all the boats passing by, wondering where they were going and where they might have been. Around ten, when he started to become restless, I handed him over to Jacinta. It was time to go if I was going to spend any time with Vivian and her new daughter before meeting Luther at noon.

I wouldn't trade living on Miami Beach for anyplace else, but the reality was that a big part of my life took place off the Beach. That meant twenty minutes to half an hour added to my travel time, in addition to the usual Miami driving insanity. I always enjoyed driving on the causeway into Miami, but when I was in a rush I begrudged the extra effort. But life on the Beach was different than in Miami—after all, Miami Beach was actually an island that ran parallel to the city. Sometimes I wondered if I chose the Beach to live on because it was a tiny island off the coast of the United States, as though, in some subconscious way, it made me feel a little bit closer to Cuba.

I wondered if I would have had an affair with Luther if I were living in, say, Coral Gables. Living in Miami Beach made me feel less constricted emotionally, more open to experience and seeking freedom. I felt as though being surrounded by water somehow lifted my inhibitions. I had changed since I moved there, and I wasn't entirely sure if it was because of my new environment or if it was something deep inside me

Traffic was light to Coconut Grove, and I got to Vivian's house in plenty of time for a visit. I pressed the call button on her gate and waited for her to let me in. This was the first time in a while I had been to Vivian's house during the day; I could see that the materials for adding the extra rooms necessary to accommodate her expanding family had already begun to arrive.

Vivian herself came outside to let me in. I had to admit, she had aged in the day or so since I dropped her off. But as she approached, I also noticed that she was radiating a sort of happiness that I'd never before seen in her.

"Margarita." Vivian leaned into the car to kiss me through the open driver's side window. "Thanks for coming to see us."

I slowly pulled into the driveway and parked next to the house. When I got out, Margarita led me to the door.

"Margarita Anabel is sleeping right now. It was a rough night. Not much rest," Vivian said, without giving me the impression that she was complaining. I was surprised because Vivian had always insisted on sleeping eight hours a night. It was something she wouldn't compromise on—even when we were teenagers, during sleepovers at each other's houses, we could almost set our watches by the times Vivian went to bed and got up in the morning.

She led me inside to the guest room, where she opened the door just a crack for me to look in. After my eyes adjusted to the darkness, I made out a dark little form lying in bed, her chest rising and falling with slow, deep breaths. I could sense that Vivian was waiting for me to say something.

"She's beautiful, Vivian, a beautiful little girl," I said, even though it was impossible to see much in the penumbra of the room.

I may not have been able to see the child clearly, but I got a pretty good look at her new bedroom. Vivian didn't live in Disney World, but that hadn't stopped her from bringing the amusement park to her house. Every wall was filled with Disney characters: Snow White and the Seven Dwarfs, Cinderella, the Lion King. There was a pink bookcase overflowing with Barbies, and an underwater scene from the Little Mermaid on the ceiling. It would be a miracle if the child slept in there every night and retained her sanity.

Vivian closed the door quietly, beaming at me. The whole ride over from home, I had debated with myself about bringing up the fact that the little girl we'd picked up at the church wasn't the one in the photograph. I knew that Vivian had been deeply shocked that night, but she had said nothing. She had apparently made a choice to accept the switch and, as her friend, it was my job to support her decision. I had no idea, after all, why the switch was made, and under what conditions. I also didn't know what Father Tomas might have told her behind closed doors in the rectory that night. Maybe the original Margarita Anabel had been too ill to travel, maybe someone from her family had appeared to take her out of the orphanage or, far worse, maybe she had died.

The lawyer in me found it impossible to accept the situation without asking questions. The way the adoption had taken place seemed pretty shady to me, but the Church was involved, and so it must have been legal. I couldn't imagine Father Tomas being involved in anything illegal. What I *could* imagine was a church so eager to find homes for children that they were willing to at least finesse certain legalities.

More than once I'd read in the *Herald* about illegally adopted children's parents showing up and demanding the child back. These situations had taken place both domestically and internationally. I hated to imagine this happening to Vivian—that a parent in Honduras would come out of nowhere and file suit in Miami to get the girl back—but these days, it was a mistake to assume much of anything.

I hadn't said a word to Anabel about my apprehensions. I figured that, if Vivian wanted her to know, she should be the one to tell her. Anabel was so blind that she might not even notice that Margarita Anabel wasn't the little girl from the picture. Vivian might even hope as much.

"Something to drink?" Vivian offered.

"Sure, *gracias.*" I noticed that Vivian had become a bit tense since I arrived. "A Coke would be great."

We walked together to the kitchen. When we opened the swinging door leading in from the dining room, I was startled to see a woman in white shirt and pants standing over the sink, washing dishes. As soon as she heard us come in, she turned around to look.

"This is Marisa," Vivian said, motioning to the middle-aged woman who, upon hearing herself introduced, broke out in a smile that transformed her expression from one of surprise to one of genuine kindness and serenity. "She's here to help with Margarita Anabel."

"Pleased to meet you," I said.

"This is my friend Margarita, the one who my daughter is named after," Vivian told Marisa. Marisa nodded, smiled, and returned to her washing. I thought that Vivian had chosen well—Marisa seemed competent, warm, and, above all, motherly.

Vivian opened up the refrigerator and took out a can of Coke. I saw that the fridge was completely full. There were little stacks of juice boxes, puddings, flan, fresh fruit, bread, eggs, all kinds of kid food. I remembered a time when there was nothing in there save for a couple of bottles of Cristal for when men came to visit. Clearly, those days were gone. I would have liked to have snooped some more, but she shut the door.

Vivian took a glass from the dish rack and poured in some ice from the machine under the counter. On the way out of the kitchen, she took a napkin from the silver holder in the middle of the table. She led me out to the Florida room, where we sat on opposite ends of the rattan sofa.

Well, I told myself, *it's now or never.*

I took a sip of my Coke and set it down on the side table next to me. I opened my mouth to speak, but Vivian interrupted. It was as if she sensed what I was about to say, and didn't want to hear it. From all the arrangements I had seen, especially the bedroom, it was obvious to me that Margarita Anabel was here to stay.

"We have an appointment this afternoon with Dr. Lopez, the pediatrician, for Margarita Anabel's checkup," Vivian blurted out, her voice obviously louder than she'd intended.

"Oh, really?" I said. "I've heard of him. My nieces went to him when they were little girls."

"Did they like him?"

"Yes, very much," I replied.

"Oh, I'm so glad to hear it," Vivian said, sounding as though I had just told her the antidote for her snakebite had arrived.

"What are you doing after that?" I asked.

"We're going to Bloomingdale's to buy her some clothes," Vivian said. "And then, on the way back, we're going on a spending spree at Toys "R" Us. It's going to be great."

"Sounds like it," I said.

Hearing all these plans, I couldn't think of anything to say. I wished Anabel was there, maybe then I could bring up the subject of the switch. But I was on my own, and I was chickening out. I could tell Vivian didn't want the truth to come out, and probably never would.

"My, you're busy," was all I could muster. I finished off the Coke in a few gulps.

Vivian beamed like a proud parent.

Well, who the hell was I to rain on her parade?

 I knew that making comparisons could be hateful but, lying next to Luther after a couple of hours of vigorous lovemaking, I realized that my past sexual experiences had basically been amateurish and unimaginative. I hadn't exactly been sexually prudish prior to Luther's arrival in Miami, but the past two hours had been a vivid demonstration of all the sensual possibilities available to the female human body. I had always known that Luther was an overachiever, and in terms of his performance in bed, he had moved to the highest percentile. It was *that* good.

It felt as though Luther had taken my body, turned it this way and that, explored and enlivened every single inch of it, and given it back to me with a fresh understanding of what its various parts did and what purposes they served. I had learned about nerve endings in places I thought were dull and utilitarian. The discoveries were exhilirating and, at times, a little frightening. Luther played my body like a musical instrument, and every time I started to lose control he would slow down and bring me back to earth before rising again to the peaks of abandon.

The first time we were together, Luther must have held back because he feared I would be frightened off by the expertise he'd gained since we were law students. He shouldn't have worried—I was his eager and willing partner. I was surprised that an American could be so daring and imaginative in bed, especially one who gave off such an impression of propriety and control. But this was Luther. He had learned an entire language to win me over, so I shouldn't be surprised by anything he did.

I lay there in bed feeling the sweat dry on my skin. I tried to remember making love with him back in Durham, when we were at Duke. I had always thought of our sex life back then as pretty steamy and passionate, but we had been in our mid-twenties and really not all that experienced. Neither of us had been virgins when we met, but we weren't all that worldly, either. Something about the passing of years, and experienced gained, made certain inhibitions fall away.

I lost my virginity my senior year in high school, to a Cuban classmate I had known since first grade. It happened during a weekend at his family's condo at the Ocean Reef Club in the Keys, while his parents were away. We planned our getaway, which included me lying to Mamá and Papa about the arrangements—I told them I was going there with a girlfriend, and that there was going to be parental supervision. Like every teenager, I was an expert at inventing stories.

I didn't really have sex with my boyfriend because I was in love with him; I did it more to satisfy my curiosity, to experience firsthand what all the fuss was about. When I thought about it, having sex when we did was completely my idea—although I was careful not to let him think that. I maneuvered the situation to ensure that he thought he was pulling off a great conquest. I certainly didn't want to be labeled a slut—and it didn't take much, back then and in Catholic school.

My boyfriend, Gabriel, was the hunky and lusty captain of the varsity soccer team at our school. He was extremely eager to be the first man to sleep with me, and couldn't get over the fact that it was really happening. The whole time in bed he kept his eyes wide open, so that he would record every instant of having me alone on the twin bed in his room, on sheets printed with soccer balls. I lost my virginity with Pelé looking down from a poster on the wall, his fists raised to the heavens in triumph. The bedside lamps had ceramic soccer balls at their bases. Looking back, it was a wonder that Gabriel didn't shout out *Goal!* at the moment he deflowered me.

The experience would have been great, but Gabriel was so much in love that he worried he was hurting me; he kept asking me how I was doing, effectively reminding me that I was supposed to be feeling pain and not pleasure. The real pain came later, when I went to a clinic in Miami and was diagnosed with cystitis. Three days of nonstop sex with a born athlete turned out to be more than my poor virginal body could take.

I suppose it was then that I learned firsthand the underlying lesson of Catholicism—that pleasure is always accompanied by pain, and that I would always pay a price for behaving badly. It was a lesson that I would learn again and again throughout my life. Sometimes it made me resentful. I didn't think Unitarians had to lug around the burden of original sin, always looking over their shoulders every time they were enjoying themselves.

I had met Luther exactly at noon on the street parallel to his apartment building. I still couldn't bring myself to use the set of keys that he had given me. I followed his car into the driveway, and we repeated the actions of our first meeting, as though already settling into a routine. As before, we didn't encounter anyone on the way in. I was starting to think of the building as sterile and uninhabited.

I had stopped along the way at Scotty's, an upscale grocery store on Bird Avenue, where I bought lunch. Like most Cubans, I'm constitutionally unable to skip a meal, even for sex. I bought some smoked salmon and its accompaniments, capers and lemon, along with French bread, a couple of deli salads, a big juicy peach, a ripe mango, and a quart of Häagen-Dazs dulce de leche ice cream. I figured it was time to reintroduce Luther to real Cuban eating. I also stopped at a cart by the side of the street where a vendor sold fresh flowers; mindful of Luther's apartment decor, I selected two dozen white roses and an armful of calla lilies. I had already paid for them when I spotted a bunch of the palest pink orchids. Deciding restraint was a thing of the past, I bought those as well. I hoped there were plenty of vases in the apartment.

When Luther saw me getting out of the Escalade with the grocery bag and all those flowers, he rushed to help me. I could tell he was touched that I had brought lunch, and he thanked me profusely. Once inside, we went straight to the kitchen. I found out then that Luther had made some preparations of his own.

First he opened a bottle of Veuve Clicquot and poured us both glasses. He scrounged around for a couple of jars to serve as vases for the flowers, while I put the meal together. I couldn't help but notice how natural our domesticity felt, the way we moved about the kitchen with ease. Once the flowers were in their makeshift vases I placed them around the apartment, most in the living room and the orchids in the bedroom. The air from the ceiling fans spread a sweet scent, perfuming the place. We left the meal on the counter for later, and picked up our champagne glasses.

"Daisy, you shouldn't have gone to so much trouble," Luther scolded me lightly as we moved to the sofa. "I was planning on ordering out."

"It wasn't any trouble," I told him. "I enjoyed it." And I had. I was no Martha Stewart, but I enjoyed planning and executing a meal.

We sat on the sofa and sipped our champagne. Luther had come straight from the office and was still dressed in a light-gray pinstriped suit over a blue shirt with French cuffs and discreet gold studs for cuff links. He also wore a dark-blue tie with a silver diamond pattern. He might have stepped out of the pages of *GQ*. Even Violeta would have agreed that he took away her hiccups. No matter how good he looked, though, this time I was determined to actually finish a glass of champagne before we went into the bedroom.

"How's your case going?" I asked him.

I wasn't particularly interested in Luther's work at the moment, but I thought we should at least have a conversation. I didn't want to turn into Mrs. Robinson from *The Graduate*—I remembered the scene in a hotel room, when Dustin Hoffman realizes they never speak, and that their assignations are composed of sex and sex only. Luther launched into a digression on the complexities of his case.

"If we aren't careful," he said wearily, "we're going to have the SEC on our backs."

I listened distractedly, perking up only when he mentioned in an offhand manner that the case would be concluded in a couple of months. Apparently he hadn't noticed my reaction, because he kept talking without interruption. I almost pointed out that, once his services were no longer needed on the case, he would be returning to New York. But I decided against it. He knew the truth as well as I did, and this wasn't a good time to talk about messy reality. I was drinking champagne in the middle of the day, in a white room that looked like heaven, looking out over the water in anticipation of great sex. There was no reason to be a masochist and ruin things. The only thing that could have possibly made me happier was hearing that Fidel Castro had died.

Luther got up and went to the kitchen for the champagne bottle; he returned with the food also. Instead of sitting at the dining room table, we put the food on the coffee table in front of the sofa and ate like at a picnic. It felt so erotic that I was barely able to keep from pouncing on him. I remembered feeling the same way on our first date back in Durham, when I had been forced to restrain myself because I had my period. Well, on this day I had no such mundane concerns.

We may have had an appetite for each other, but that didn't stop us from devouring the entire meal. We spoon-fed each other dulce de leche ice cream straight from the container. Luther said he'd never had a better lunch—probably a white lie, but I liked to hear it. Along the way, we made a serious dent in the Veuve Clicquot.

There was little mess to clean up, so we were free from getting too domestic. And we were in no mood to start loading up the dishwasher.

Luther took me by the hand. "Come on, Daisy." He led me into the bedroom and turned down the covers on the bed.

He carefully undressed me for the second time in a week and carefully put my clothes on the dresser. Then he took off his own clothes and slipped in next to me. We still hadn't touched. Luther propped himself up on one elbow and turned to look at me; his blue eyes shone so brilliantly they seemed almost unreal.

"I can't believe you're here, Daisy," he whispered, his voice heavy with emotion. "I still can't."

He didn't seem to expect a reply, so I moved closer and kissed him. A couple of hours later I realized I must have dozed off after lovemaking. I opened my eyes to see Luther staring at me, his expression serious. The air in the room felt suddenly heavy.

"Daisy, I need to talk to you," he said.

"Luther—"

"I know it's been a shock, my coming back into your life," he said quickly, before I could stop him. "I understand that you need some time to adjust. But you have to realize—I've been thinking about you, about us for a very long time."

My heart sank. I was still enjoying the afterglow of everything we'd done together, and I didn't want the spell broken by a heart-to-heart conversation about the state and future of our relationship. It felt too early, and I didn't want to face making the inevitable choice between Luther and Ariel. The moment I started to consider the future, my thoughts cascaded down.

"I know, Luther," I said. "You explained all that when we were sitting together at Dinner Key."

I started to kiss him again, mainly to keep the conversation from progressing into territory I didn't want to think about.

Luther gently pressed me away. "Daisy, please. I'm serious. I really want to talk about this."

I chewed my lip and tried to look at him.

"I love you, Daisy," Luther said. I felt him tense up. "I love you, and I want to marry you."

I might have killed to hear him say that years ago. We had talked about getting married at Duke, but only in the abstract, in the same way we talked about prospective job offers. Thinking about it, I felt a quick surge of irrational anger.

"Why the hell didn't you tell me that years ago?"

The words came out before I could stop myself. But they carried truth. It was as though we had stepped into a time machine, into a possible future. But I had changed; my life had taken on weight and irreversibility; I had created a new life in Marti. Luther's voice echoed like a ghost's.

Luther rested his forehead on his hand, miserable. "I know. I realize now I should have." He reached over and took my hand. "Trust me when I tell you I've been beating myself up for years about it."

A terrible sadness came over me as I thought about marrying Luther right out of law school. I considered the life we might have led together, but then I thought about Marti. Marti, my angel, the spitting image of his father—he never would have existed. It was impossible for me to look at Marti and not also see Ariel. I wondered if it would always be that way.

"Luther, my life is too complicated now," I said gently. "You know that. I can't just walk away from everything and marry you."

"Look, Daisy, I let you get away once," Luther said. "I learned my lesson the hard way. I'm not going to let it happen again."

Luther pulled me closer.

"This is too much, it's happening too fast," I said. "I need time to sort it out. You can't expect me to unravel my entire life at a moment's notice just because you ask me to."

The whole thing—the white room, the bed, the trees, the sea, and Luther—was becoming too surreal. Luther had come back into my life just days before, and now he was talking about getting married. It was easy for him—he didn't have a wife, and a child, and other lives to completely disrupt. He had also been thinking about the situation for years, while I'd just realized I still had feelings for him.

My life was starting to feel like a train moving down a steep mountainside without brakes—I was still on the rails, but I didn't know how much longer I could keep it up. I had to admit that being with Luther felt right. But the cost of following that feeling could be total devastation. I knew what divorce could do to children, and I hated to think of Marti growing up with that kind of pain and uncertainty in his life. I had made the decision to marry Ariel years ago and, just because Luther had come back into my life, I shouldn't forget that that commitment had meaning. I had taken vows, and I had lived for years in what I thought was happiness and contentment.

Ariel would be so shocked.

"Take all the time you need, Daisy," Luther said softly. "I understand how difficult this is, how crazy it seems. Just remember one thing. We belong together. We always have. You know it, and I know it. It's just the way things are. We got sidetracked somewhere along the line, but eventually we're going to have to make things right."

Dios mio. The gringo was right.

[32]

"How long has it been since the three of us got together, Maggy?" Anabel asked, as we walked up the driveway to Vivian's house.

Anabel and I had decided that it was time that we formally welcomed Margarita Anabel into our world. Earlier that week we had announced to Vivian that we would be coming by to visit and to see her daughter. Of course, I had already met her, but not under the most auspicious of circumstances—once in the car when I had driven Vivian to fetch her, and the other when the baby was sleeping, so I felt I had not really met her. I was almost resentful I was going to have to give up one of my precious afternoons with Luther to visit Vivian, but this was something I had to do.

I had not mentioned anything to Anabel about my suspicions surrounding the adoption, figuring that she was so blind that she could not even match the child in Vivian's home to the one in the photograph we had been shown at Greenstreet's a few weeks ago. It was up to Vivian to say something, if she felt it necessary.

That afternoon Anabel had outdone herself in choosing her outfit, and, given her history, that was quite a track record. I had driven over to her house to pick her up, so we would go in one car. I think I was still in shock when I saw my friend emerge from her house dressed in several different shades of yellow, looking like a demented chicken who had escaped from an Easter basket. I resisted the temptation to reach for my sunglasses to ward off the glare. Anabel was wearing a skin-tight pair of canary yellow jeans with an even brighter-colored T-shirt on top. I know it was probably my imagination, but I thought I could discern a fluorescent yellow brassiere under her shirt.

For some unfathomable reason, Anabel had decided to sport a lime-colored straw hat adorned with daffodils. Apparently, the flower motif had greatly appealed to her, for both her platform shoes and belt also had variations of the same flower. As Anabel got into the car, I could swear I was able to smell the scent of daffodils, whatever that might be, emanating from her.

I was so stunned at my friend's appearance that I was rendered speechless for much of the ten-minute drive over to Vivian's house. However, Anabel did not seem to notice, because she chatted on about inconsequential matters all the way. I knew Anabel well enough to realize that something was worrying her. I also knew not to press, as she would eventually get around to bringing up whatever it was that was troubling her.

Sure enough, just as we pulled into Vivian's street she suddenly stopped telling me a long-winded story about the triplets' swimming class at Waters-R-Us, and asked, "Maggy, what do you think about Vivian going out and adopting this child?" Anabel reached over and grabbed my right elbow, surprising me with her intensity.

My heart thumping, I took my eyes off the road for a second and looked at her squarely. Anabel's huge blue eyes zeroed into mine as might a laser that had located its target. It was almost impossible to believe that eyes with a gaze as powerful as hers could be lacking sight. Not wanting to cause an accident, I looked back at the road and concentrated on my driving. Clearly, Anabel did not expect a reply, for she continued: "She kept such an important secret from us! Us!" Anabel shook her head in disbelief. She could not keep the anger out of her voice. "Her best, closest friends! You know the rule we have always lived by, ever since we were eight and played on the soccer team. We have no secrets from each other—we never have, and never will."

I shrugged, trying to appear as nonchalant as I could, even as I felt myself beginning to break into a light sweat. I had been on the receiving end of Anabel's anger a few times, and therefore knew from painful personal experience that my pint-size friend was nothing to be trifled with.

"Well, at the lunch, she explained to us the reasons why she had done it." I knew my answer was weak, but just then I did not feel comfortable discussing Vivian, especially since I had such a momentous secret of my own.

Mercifully, just then we arrived at Vivian's house, so the conversation ended. I had sensed that Vivian's actions had bothered Anabel, as they had me, but I had not realized exactly how much until she spoke. I knew my answer had not satisfied Anabel, but there was nothing to do except to park the car and go inside.

As this was a formal visit, Anabel and I had come prepared. We were both clutching oversize packages, large boxes wrapped in the distinctive shiny gift-wrapping from F.A.O. Schwarz, the upscale toy store. I noticed that our boxes were almost identical in size, and hoped we had not bought the same gift, a miniature Victorian wooden dollhouse. Oh well, Vivian could exchange one, if not both of them. She was good at that.

Holding the present in front of me, I was having trouble balancing myself on the high heels I was wearing as I walked on Vivian's pebble-strewn driveway. Anabel, with her three-inch-high platform shoes was not faring any better. Still, however, I was grateful that I had an advantage over Anabel, for, unlike my friend, I could actually see where I was going.

Vivian must have been watching our approach from one of the windows facing the street, for she opened the door as soon as we arrived at it. I was shocked to see how worn out she looked. All I could hope for as I kissed her hello was that Anabel could not see the deterioration of our friend's physical appearance that had taken place since the baby's arrival. Even her roots were showing. Had Vivian skipped her twice monthly touch-up at Great Locks? I was truly worried.

"Margarita! Anabel!" Vivian greeted us effusively, kissing and hugging us, as if we had not seen each other in years rather than days. "It's so wonderful to see you!" It must have been true, for she had not made any comment on Anabel's outfit.

Anabel and I looked at each other with alarm. Even though Anabel could not clearly see Vivian, she knew our friend would have never physically touched us voluntarily. Vivian was certainly not known for being demonstrative, especially to women. We had been friends for almost thirty years, yet I could not recall our ever having been this awkward with each other.

"Where's the baby?" I asked, holding the present out to Vivian. "I can't wait to see her and give her this!"

"Me, too." Anabel chimed in, holding out her own present.

We trooped into the house, single file, as if going to some sort of ceremony. Vivian led us to the Florida room, where we stood in the doorway, looking in at Margarita Anabel, who was sitting in the middle of her playpen, dressed in a pair of not-too-clean pajamas even though it was now afternoon, quietly playing with one of the dozen or so toys surrounding her. I could not help but notice that the room was a mess, with toys and clothes strewn everywhere.

"Is Marisa here?" I wondered if it was the housekeeper's day off, and that was why the house was in such disarray.

"Actually, she's not working here anymore," Vivian mumbled as she walked past us on the way to the playpen. She bent over and picked up Margarita Anabel, who promptly began to wail.

The more Vivian tried to comfort her, the louder the child's screams became. "She'll quiet down eventually." Vivian explained. "Sorry."

Anabel and I just stood there helplessly, holding on to the presents for dear life, as we watched our friend try to shush the screaming child. By then, the little girl was screaming so loudly, and her face had gotten so red, that I was afraid she was going to have a stroke.

Hoping my eardrums would not rupture as a result of the blood-curdling screams, I was beginning to understand why Marisa had quit. "Maybe she wants to stay in the playpen," I suggested. If that did not work, I was going to suggest Vivian give her a Valium, of which I knew she kept a stash in her medicine cabinet. Anything to get the child to shut up.

Vivian placed her back in the playpen, and the child quieted down instantly. Observing this brief, but loud, interaction between mother and daughter, it was not difficult to see who was the boss in the outfit.

"Well, sorry about that." Vivian took the presents from us and led us into the kitchen. She opened the door of the refrigerator, rummaged around a little bit, and took out a bottle of Cristal. Without saying anything to us, she popped the cork and poured healthy servings of the golden liquid into flutes she took down from a cabinet. Just like old times—drinking champagne at three o'clock in the afternoon.

"To motherhood!" she toasted, tipping her glass in the direction of the Florida room before draining it. She finished hers before Anabel and I had even had a chance to taste ours, and quickly replenished her glass. "I know it'll get better, but until then, *mierda!*"

"What happened to Marisa?" I could not resist asking.

"She quit." Vivian explained without elaborating further.

Anabel put her glass down on the counter and stood next to Vivian. "When was the last time you went to the office?"

Vivian shrugged. "I don't know, a few days."

I was almost certain that our friend had not been to work since the morning she had brought the child home, and I could see from Anabel's incredulous look that she thought the same. We stood there in the kitchen, sipping our drinks, when the child in the next room began to cry again.

"Look, Vivian, you need help with the child," I began. "Would you like for me to ask around and try to find a replacement for Marisa?"

The screaming got louder. Anabel turned and started to walk toward the Florida room. "Maybe she's hungry."

Vivian looked at us, her eyes blazing in anger. "I can manage very well by myself, thank you." She put down the empty champagne flute, and declared, "You both have children, so you think you know everything. You're so smug about how well organized your lives are, and how well you manage motherhood. You come in here to check out how I'm doing, to find fault with me. You resent me now that I have a child, too."

Anabel and I just stood there, speechless. What the hell was Vivian talking about? Where had all this anger and resentment come from? What was happening to our friend? When was the last time she had slept? The circles under her eyes were not even bags anymore. They were more like steamer trunks.

"No, Vivian, no," I protested. "We came here to celebrate your daughter."

Vivian would not buy it. "No, you just came here to show off what great mothers you are, how much you know about children, and how little I know."

"Vivian, please let us help you." Anabel pleaded, even as the screaming in the next room turned into howls of rage. "Everyone needs help with children."

"Well, I don't! I know exactly what I'm doing. I don't need any help. I can manage just fine without you." Vivian then added, "Maybe you'd better go now."

I could not believe Vivian was kicking us out of her house. I took Anabel's arm and escorted her to the front door. Without saying a word, we let ourselves out and walked toward the car. What had happened back there was like a bad dream.

It was only when I had driven for a few minutes that Anabel spoke. "See, I knew she should have told us about the adoption. We could have helped her."

We continued in silence until we arrived at her house. Then, just as she was getting out of the car, Anabel declared somberly, "Secrets are bad. Vivian should have told us what was going on in her life. We would have helped her through this."

My heart beat faster as I watched Anabel walk toward her house. What price was I going to pay for keeping my secret?

For the weeks that remained in July my life slipped into a distinct pattern, one that I welcomed without difficulty. After a few days of juggling my schedule I found that I was able to balance the three main components of my life: time with Ariel and Marti, days in which I went to the office for work, and afternoon rendezvouses with Luther. Sometimes I even managed to see my family and friends, but not regularly. For the time being, I had more pressing concerns.

Mercifully, Vivian had come around and apologized to Anabel and me, claiming it had been sheer exhaustion which had made her act that way, and she accepted our offer to help. She had been so ashamed of her behavior that Anabel and I forgave her. We knew what it was like to be so tired from caring for children that one acted in ways that were out of character.

In spite of having been kicked out of the house in such an unceremonious manner, Anabel had found her a housekeeper the following day, a strict no-nonsense experienced mother of ten who knew exactly how to manage Margarita Anabel, and, in no time at all, Vivian was back on track. I had made her a present of a full day at the spa connected to Great Locks, and, once she had been tinted, manicured, pedicured, and massaged, Vivian was back to her old life.

The matter of why Vivian had arranged for the adoption without discussing it with us was not brought up again. Maybe we would discuss it later, but for now, we were not about to risk another blowup. I, of course, did not press that issue, as I had my own skeletons in the closet as far as secrets were concerned.

Every so often I would go by her house and stop in for a brief visit, but never did I see the presents that Anabel and I had brought over that fateful day. I was reasonably certain that the two wooden dollhouses were back on the shelf at F.A.O. Schwarz, but I was too busy with my own life to follow up and check.

Three times during the week I would meet Luther at his apartment. I always stopped off at Scotty's to buy lunch, paying cash so I wouldn't leave a paper trail for Ariel to discover. After eating, Luther and I would retire to the bedroom. I was probably becoming too used to drinking champagne at lunchtime. The more time Luther and I spent together, the more comfortable we were with each other and, although our attraction was probably growing with each encounter, our frantic urgency to make love all the time began to diminish. It was a welcome development. Our relationship was becoming more natural, sensual as well as sexual, and definitely more relaxed.

We shut out the rest of the world during the time we were together, retreating into one of our own making. Once in the apartment, we turned off our cell phones, removed our watches, made sure Luther's phone ringer was switched off. Our time together felt precious, and we wanted to be able to concentrate on each other without all the distractions of the everyday lives we were both escaping from. The apartment's decor reinforced the feeling that we were in our own little cocoon, with the billowing white fabric framing the treetops and the gently undulating ocean outside the windows. Luther said that at night when he came home alone the place made him feel like he was on a deserted island. To me it felt heavenly, as though I was living up in the clouds and listening to the music of nature.

I could still talk to Luther about anything, the way it had always been. He was understanding, helpful, and in no way judgmental. As open as we were together, though, there were some topics that we didn't touch—such as the state of my marriage, and the fact that the case that brought him to Miami was going to conclude soon. The future became a sort of taboo between us, and we lived as though under a divine order not to discuss it.

We did discuss the career deadline I was facing, and how I had just weeks in which to decide what I was going to do. I told Luther all about the firm, the various players I had to deal with, and the importune complication of the immigration attorney waiting to take my partnership in anticipation of my resignation. I was showing up regularly and holding back the threat, but I knew plans had been made to replace me. The partners were waiting to hear my decision, but, clearly, their patience was wearing out.

In Luther's mind, there was really no point in my agonizing about the decision. He felt I'd already made the decision subconsciously, and that I was processing it. I wasn't so sure I agreed with him. I'm a Catholic, but I didn't take great pleasure in torturing myself. Luther listened to me lay out the pros and cons of the situation for about an hour one afternoon.

"Look, you should really go back to the firm," Luther finally said, after listening in silence. "You know that's what you want. You don't want to stay at home all day. You're not made for it, and you'd go crazy. You need the challenge and the stimulation of your work."

"You're right," I agreed.

"For Christ's sake, it's such a gender thing," Luther added. "No one's pressuring any of your male partners to raise their kids full time and leave their partnership."

"I'd like to see their reaction if someone suggested it," I said.

"So what you need is to figure out a practical way to make your life bearable," Luther said, lightly touching my hand. "You burned out before, right? Why?"

"Because of the hours," I said. "And the pressure of coming home to Marti, not to mention always feeling like I was coming home too late and never spending enough time with him."

"Okay." Luther paused. "From what I hear, your firm isn't that much different from mine. You're a partner, so you have clout. You need to adjust your hours and not get sucked into a frantic schedule like you did before."

"But there are other considerations," I said. "I'm the first Latina partner. I have to think about—"

"You have to think about your own well-being," Luther said, "and let all the bullshit sort itself out. You put a lot of unnecessary pressure on yourself. Really, you can basically say: I'm back, and this time I'm not going to get burned out. I'm a partner, and I get to call the shots."

Luther had seen how hard I worked at Duke, and he understood how much being a successful lawyer meant to me, and how much it cost my identity and self-worth to give it up. Luther had all kinds of constructive suggestions: get a full-time paralegal assigned to me, start looking into preschools near the firm so I could see Marti in the afternoon when he was old enough to start. He stopped short from suggesting any rearrangement of my domestic situation.

I knew that Luther wasn't exactly a disinterested party to my life, but he was able to distance himself enough to offer practical advice—and advice that was made with my own interests in mind. With Ariel, it was impossible to talk over the situation at the firm: His bias was so strong, I knew it colored anything he might say. It wasn't that Ariel was incapable of being fair and impartial; it was that he wanted me to stay home so much that he was incapable of separating his desires from what might be best for me.

Talking about the matter with Luther, I felt a stinging pang that I was being disloyal to Ariel. But then, I reminded myself, I was already betraying him as deeply as a wife could. During the days when I didn't see Luther, I was spending hours at the office—and I wasn't always telling Ariel about it. After I took my leave of absence, I promised Ariel I would only go to the office sporadically, when my services were needed on an emergency basis. Now I was slipping back into a regular schedule and, by working hard to keep my profile as high as possible, I was refamiliarizing myself with the office culture. In the month of July I had managed to betray Ariel in two different ways. I couldn't even blame my behavior on hurricane season, because there were no big storms out there waiting to hit South Florida.

I knew I was living in denial. As pleasant as my juggling act had been, I couldn't continue having a secret life forever. Ariel was no fool, and sooner or later he was going to figure out that I was changing. He still seemed to assume that any preoccupation on my part was the result of my trying to sort out my professional life. Since he hadn't brought up the subject lately, he must have thought the best strategy was to leave me alone to make the "right" decision without his meddling. Maybe Ariel, like me, was practicing a particular form of denial.

Meanwhile, I had to admit, he was being the perfect husband, even more thoughtful and sweet than usual. It made me feel horrible at times for what I was doing behind his back. Not only was I spending time with my lover, I was going to the office regularly and keeping it from him. For some reason, Ariel hadn't been very interested lately in how I was spending my days. If I didn't volunteer information, he generally didn't ask. It was a strange time, and because of his lack of interest I had to do very little lying.

I was also more sweet and considerate around the house in the evenings, a departure from my normal slightly acerbic personality, and surely compensation for my sneaking around during the day. Sweetness didn't come naturally to me, and sometimes it felt like an act. If Ariel noticed the change, though, he didn't say so. He couldn't attribute any change to my time of the month because the stress of the past weeks had made my period late. It was a relief, really, because I didn't want to be out of commission for even a few days. Luther's return to New York was looming, and our every minute together counted.

There was another factor that I couldn't deny, which was Ariel's increased amorous attention. We'd always had an active sex life, but lately he'd been more energetic than ever, wanting to make love more often and in more adventuresome ways. He was approaching our sex life with even more than his usual gusto and focus—two attributes he had never lacked in the past. Prior to Luther's reappearance in my life, I would have welcomed this new ardor, but for the moment it just complicated my life. When I was with my lover, I felt unfaithful to my husband; when I was with my husband, I felt unfaithful to my lover. I had never imagined life could be so complicated.

This last development put me in an awkward position more than once, because if Ariel wanted to make love on a day that I'd spent with Luther, I wasn't really in the mood. Obviously I couldn't say so, though. The days when both my lover and my husband were particularly inspired were physically draining. And I couldn't let on to Ariel that I felt like a sex machine.

I never discussed with Luther the intimate aspects of my life with Ariel; if anything, we pretended that life didn't exist. Since I never saw Luther on the weekends, I tried to make sure Ariel became sexually inspired on Saturday and Sunday. The days passed, and I kept juggling my secret life. At times I could sense myself calculating, plotting, and I felt an inner coldness developing that scared me.

I began to wonder if this shrewd aspect of my personality had always been there, and had only surfaced when the situation required it. Or was it like a virus, stirred up by circumstance? I was always calculating and cool in my professional life—every attorney had to be. But now my personal life was calling on the same skills.

Time was passing, no matter how much I worried or tamped my fears down with denial. Things were going to change, I knew it.

At least I thought I knew. For an intelligent woman, sometimes I could be very stupid.

 It was the last week of August. I never used to think about time passing. But now my life was all about time—time hidden, time spent, deadlines and pressure. In the early morning hours sometimes I felt like Captain Hook in *Peter Pan*, hearing the ticktock of the clock in the crocodile's stomach wherever he went.

Unless something changed, Luther would be leaving Miami within the week—exactly at the same time I was supposed to announce my decision to the firm. I had tried to ignore the hard choices in my life, losing myself in juggling priorities, schedules, and loyalties. It was frightening how easily I was able to keep each part of my life discrete from all the others, and how good I had become at not facing reality.

I should have realized there was going to be a price to be paid for my actions. There always is when someone does something wrong. It was one of the few things I could say for sure was true.

Ariel was consumed by his personal-injury case, the one involving the water-delivery driver suing his employer and everyone else he could drag in. Ariel spent a lot of hours at the office, leaving early and coming home late, sometimes after dinner. Ariel had kept these kinds of hours before when working on an important case, but never for such an extended period of time. It didn't occur to me to question his behavior, and I believed him when he said he was at the office. Every time I phoned him there, he picked up.

Normally I would have said something to Ariel about neglecting to spend time with Marti, but I was busy with my own agenda and, of course, Ariel's long hours made things a hell of a lot easier for me. I was busy every day either with Luther or with going to the office. I was relieved that Ariel and I weren't spending much time together, because we were spared the usual chitchat about how we had spent our days.

When Ariel *was* home, he didn't even seem to notice that we weren't communicating as much as before, and that we only achieved any closeness when we were in bed making love. I thought that maybe he was unconsciously avoiding me, not wanting to discuss what I was going to do with my job. If so, I realized he was trying to be considerate and not influence my decision with anything he might do or say. Probably also he was simply working so intently on his case that he didn't want or need any distractions for the moment. It didn't matter much. In those days, I was happy just to be left alone.

I started feeling more and more guilt about my infidelity to Ariel in those moments when I allowed myself to stop running and examine my emotions. When Ariel lay in bed after we vigorously made love, he would softly snore next to me, with his features relaxed and his body at ease. He was a sound sleeper, the picture of a man whose world was right and who didn't have a care. He said he seldom dreamed, never had nightmares and, once asleep, hardly ever stirred in bed.

No woman could have asked for a better husband and father than Ariel. The man loved Marti and me with every bone in his body. I knew that he would have died for us. He was a great provider, and never denied us a thing—in fact, he delighted in spoiling us rotten. He drank in moderation, and his only vice was a fondness for Cuban Montecristo Numero Uno cigars, which were smuggled into the U.S. in defiance of the embargo. He was smart, he was funny, he always knew what I was talking about and was always ready for a laugh.

I couldn't come up with a clear answer that explained why I was betraying him. Before Luther came to Miami, the idea of getting involved with another man was the furthest thing from my mind. I wondered, if not Luther, would I eventually have had an affair with someone else? I liked to think not, that Luther had come at the right time and that I had been particularly receptive to him as a result. I didn't think I would have ever been unfaithful to Ariel with anyone else. Luther had been the great love of my life, and I was his. We hadn't recognized it at the time, at Duke or in the years that followed. Maybe we wouldn't have been ready then, even if we'd tried to stay together and get married. It might even have been a huge mistake, and we might have ruined things forever between us. I could drive myself crazy with all this speculation and navel-gazing, but I craved an explanation for what had happened to me this summer. The sun kept beating down, the sidewalks baked, and I felt myself drifting.

Although I spent much of the day in air-conditioning, I felt the heat getting to me. I started to feel tired all the time, even after a long night's sleep. I didn't think anything of it.

But one morning I experienced a symptom I couldn't ignore. It was the morning after a day in which I'd been with both Luther and Ariel, and I felt a painful burning sensation when I went to the bathroom for my morning pee. My bladder was so full that I had to empty it, but by the end I had tears in my eyes. Luckily, Ariel had already left for the office, so I could deal with my problem without him knowing.

I realized that my behavior had finally caught up with me. I had contracted the "honeymoon disease"—cystitis, the result of indulging in too much sex. I cursed under my breath because I realized that I would be out of commission while I took medicine to clear up the infection. The time left for Luther and me was rapidly dwindling, and the idea of abstaining from sex for at least several days seemed like an unendurable hardship.

I lay in bed, trying to think clearly despite the pain radiating from between my legs, and considered my options. I thought about going to one of my family's pharmacies, the one on Calle Ocho. I knew the pharmacist, Rodrigo. He'd worked there for decades, and I might be able to beg him for medicine to take care of the problem without a prescription. I knew he would do it, but I also knew that I couldn't trust him to keep quiet. Rodrigo was already privy to too much information about our family, since he filled all our prescriptions from birth control pills to Marti's antibiotics when he became sick. Rodrigo would probably tease me about having too much sex with Ariel while filling the prescription. He was a good friend, but I couldn't trust his discretion. He was totally loyal to my family, but that might make him more likely to blab to Mamá.

No, I would have to go see my regular ob/gyn, Dr. Kennedy, to get this deal over with. I looked over at the clock on my bedside table and saw that it wasn't even eight yet. It was going to be agony waiting until nine for the office to open. I considered getting in my car and driving there in hopes that I could somehow be worked in between patients, but I decided against it. I could end up sitting in the waiting room for hours.

I felt terrible, but I received some pity for my sins when, at precisely nine, I called the doctor's office. The nurse who answered told me that there had just been a cancellation, and said that an appointment was mine if I could get there by nine thirty. I didn't even take a shower. I put on a skirt, a T-shirt, and espadrilles, then darted for the door.

Dr. Kennedy's office was in the Grove, and traffic was light, so I made it right on time. I found an empty parking space across the street from the Mayfair House Hotel, right next to the doctor's office, but as I bustled away I suddenly realized that I had forgotten to put money in the meter. Knowing the merciless restrictions in the Grove, I would surely find a ticket waiting for me. I was in such pain by then, though, that I would rather take the ticket than have to retrace my steps. I would have paid five tickets without complaining, if only I could get a little relief.

I arrived in the office completely out of breath, and cringing with each step I took. I didn't want to seem overly dramatic, but keeping my composure was becoming increasingly difficult. Once inside, I signed my name on the clipboard by the frosted pane of glass that separated the nurse's station from the waiting room. A couple of minutes later the partition opened and one of the nurses—a bored, gum-chewing twenty-something who looked barely old enough to be out of school—glanced at the paper where I'd written my name.

"Margarita," she said. I hated to be called by my first name by strangers, especially when they were a dozen years younger than me.

"Right here," I said weakly.

"Sorry, but Dr. Kennedy's been called away on an emergency," she explained. "He had to go to Baptist Hospital to deliver a baby."

I felt my eyes tear up, and struggled to keep myself together.

"When will he be back?" I asked.

The nurse just shrugged. "Don't know." She chewed her gum, looked at me, and seemed finally to notice how much pain I was in. "You know, Dr. Macia is here. She can see you, if you're not able to wait for Dr. Kennedy."

I had no idea who Dr. Macia was, but I had gone from hating the young nurse to wanting to kiss her.

"That would be great," I said.

The frosted glass door slammed shut. I got up and found myself in too much pain to sit down again. The waiting room was empty save for me, so no one was there to mind my pacing around and grimacing. I loved Dr. Kennedy—he had been my ob/gyn ever since my freshman year at Penn, when the family pediatrician said he could no longer see me, since I'd just turned eighteen. I thought that it was going to be a little strange, having a female doctor examine me. I was so miserable, though, that I would have seen Attila the Hun if he'd been able to help me.

I kept pacing, trying to distract myself from the burning inside me. I thought about all the prenatal visits to this office when I was expecting Marti, and how I'd never really looked around at my surroundings—I'd been too tense with expectation. It had been a blessing, really. Now that I had a good look, the place resembled nothing more than an adolescent girl's fantasy, with light pink, striped wallpaper, rose-colored upholstery on the sofa and armchairs, a flowery red carpet, and lavender checked curtains tied off with white eyelet sashes. Even the window shades glowed with a rust color. Maternity and parenting magazines covered all the pink-stained tables in the four corners of the room.

It was bizarre to see the place as it really was, and I realized that I had never been alone in the room before. I couldn't fathom any reason for decorating a room for grown women as though it was a nursery for little girls. Maybe some misguided decorator had thought that female patients would be more comfortable in a room that evoked their childhood. Instead, standing there alone, the room looked infantile and depressing to me. If my condition hadn't made me sick, my surroundings would have.

Suddenly the frosted glass snapped open and Nurse Lolita called out to me. I moved as fast as I could to the door when she opened it, and went to a bathroom when she directed me to pee in a plastic cup.

"Open the little door next to the sink when you're done," she said with some distaste. "Just push the cup through. The lab's on the other side. And don't forget to write your name on the cup—there's a pencil right here."

The very idea of urinating filled me with horror, but I knew I was going to have to get through it. The burning pain was almost unendurable, but I somehow managed to follow the nurse's orders. When I was finished, I washed my hands and opened the door, waiting to be escorted to the examination room. I looked at my watch. If Dr. Macia worked like Dr. Kennedy, I would be out of there, prescription in hand, in about twenty minutes.

Instead, a second nurse came to get me.

"I'll take you to the lab," she said.

"What for?"

"Dr. Macia has ordered a blood test," she explained.

I just needed some antibiotics, but I went along without protest. I figured this was just the doctor's way of dealing with patients she'd never seen before—after all, doctors were sued every day, and I was an attorney. It wouldn't be the first time my occupation made someone paranoid.

The lab technician was doing her best to carry on the proud tradition of Count Dracula: She took about five gallons of blood from a vein in the crook of my arm. She was so enthusiastic, I was surprised she hadn't just gone for a bite from my neck. When she was finished, she slapped a Band-Aid on my arm and gave me a big smile. The nurse returned and escorted me to an examination room. I was totally miserable, my arm throbbing and my insides burning, but I kept telling myself that it would all be over soon.

Inside the examination room the nurse ordered me to take off all my clothes; she then handed me a pink paper robe that had a red plastic strap to tie around my waist. I wasn't going to be walking down a Paris catwalk in that outfit anytime soon. The nurse then took my blood pressure and asked me questions about my general health. I fought off the urge to just ask her for a prescription so I could be on my way.

"The doctor will be with you shortly," the nurse said, signing her papers and nodding officiously. I sighed, resigning myself to a long wait. Apparently Dr. Macia didn't work as quickly as Dr. Kennedy. To distract myself from the pain, I busied myself folding my clothes.

There was a magazine rack on the wall near the bench where I waited. I leafed through a couple of celebrity gossip rags, then opened the blinds and watched the traffic on the street below. So much time passed that I was almost tempted to open up one of the parenting magazines, but I was spared that brand of torture by Dr. Macia's arrival.

At first I couldn't believe the person who had stepped in the door could possibly be a doctor. She looked too young to buy a drink. She was tiny, with short black hair and bangs, no makeup, and she wore plain blue jeans under her white lab coat. She came in holding the clipboard containing my chart, which she looked at as though it contained incriminating information.

"I'm Dr. Macia," she said without looking up.

"I figured that out," I said, my voice tight with pain.

Dr. Macia seemed oblivious to sarcasm. As for me, sitting there in my pink wraparound, the throbbing between my legs, having come there without a shower, I felt ready to apply for Social Security. I had never imagined that I would long for old Dr. Kennedy.

"Please lie down." Dr. Macia indicated the examination table. I carefully did as I was told, feeling anxious about the prospect of having a woman put her hand inside me. I gritted my teeth and tried to have an out-of-body experience as the doctor poked and prodded around. I had to admit, Dr. Macia had a gentle way about her. As soon as she was finished, I sat straight up on the table and tried to arrange my robe to cover myself as much as possible. It was a futile gesture—the young doctor knew me physically by then about as well as anyone could—but it made me feel better.

Dr. Macia took off her white surgical gloves and washed her hands in the sink. After she had scrubbed her skin raw, she dried her hands with meticulous fussiness. She then picked up my chart and read through the top page for what seemed like a long time.

"It's just as you thought, Mrs. Silva," she said. "Cystitis."

Dr. Macia looked up from the page and, I sensed, saw me for the first time as someone other than a name on a chart.

"So I'll need antibiotics," I said.

"No, no," she replied, frowning. "Because of your condition, we can't treat you with antibiotics."

When I heard the word "condition," I wrapped the robe a little tighter around my body.

"I don't understand," I told her.

Dr. Macia looked again at the chart. "Because of your pregnancy, we can't use antibiotics," she said. "It's too potentially dangerous."

"My son is three years old," I told her. "He hasn't breast-fed for years. I can't see how it would make any possible difference."

Dr. Macia blinked. "I know you have a son," she said. "But I'm talking about your current pregnancy."

"I—" I stopped myself. "I don't know what you're talking about. I'm not pregnant."

"Yes, you are." Dr. Macia tilted the chart so I could see it, then pointed to a box in the middle highlighted in pink. "I have the lab run a pregnancy test on all patients as a matter of routine. Yours came up positive."

Dr. Macia took out a round plastic card and consulted it. "Let's see now, you told the nurse your last period was on June 8. That makes you six weeks pregnant. Your delivery date will be March 8."

Delivery date! I would have hoped I was dreaming, but the nauseating pain I felt ensured that this was real.

"I'm on the Pill," I insisted. "I take it without fail, so I can't be pregnant. Your lab made a mistake."

Dr. Macia's expression darkened, as though I had impugned her professional credibility.

"I take it you weren't aware of the pregnancy until now," she said.

"Aware of . . . no!" I sputtered. "I wasn't . . . this doesn't make any sense. There's been a mistake."

"I'm afraid not," Dr. Macia said. "You're pregnant. I can see this is a shock, but you're going to have to deal with it."

I was still unwilling to concede defeat. My lawyerly instincts were too strong. "I take the Pill every day!" I cried out.

Dr. Macia's expression betrayed her lack of patience with me. She had other patients to see, and that day she was carrying Dr. Kennedy's load as well as her own.

"There is a statistical failure rate with the Pill," she said. "Surely you know that."

Dr. Macia began writing on her prescription pad, leaving me sitting there in shock. I was numb when she handed me two slips of paper.

"The first is for the infection," she said. "The other is for prenatal iron pills—your red blood count is on the low side."

"Thank you," I said quietly.

"You've had a child, so you know about diet and abstaining from alcohol," Dr. Macia said. "Make an appointment with Dr. Kennedy so he can follow your pregnancy. When you see him, he can explain all about the Pill's failure rate."

I must have looked particularly forlorn, because Dr. Macia paused on her way out.

"Congratulations," she said in a strangely shy manner. "And good luck with your second child."

With that, she was gone. I thought that my profession had probably made her act coldly toward me, and I tried not to take it personally. I hoped it wasn't the generation gap. The thought was too depressing.

I got dressed in slow motion and went back out to the reception area. I paid the bill with a check—there was no way I was going to put it through the insurance company for reimbursement.

Wait, I thought. *I'm pregnant. I can't hide that.*

I left the office and crossed the street as though walking in a fog. Once inside my car, I sat behind the wheel for about a full minute until I was composed enough to drive.

I looked out at the windshield wipers. Amazingly, there was no ticket tucked under there, even though I hadn't filled the meter.

Well, it was about time I caught a break.

 First things first. After I left the doctor's office, I drove straight to the nearest Eckerd's to get my prescription filled. I was so shaken that I felt cold, and I shivered. My hands shook so much that it was hard to drive; still, my survival skills took over, and I managed to avoid getting into an accident. I felt myself shift into autopilot, as though I barely inhabited my body. I was able to go through the motions of living, but through it all I felt a cool, serene sense of detachment.

There was a full-length mirror just outside the drugstore. I stopped, surprised to see that I looked normal despite all my inner turmoil. I couldn't understand how that could be. My world had been turned inside out, but there was no visible evidence for me to see.

"We're really backed up," said the pharmacist, a middle-aged man in thick glasses. "It's going to take about two hours to take care of this. You really should have had your doctor phone it in in advance."

All the tears I had held back in the face of Dr. Macia finally came out. I stood there, my head dropped down to my chest. I must have looked sufficiently pathetic, because the pharmacist looked around in dismay.

"Wait there," he said. "I'll take care of you right away."

Five minutes later I paid cash for the prescription. I clutched the precious white paper bag and asked for directions to the ladies' room. I hobbled to the back of the store, locked myself in a bathroom stall, and applied the prescription unguent to myself. I felt relief almost immediately—so much that I forgave Dr. Macia for being brusque with me.

I was able to walk out to the car without wincing in pain, a definite improvement. I started up the Escalade and headed instinctively for Dinner Key Marina; once there, I drove east, toward the docks. I parked in the same restricted space as I had a few weeks before, got out, and seated myself on the same bench where Luther had professed his love for me.

I looked out over the water, hoping it would restore some sense of peace to my spirit. It was only midmorning, and not as hot as the afternoon I met Luther, but I knew it was only a matter of time until waves of heat would emanate from the sidewalks.

Listening to the water lapping against the hulls of the boats, I felt myself calming down. Dozens of pelicans perched haughtily on the channel markers, preening themselves in the ocean spray. They must have already had breakfast because they showed no interest in the schools of fish skimming the water's surface, their silver scales flashing in the bright sun. Seagulls squawked as they flew past, swooping in formation, heading out to sea. I watched a couple of men working on a boat, scraping barnacles from its side and rinsing off the hull. Some people were fishing, and from somewhere nearby a transistor radio sent tinny music across the morning quiet to where I sat.

I could have stayed there for hours, just taking it all in, but I had to deal with my problems. I remembered Dr. Macia talking about the Pill's failure rate. I was a believer in statistics, but I never really believed the law of averages applied to me. When Ariel and I decided to start a family, I simply stopped taking the Pill and got pregnant a month later. There wasn't anything complicated about it, or anything that required much thought. As long as I took the Pill, I assumed, I wouldn't get pregnant. The moment I stopped, I had.

And in all the years I had taken the Pill, I had never even missed a single dose.

During the past six weeks I had been engaging in a lot more sex than usual, but that shouldn't have been a problem for the Pill. It was designed to protect against pregnancy whether a woman had sex once a month or several times a day. Ariel was obviously capable of fathering a child, and Luther was very virile, but it shouldn't have mattered.

I bit my lip and reached out to either side to hold on to the bench as a wave of anxiety washed over me. I didn't know who the father of my baby was. It was a fifty-fifty possibility either way. I had had sex with Luther and Ariel about the same number of times during the time in which I'd conceived. Unless I submitted them and the baby to DNA testing—and, believe me, I didn't see that happening—it wasn't likely that I would ever know. I realized I was going to spend the rest of my life watching the child, looking for traits that might identify who the father was.

Terminating the pregnancy was out of the question. I may not have been a churchgoing, confession-making, Communion-taking Catholic, but I didn't believe in abortion. I realized that I was selective about which of the sacraments I followed, and I had seriously messed around with the Ten Commandments, but abortion was an act I simply couldn't ever commit. I may have been somewhat of a lapsed Catholic, but I wasn't so far removed from the Church's teachings that I could abort a child. Like it or not, he or she was part of me now.

It was starting to get hot, and a sheen of perspiration appeared on my forehead. I looked at my watch and was surprised to see that an hour had passed since I sat down. So far I hadn't figured anything out, or thought things through. All I had done was feel sorry for myself, and run over the increasingly familiar ground of my predicament. I had to snap out of it because I was going to have to be very careful about what I did next.

The fact that I was pregnant wasn't really sinking in; it was like a persistent knocking at the door that I couldn't bring myself to answer. I didn't feel pregnant, nor had I exhibited any of the symptoms of my condition. I ran my hand over my belly, which felt as flat as before. My breasts weren't sore, and I hadn't experienced any morning sickness. I had been tired lately—exhausted, really—but that was a natural consequence of the stressful and duplicitous life I had been leading.

I had to accept the fact that I was going to be a mother again. *A baby*. I hadn't planned it, so I had a hard time understanding and accepting it. I knew how my mind worked, and I wasn't about to refuse the gift of at least a short period of denial.

I stretched and yawned, closing my eyes to the sun. And, in that moment, I realized something. I didn't know how, I didn't know why, but I suddenly understood that my getting pregnant hadn't been an accident. I knew that I didn't belong in that tiny fraction of women who get pregnant while on the Pill. I couldn't say why I was so sure of this, but I would have bet everything I had that it was true. I needed to know what had gone wrong, and how I had ended up this way. I needed something concrete before I could make any decisions.

The batch of pills I was taking when I conceived might have been defective. I wondered if that was possible, and how I could find out about it. There was no way the drug manufacturers were going to admit that there might be something wrong with their product, especially once they learned that I was a lawyer. They would hide behind statistics, and invoke that small possibility that the Pill can fail. They could even call Dr. Kennedy as a witness, and have him state under oath that he'd quoted me the insignificant failure rate for birth control pills. No, contacting the manufacturer would get me nowhere.

I stared at the pelicans, as though one of them was going to fly over and give me some insight. They were no help; they were getting ready to go fishing, and were flapping their wings in anticipation.

I remembered waking up this morning. I had thought I had tough decisions to make. Sorting out my marital and professional lives, it turned out, was easy in comparison to dealing with this child. I could have hung my head. I was pregnant and didn't know who the father was. It felt like divine retribution for the way I'd been carrying on, and the Catholic inside me said I had gotten what I deserved.

Once, years ago, I had gone to Dallas to take a deposition for a case and stayed in one of the chain hotels that caters to business travelers. The window of my room faced a giant billboard that lit up during the night. There was no ignoring it, and I could close my eyes and see it in vivid detail years later. It depicted a giant sperm, its head pointing up toward heaven, its wiggling tail pointing downward. The caption read: "Pregnant? Don't know who the father is?" It turned out to be an advertisement for a company that provided DNA tests to determine the paternity of children. I had found the image sad and depressing, and hated to think about a world in which such a service would even be necessary. But now it made a lot more sense.

I felt like a teenager who'd been fooling around with two guys and had gotten caught. It was a terrible feeling, and I burned with shame. I was a professional, married woman, the mother of a toddler. This was the kind of thing that happened to someone else, not me.

God, I thought about Ariel finding out. And Mamá. And even Marti, and my eyes filled with tears when I wondered what he would think of me when he was old enough to understand.

I decided two things: I was going to stop putting myself down, and I was going to figure out what had gone wrong. Then I could move on and deal with the situation.

Because, like it or not, that was what I was going to have to do.

Arms outstretched to greet me, Rodrigo came out from behind the counter at the Calle Ocho branch of Santos Pharmacies.

"Margarita," he said in his raspy voice. "It's very, very good to see you."

It was a little strange to be hugged by Rodrigo, since his face came up to my midsection. Somehow he always managed to make sure his head ended up between my breasts. When I was a teenager I thought he was a dirty old man, but I had since realized that this was simply how he greeted women—especially young and pretty ones. Anyway, he was in his eighties and there was no point lecturing him on the fine points of political correctness.

Rodrigo was a skinny, wizened old man, a widower whose wife had died almost fifty years ago; he had loved his Zoraida so much, the story went, that he never even looked at another woman after she died. He had no children, and he had unofficially adopted us Santos children as his own. My brothers and male cousins all adored him, especially when we were adolescents, because he was a never-ending source of seriously dirty jokes.

Save for when I was away at college, I couldn't recall a time in my life when I went more than a few weeks without seeing Rodrigo. He had worked for my family back in Havana, at the Santos pharmacy on the corner of Galiano and San Rafael. When Fidel Castro came to power and the stores were nationalized, Rodrigo went into exile with my family. At one point he even lived with my grandparents while he was studying for the exam to validate his pharmacist's license in America. The minute the ink was dry on the license, Rodrigo was back behind the counter of a Santos drugstore.

"Hola, Rodrigo. Cómo estás?" I hugged him back, feeling his skinny body through the folds of his heavy white cotton pharmacist's smock. With his tiny, wiry build, he reminded me of a jockey.

"Bien, bien, muchachita." Rodrigo stepped back, squinting, with his head tipped back to take a good look at me. "You are as beautiful as ever."

"How's Perrita?" I asked, referring to his constant companion, a mangy mutt he found in the alley behind the store after locking up late one night about a dozen years ago.

Perrita was a mix of breeds, so everyone always said her mother must have had one hell of a Saturday night many years ago. She barely weighed twenty pounds, with dark brown fur and white splotches, and she was missing her right eye, her left ear, and most of her tail. She walked with a strange kind of gait, tilting to one side like a sailor trying to keep his balance on the deck of a ship during a storm. Perrita was clearly a dog with a colorful past. She went everywhere with Rodrigo, and spent many of her days sleeping in a well-worn armchair behind the pharmacy counter, never more than a few feet away from him. Normally, no one would have objected to Perrita accompanying Rodrigo to work, but in the last year or so she had developed a very unattractive trait—she farted constantly, and the smell of gas circulated around the store, borne on drafts from the air-conditioning. It was actually pretty funny to watch the expression on a customer's face who caught a whiff of one of Perrita's farts, then looked around suspiciously to locate the culprit.

The cause of the problem was obvious to everyone. In all the years he'd had her, Rodrigo fed Perrita only Cuban food. It wasn't the easiest to digest, and now that the dog was getting old, it was wreaking havoc on her intestines. Everyone at the pharmacy had, at one time or another, tried to give Perrita Purina Dog Chow or some other brand suitable for older dogs. But Rodrigo wouldn't hear of it, claiming that she was a Cuban dog with Cuban taste—and that she should never be fed gringo dog food made from the carcasses of dead horses.

No one dared speculate aloud what might happen to Rodrigo when Perrita passed away, since she was so important to him and had been in his life for so long. No one knew how old she was; there was no way even to guess how much more time she had. Until the sad day when she would pass away, the other employees and the customers would just have to deal with her noxious gas.

Rodrigo beamed, his nut-brown face glowing with pride and affection. "Perrita is great, really fine. And Marti?"

I smiled. Obviously, Rodrigo felt we were discussing our respective children. For him, the gaseous Perrita was certainly on the same level as the little boy Marti.

"He's growing fast," I said. "Soon he'll be starting playschool."

"Time for another, eh?" Rodrigo said, actually winking at me. His eyes went straight to my belly, and I decided to stop making excuses for him. He *was* a dirty old man. I moved a little to avert his stare. Rodrigo was undeterred. "A little sister for Marti, maybe?"

"You think so?" I asked, surprised by the coincidence of his comment—not to mention his open appraisal of my body. I knew he meant no harm, and was a trusted family friend, but he had been a widower for far too long.

"*Sí.* Yes, yes."

And, if it were possible for someone nut-colored to blush, Rodrigo's face turned bright red. He dipped his head, muttering to himself, and stepped away to rearrange some of the condoms displayed in front of the prescription counter. His hands shook slightly, and all of a sudden he seemed to realize that he was fiddling around with male contraceptives in front of me, which sent him into a minor spasm of coughing, pretending he hadn't been rearranging condoms and, finally, rearranging the condoms again. This shifty behavior was totally out of character for Rodrigo. He had always seemed like part of our family and, as our pharmacist, he knew about many of our private affairs. Believe me, someone who fills your prescriptions knows a lot about you.

I stared at Rodrigo, suddenly suspicious. I had come to ask him about birth control pills, and now he was obviously hiding something from me.

"Rodrigo, what's going on?" I asked him, moving between him and the counter so he had no escape from me. "Tell me—why are you acting this way? Is there something you want to tell me?"

The old man didn't answer. Instead, he moved over a few feet and pretended to be absorbed in the row of thermometers next to the condoms. He knew something I didn't. The lawyer inside me bared her teeth.

"Rodrigo—" I began.

"Listen, Margarita, I have a lot of prescriptions to fill," he said nervously. "So, if you will excuse me, I have to go."

He got on his tiptoes to kiss me good-bye. I had to think fast, or I wouldn't get anything from him.

"Rodrigo, I have a huge favor to ask." I gave him my most winning smile and slid my hand into his. I put my other hand on my belly and rubbed it, then leaned over and whispered into his ear. "Lately I've been putting on weight. Not much, just a few pounds, but my clothes are getting tight. I want to do something about it."

Now Rodrigo broke out in a huge smile of relief. The man's face was like an open book, embarrassingly easy to read. As soon as I saw his reaction to what I had told him, I felt cold inside.

"Remember after Marti was born, when I was having trouble losing the weight I gained during my pregnancy?" I asked. His smile disappeared. "You gave me some diet pills, some really strong ones. I lost the weight fast."

Rodrigo's smile dropped. "Yes, I remember. I gave you Phen/Fen." He shook his head. "That's off the market now. Some women had heart trouble when they took that. Their valves didn't work right. Some women died, and there were really big lawsuits. Millions and millions of dollars."

"I heard about that," I told him. "But there's been new information that maybe Phen/Fen wasn't responsible for the deaths. I've done a lot of reading on the subject, and I've never believed those pills were really dangerous."

"Margarita, I don't know," he said, troubled.

"Rodrigo, you kept some of those pills, right?" I pressed him. "You didn't send them all back, or destroy them, did you?"

Rodrigo pulled his hand from mine. "Margarita, why are you asking me about the Phen/Fen?" he asked. "I've known you for a long time, and I can tell when you want something from me."

I leaned over him. "If you have any of those pills left, I want them," I said. "They worked so well for me before, and I want to take them again. There's nothing wrong with my heart. Those pills won't do anything to me except help me lose weight."

A horrified look came over Rodrigo's face; he rubbed his hands against his smock, suddenly agitated.

"No, you can't do that!" he exclaimed. "Margarita, you can't take any diet pills!"

I knew it. He was hiding something from me.

"Why not?" I asked him. "They really work, and I want to lose the extra pounds. I've been exercising, but it doesn't seem to be making any difference. So why not take them?"

"Margarita, no," Rodrigo said, almost sadly.

"Well, maybe not Phen/Fen." I softened my stance a little. "But do you have anything else you can give me?"

Rodrigo shook his head violently from side to side. "No, no. I won't give you anything."

I hated to use the old man in this fashion, but it was obvious he wasn't telling me everything I needed to know.

"I don't understand," I said. "You've given them to me before without a prescription. All I ever had to do was ask. You said that yourself."

Rodrigo moved toward the pharmacy counter door. "I'm sorry," he said. "I just can't."

I shrugged. "Okay, I guess I'll just go to Montez's, then."

At the mention of a rival drugstore, also Cuban-owned and which was known to dispense pills without a doctor's prescription, Rodrigo stopped in his tracks.

"You can't do that!" he said.

"Why not?" I challenged. "I'm determined to lose weight, and I know the diet pills help me. Frankly, I can't understand why you won't help me all of a sudden."

It was painful to watch Rodrigo wrestling with his conscience. On the one hand, he obviously wanted to do what was right. But he was trying to figure out how to keep from revealing the truth to me. Apparently, morality won out over confidentiality. Rodrigo nervously ran his tongue over his teeth and looked around, making sure no one was around to listen.

"Because, Margarita, you can't take that kind of medication in your condition." He stammered, and spoke so softly that I had trouble hearing him. The man was obviously suffering, and I was responsible. Too bad. I had taken a big bite of his ass, and I wasn't letting go.

"My condition?" I repeated. "What condition are you talking about?"

Rodrigo sighed and took a deep breath. I knew I had him then.

"I'll get fired if it gets out that I told you this," he said.

I felt like picking him up and shaking him until the answers tumbled out of his mouth.

"Told me what, Rodrigo?"

He took my hands in his and looked up into my face. His old eyes shone with emotion.

"You're not gaining weight because you're eating too much, or not exercising," he said. "It's because you're having another baby."

There, he had said it.

There was only one way he could have known that information. In spite of my shock and disappointment, part of me felt an eerie sense of relief from having my suspicions confirmed. My instincts had told me to come to Rodrigo to ask him about the Pill, since he was the one responsible for filling my prescriptions. I hated to lie to him, but I had to.

The pieces fell into place in my mind. They shouldn't have messed with a lawyer. Now all I needed was for Rodrigo to fill in the blanks.

"Tell me what happened," I gently ordered him. "I promise that I won't get you in trouble with my family."

"I'm sorry, Margarita," he moaned.

"Don't worry about it," I said. "Just talk. Tell me everything."

There was no point accusing Rodrigo of betraying me, because it was done. Now I just wanted the details of what had transpired.

And, with that, I listened to the story of how I was betrayed by my mother and my husband.

 I was so drained after talking with Rodrigo that it took all my strength to walk out to the car. My eyes wandered all over the console and rested on the clock, but I was so distraught that it took a while before the neon green digital numbers registered in my mind. I realized with a shock that it was already past one o'clock, and I hadn't even taken a shower or had coffee. My whole life had been up-ended in the span of a few hours.

Listening to Rodrigo explain exactly what had happened—what he had done, and why—I was devastated by the enormity of the be-trayal I'd suffered. When I saw Ariel and Mamá so buddy-buddy at the family dinner, I should have suspected they were cooking up something. Never in a hundred years, though, would I have thought they would resort to such low-down, dirty means of making sure I quit work and stayed home with another baby.

And they thought I would never find out.

I knew that Ariel and Mamá had always been in agreement, think-ing they knew what was best for me, but to stoop as low as they had was inconceivable to me. They had infantilized me, making decisions for me as though I was incapable of making them on my own. They had talked to me like I was a child before, and I had gone along with their little jokes, thinking them harmless. Now I saw that my laissez faire attitude had been a huge mistake.

I had maintained my composure while talking to Rodrigo, but the truth was that I felt traumatized, almost as though I was learning someone in my family had died. The tragedy had taken place, nothing could be done about it, and there was nothing left but to learn the particulars. I felt like a voyeur of a scene in which I was the main actor, and it was a horrible sensation.

Rodrigo had, of course, sworn me to secrecy, telling me that not only would Mamá fire him if she learned he had talked to me, but he would also be permanently expelled from the Santos family inner circle. Mamá had known exactly what she was doing when she threatened the old man with banishment from our family. We were the only family he had left.

Once he started talking, there was no holding the old man back. Mamá had told him how tired I was of working, and how I really wanted to resign from my job and have another baby but I worried that I would be letting down my partners at the firm. She told him how I felt that, as the only Cuban woman partner, I worried I would be setting a bad precedent if I quit for no reason. She told him how I talked about having worked too long and hard to just walk away from my job.

To put it another way, she used my own thoughts and concerns against me.

Mamá told Rodrigo that getting pregnant would give me a perfect reason for resigning—which is what I really wanted to do, but wouldn't admit to anyone. She had actually told Rodrigo that there were problems between Ariel and me because of my job, and that having another baby would keep us together. Mamá, she explained, was being a good mother by helping me with my dilemma.

Rodrigo, a Cuban man, understood this reasoning perfectly. They were speaking the same language, and he agreed wholeheartedly that it would be best for me to get pregnant right away. And, after all, who knew what was best for me, if not my husband and mother? As a pharmacist, though, he knew he would be breaking the law by going along with Mamá's proposal. The fear of being banished from the Santos world was stronger in the end than the oath he had taken upon becoming a pharmacist and, in the end, he bought into her argument and overcame his initial hesitation about going along with the plan.

I knew how persuasive Mamá could be, and I wasn't surprised she had managed to browbeat Rodrigo into breaking the law. And that was why, when I went to get my last batch of birth control pills, he had substituted placebos for the real thing. It was clear to me that Rodrigo was convinced he had done what was right for me. Talking about what had happened, it all made perfect sense to him.

I had never felt so alone in my life. There was no one I could confide in, or consult with. Close as I was to Vivian and Anabel, I couldn't go to them for help. I would trust them with my life, but this was information that I simply couldn't share with them. I wasn't able to tell them about the affair with Luther, and I didn't think I ever would. They both liked Ariel, although in the beginning when we had begun dating, they had been suspicious of him and his motives toward me, but those had dissipated as the years passed and he had convinced them of his honorable intentions. I knew that they would take Ariel's side in this situation, especially as I could not tell them the whole story. And there was no way to understand the problems I faced without knowing about the affair.

After the first conversation with them in Starbucks when I told them Luther was in Miami, I hadn't mentioned his name to them again. They would also be hurt that I hadn't confided in them—although, I reminded myself, Vivian had adopted a child without saying a word. Maybe the time for confidences was over. It was a sad thought, but there was no way I could go to Vivian and Anabel for help.

Sometimes, I realized, we're simply alone in life. And this was certainly one of those times. I got into this mess—with some help, admittedly—and I was going to have to sort it out. Maybe all that was left to me was heavenly consultation.

A full ten minutes passed before I felt sufficiently composed to start the car. I drove without really thinking toward the Ermita de la Caridad, the shrine in Coconut Grove dedicated to the Virgin de la

Caridad del Cobre, the patron saint of Cuba. I turned east off South Bayshore Drive, almost in a trance, and pulled into the drive leading to the shrine. The shrine was a holy place for exiles, a round building sitting just yards from the waters of Biscayne Bay.

I had gone there before for solace, but it had been a long time since my last visit. My hands shaking, my breath coming in ragged gasps, I felt I was going to the only place left to me.

I circled around the building and parked in a slot directly in front of the water. The wind off the bay was blowing so hard that I had difficulty opening the car door. The shrine was unlocked, and I went inside without any problem.

The church was empty—no surprise, since it was midday and the middle of the week. I walked slowly until I faced the altar, where I knelt, crossed myself, then slipped into the first pew. I focused my eyes on the statue of the Virgin de la Caridad del Cobre, a small mulatto figure placed in the center of the altar. She was dressed in her usual white raiments, with cascades of pearls framing her visage.

Peace. Just for a moment it washed over me like cool water.

The instant I came into the Ermita, I felt connected with my Cuban roots. The building was a testament to the exile experience, and to its heroes and heroines. The wall behind the altar contained a mural depicting the important scenes from Cuban history. Although Fidel Castro had been in power for more than forty years, the paintings of Cuban men and women who had contributed to Cuba's five-hundred-year history served as a poignant reminder that the sum total of the island's history was stronger and more powerful than any single dictator. The nightmare will pass, the mural said to me, and hopefully we will have learned something from that tragic and painful lesson.

Although I consulted Violeta and trusted her judgment, my problems had become too big for her. I went to the Virgin sparingly, not wanting to overburden her with my troubles. She was small, barely a foot tall, but for Cubans she towered in importance. She was a confidante, a quiet force that held our lives together. I was no different than my twelve million compatriots here in exile and on the island; I always felt she spoke to me directly, and more than once I thought I actually saw her lips move.

I made myself comfortable because this was going to be a long conversation. Although she surely knew all the facts, I looked into her eyes and explained what I had done.

I knew my affair with Luther had broken the vows I had taken during the sacrament of marriage. There was no excuse or reason for what I had done with Luther. I was happily married to Ariel, or so I had thought. Even though something must have been wrong, inside me or between us, I had still betrayed a good man, one who loved me. It was unforgivable, and something that I was going to have to live with for the rest of my life.

But Ariel wasn't without blame. He'd conspired with my mother to force me into leaving my job, and he'd violated my right to choose how I lived my life. These weren't the actions of an honorable man. Clearly he thought I would never find out what he had done, but he and Mamá had underestimated me. Ariel obviously didn't know about Luther. Now Ariel and Mamá's plot to get me pregnant had created the possibility that I was carrying Luther's baby.

And Luther, approaching me, declaring his love when he knew I was married with a family. He was thinking only of himself when he showed up in Miami and came back into my life. Of course, I hadn't resisted him.

No one was blameless. And now it was time to deal with it. The Cuban and American sides of my life had come together, created sparks, and now threatened to destroy my life. I couldn't let that happen. I had one child, and a second was on the way. And that's all that mattered. I couldn't worry about Ariel's feelings, or Luther's, and I sure as hell wasn't going to worry about Mamá's.

My eyes wandered over the Virgin's face, from her eyes down to her lips. Then I saw them move.

"Tell me," I said. And I began to hear what she said.

As soon as I heard Ariel's car pull into the drive-way, I sprinted over to the bedroom and lay down on the bed. An hour before, I had telephoned him at the office and asked him to please come home as soon as possible. This had been the first time I could recall ever hav-ing made such a request, so it was understandable that Ariel sounded first curious, then annoyed that I would not divulge what was on my mind. I suspected he knew but was not giving that away, experienced lawyer that he was.

Ariel kept calling for me as he walked through the house. Calmly, I waited until he was at the doorway of the bedroom before answering him.

"Oh, hi, Ariel." I opened my eyes as if I had just woken up. If I ever wanted to find out if I had any acting skills, now was the time. "I must have fallen asleep."

Even though I was fuming at his treachery, I had to admit that Ariel looked attractive, in his olive-green linen suit, his face tan from riding in the car with the top down.

"Margarita, is something wrong?" He asked, as soon as he saw me lying there. "Are you sick?"

"Ariel, come here." I sat up, and patted the place next to me on the bed. "I have to tell you something."

My heart sank when I recognized a look in Ariel's eyes that he got when he was in the courtroom about to cross examine a witness, indicating he was circling in, ready for the kill. He knew what I was going to say, but was waiting to see how I would do it. That one single look confirmed what Rodrigo had told me, and was all I needed to go through with my charade.

I took his right hand and held it between mine. "Ariel, today, I went to see Dr. Kennedy for a checkup." Ariel knew perfectly well the name of my ob/gyn, so as soon as he heard it, he could be fairly certain of where I was headed. "I got some news," I began.

Ariel frowned, not wanting to give anything away. "What kind of news, Margarita?" He began stroking my hair. "Is there a problem?" I wanted to pull away, but managed to keep my composure. The only way my plan—and the Virgin's—was going to work was if I played it convincingly. No doubt about it, I was going for the Oscar. I just had to keep thinking of Marti.

"I just found out today that I'm having another baby," I stated flatly, careful to keep all emotion out of my voice. I did not want Ariel to have any idea how I felt about the situation.

Ariel leaned over and kissed me. "A baby! Oh, Margarita, that's wonderful! A little sister or brother for Marti."

I refrained from making any kind of comment, but, instead, I waited a minute before speaking. "Well, Ariel, as you know, I'm on the Pill, so this is an accident."

Ariel squeezed my hand, and kissed me again. "Aren't you happy, *querida?* We've talked about having another child."

It was all I could do to restrain myself from hurling accusations at him. "Yes, but we agreed it would be planned, and not an accident." I lay back on the bed. "I still have not decided what I'm going to do about going back to work." I closed my eyes. "This is not the way to have another child."

"Margarita." Ariel lay next to me and stroked my hair. "It was just meant to be."

My eyes still closed, I ventured into dangerous territory. It was now or never. "I know I took the Pill without skipping any day. I became pregnant in spite of that." I took a deep breath. "The only explanation possible is that the pills were defective."

I could feel Ariel beginning to squirm next to me. Good. "Well, Margarita, there is a failure rate associated with birth control pills. You know that."

I opened my eyes as I sat back up in bed again. "Right after I came back from Dr. Kennedy's office I went on the Internet and looked up the track record of the brand of pills I take."

Now Ariel was openly concerned. And, based on his knowledge of me, he was right to be. He knew that once I set my sights on a malfeasant, they were history. "Why?"

"Because I'm going to look into suing them for selling a defective product," I announced gravely. "Oh, yes, by the time I'm done, that company is going to regret ever having manufactured those pills."

Ariel was silent as the significance of my words sank in. We both knew that once I embarked on that road, there was no turning back. The minute I filed the lawsuit, the attorneys for the pharmaceutical company, in order to defend itself, would unleash its teams of investigators, who would swarm over every aspect of our lives. It would not take long for the trail to lead them to Rodrigo, and expose his role in the pregnancy. Not a pretty picture to say the least.

I went on a bit further, detailing what legal strategy I was thinking of following. The more I spoke, the paler Ariel became. The tan that he had been sporting earlier was a distant memory. Seeing his reaction, I decided to lay it on thick and go for the jugular. I certainly had not behaved like Mother Teresa, but he had acted in a despicable manner.

Ariel listened as much as he could, but then, apparently, it all became too much. After considering the horrific scenario I was laying out in front of him, Ariel decided that the best approach would be for him to come clean and confess.

Now visibly perturbed, he looked at me squarely in the eyes and said. "Margarita, you are not going to sue the pharmaceutical company. Those pills were not defective."

I let him sweat before speaking. "I am devastated, Ariel, by learning what you've done. I have to say, I'm not necessarily surprised at my mother's actions, but *you*! You have betrayed me in the worst possible way." I must have been a better actress than I thought, for I could actually feel my eyes water.

And once Ariel began to panic at the very real possibility that I might leave him, I stated the terms and conditions under which I would stay, the ones I had worked on earlier that day while consulting with the Virgin in the Ermita de la Caridad.

As I listened to Ariel swear to me that he would abide by our deal, I was positive that I could see the Virgin looking at me from the bay window, a big grin on her face. We Cuban women certainly know how to cut a deal, especially when we were playing with weak cards. I had come out on top in a bad situation.

Gracias a Dios!

After having settled my business with Ariel, I decided that I could not postpone speaking with Luther. Therefore, the very next day, as soon as Ariel left for the office, I picked up the telephone and punched in a familiar number. Luther answered it on the first ring, almost as if he had known I would call just then. When I told him that the reason for my call was to see if he was free to meet that afternoon, the relief at hearing from me was palpable, making me feel instantly guilty. I had been so engrossed in my own situation that, the truth was, I had not really thought about how my not being available to see him had affected him.

After quickly asking each other how we were, we agreed to meet at noon at the apartment. Luther sounded so excited at the thought of us getting together again that I just hung up without saying good-bye. Clearly, he did not suspect anything was amiss.

As I drove toward the apartment in the Grove, I could feel my heart beating faster every mile I traveled. I fiddled with the radio, tuning in to this station and that in an attempt to distract myself from picturing what lay ahead of me.

Just as always, I stopped off at Scotty's and picked out some tantalizing tidbits for our lunch. I wanted this meeting to be special, memorable. Once I had finished, I got back into the Escalade and headed for the apartment. I had scheduled my time perfectly, for Luther was turning into the driveway of the building just as I arrived here.

We followed the same routine, as if there had not been any interruption at all. At that point, I could have done it in my sleep. Luther and I were perfectly formal and correct with each other, so much so that a stranger observing us would have been hard pressed to say that we knew each other at all, and, of course, much less in a biblical sense.

That day Luther looked particularly attractive, in a tan cotton suit, with a blue shirt underneath that matched the color of his eyes perfectly. While we waited for the elevator, I could feel myself start to melt, and by the time we walked down the hall toward the apartment, my knees were so weak you could have picked me up off the floor. I somehow managed to restrain myself from jumping on him. If he felt the same way about me, he disguised it with perfect WASP control.

It was only when we had closed the door of the apartment behind us that we touched each other and, only then, after having put the package of groceries down on the kitchen table. The time we had spent apart had only served to make us hungrier for each other. By mutual consent, we skipped the champagne and went straight to the bedroom. I thanked God that the antibiotic cream had worked so well that I could fully enjoy our lovemaking.

Afterward, as we rested, spent and sweaty, the realization that I would never again have a lover as skilled as Luther in my life hit me, making me very sad. Luther must have sensed the change in my mood, for he turned to me and asked. "Daisy, what's up?"

Instead of answering, I asked him, "Luther, could we have some champagne now?"

Sensing something was amiss, Luther did not comment, but instead did as I asked. He got out of bed and walked toward the kitchen. As I watched him cross the room stark naked, admiring his body, I almost wept at the thought I was not going to see it again. I was fairly confident nobody would admire it the way I would, nor enjoy it in quite the same way.

I could hear familiar noises coming from the kitchen as Luther readied the champagne and glasses. Even though I should not have been drinking because of the baby, there was no way I could have this conversation totally straight. I determined to have only a few sips, enough to take the edge off. Besides, I really did not think a glass of champagne would be that harmful to the baby. It was only when overdoing the drinking that it really had calamitous effects. Still, better safe than sorry, so I would be cutting back drastically—but after today.

Luther came back carefully holding the silver tray with the bucket and glasses in front of him. I could just see the orange-colored top of the bottle of Veuve Clicquot poking out. What a wonderful sight that was—a naked man, especially one built like Luther, bringing such a lovely offering to me.

Luther placed the tray on the bed, and began opening the bottle, carefully twisting off the cork. It certainly would not do to have the cork hit an inappropriate place on his body. He poured the golden liquid into the glasses and handed me one. Sitting up in bed facing each other, we tipped our glasses in a silent toast and sipped the delicious drink.

"Okay, Daisy." Luther put his glass down on one of the bedside tables, and took mine and did the same. He then took both my hands in his and looked into my eyes. "What is it?"

Gazing into his blue eyes, I knew this was going to be much more difficult than I had thought. Still, it had to be done, for Marti's and the baby's sake.

"Luther, I don't think we should see each other anymore," I began. I pulled my hand from his and reached over for the glass of champagne on the bedside table. I took one long swallow and decided there was no perfect time to say what I was going to say, so I might as well get on with it.

"Luther, you know how much I love you." Luther nodded warily, instantly sensing that this was not going to be a pleasant conversation. "These months this summer with you have been the happiest of my life." Luther began breathing a bit easier. Seeing his reaction, I decided I had better hurry, or he was going to get the wrong impression as to where this was going.

"As much as I love you, I believe that we do not have a future together," I stated straight out. I held out my arms, and waved them around the room, and then pointed toward the living room. "This has been a fantasy. A wonderful, terrific fantasy, but a fantasy nevertheless. This is not real life. We come here in the afternoons to have lunch, drink champagne, and make love." Luther just looked at me as if I had just told him that Santa, the Easter Bunny, the Tooth Fairy, and Tinker Bell did not exist.

Knowing from experience that champagne has been known to make me change my mind, Luther reached for the bottle and poured us two more very hearty servings. "What are you telling me, Daisy?"

The look in his eyes was such that I almost backed out of what I was going to say, but only the image of Marti's face gave me the strength to keep me going. "I have family responsibilities—I have a son, and I have to think of him." I threw Luther a face-saving explanation. I wanted and needed to part as friends with him. I have never believed in burning my bridges. I took a large sip of champagne and continued. "The more I see you, the deeper I am becoming involved with you."

Luther seemed perplexed. "What's the matter with that?" he quite logically asked. "I've told you how I feel about you, that I'm willing to move down here for you." His eyes flashed. "Daisy, I even learned Spanish for you, for God's sake!" He reached over and touched my cheek with his right hand. Do you know how difficult that is for a gringo?"

Luther was breaking my heart. "I know my love, I know." I kissed him softly. "But I have responsibilities." We both knew what I was referring to.

"I'm willing to assume those responsibilities," Luther pointed out. "I am, I told you that."

"I know, and I am very, very grateful, but I don't think that would be right," I said. "Miami is not a natural environment for you; you would be here for me, and that would be very difficult. Ariel would fight me for Marti, and I could lose him."

"But, Daisy, if we love each other—" Luther put his arms around me, "—we could fight him; we could. I lost you once before, I cannot let you go again."

It took all the strength I had to continue. "Luther, I'm sorry. My mind is made up. My life is here in Miami, with my husband and son." Every word was being wrenched from me. "You are the love of my life—you always have been and always will be, but sometimes in life things don't turn out the way we want them to."

"Daisy, we are not two characters from *West Side Story*—just because you're Cuban and I'm American. We can work something out. I know we can." Luther was trying his best to convince me. "We're mature adults; we can make it work."

I shook my head and began to cry. I felt like an actress in a really bad soap opera. "I'm so sorry. I can't risk losing my son." Just then, I came very close to telling him about the baby, but I knew that if I had done that, he would have persuaded me to stay with him. And, if there was something I was persuaded about, it was that that would have been wrong. I could not blame him for doubting my logic, as even to *my* ears the arguments I had given him had been pretty flimsy. But, of course, I could not tell him the whole truth. That was impossible. "I'm so sorry," I repeated through my tears.

Luther realized he was fighting a losing battle. He could not win against motherhood. All he could do now was to make our parting sweeter. He was nothing if not an optimist, and considered the possibility that maybe I would come around in the future if we left off on a positive note.

"Come here." He pulled me to him, as we lay back on the bed. "If you are really convinced as you say you are, maybe this will make you come back to me, Daisy." He began playing with me in a way he knew would give me the most pleasure imaginable. "I know you'll be back, Daisy. I'm a patient man."

And, as it was going to be our last time, Luther applied himself wholeheartedly to the matter at hand. The man was an overachiever, no question about that. He explored my body with a thoroughness not even a CAT scan could have achieved. After that day, I could have applied for a job as a contortionist in the circus. Never in my life had I felt so supple. If we were to have continued our relationship, I would never have to worry about osteoporosis.

At the end of our encounter, feeling the way I did, I could have agreed to almost anything Luther proposed. Anything except for the one thing he wanted. That I could not give him. I had my children to consider, and I was, above all, a Cuban mother.

[**39**]

EIGHT MONTHS LATER.

The lights in the delivery room were blinding
white, making my eyes hurt whether they were
open or closed. To distract myself from the excruciating pain below
my waist, I kept them open so I could look around. I was freezing
cold despite all my exertions over the past few hours, but when I
pointed that out to one of the bustling nurses, she told me it was necessary to keep the birthing room cool. She said she would bring some
extra blankets to cover me up, but she seemed to have gotten busy
and forgotten me. I felt as though I was on an endless flight; I had
asked the flight attendant for a blanket hours ago, and she had promised to bring it but never quite managed to tend to me.

Marti's delivery had been relatively easy, so this one, long and
brutally painful, was a real surprise. Dr. Kennedy saw that I was suffering about as much as I could take, so he administered an epidural
as well as a hefty dose of Demerol to dull the pain. I watched the
medicine being added to the drip hanging next to me, and blessed the
fact that I had chosen an obstetrician who believed in the power of
pharmaceuticals. After a quick injection into the base of my spine, I
felt my mood change dramatically.

All of a sudden I was floating on clouds, warm milk running through my veins. I welcomed the painkillers, although part of me felt I didn't deserve the relief. I deserved to suffer for what I had done.

I lay on the table in the delivery room, sensing all kinds of activity going on around me, my body being pulled and pushed every which way, but I didn't care and was no longer paying attention. I was off in another world. Dr. Kennedy left, came back, and was saying something to me. He was at the foot of the table but I couldn't really hear him; there seemed to be yards and yards of green cotton fabric separating us. There seemed to be about a dozen people working in the room, talking to each other, talking to me, but I didn't even bother to count them. I was past caring what I looked like, and what they had seen of my body. I was way beyond any kind of modesty.

My emotions had been conflicted about that day—March 8—the very day Dr. Macia had set for my due date. I always was punctual for a Cuban. It was a day that I had both welcomed and dreaded.

Floating off in a sea of pharmaceuticals, I replayed the events that had led me to that cold steel table, with my private parts opened up for the world to see. I replayed the moment when I got the news from Dr. Macia, then the encounter with Rodrigo at the Santos drugstore, when I found out about Ariel and Mamá conspiring to substitute placebos for my birth-control pills.

And if I closed my eyes tight enough, I could hear my voice at the Ermita de la Caridad, and see her lips moving. The Virgin hadn't let me down.

I know you can't negotiate with the Virgin, but I felt she had made an exception in my case. Maybe it was my sheer desperation that had compelled her to help me. She must have believed my pledges that I would do whatever she asked if she would only give me guidance, help, and support.

It ended up taking three visits to the Ermita over the course of three days for me to understand what the Virgin was saying. By the end, though, I was confident of what I should do, and what she demanded of me in return. It was a hard bargain. First of all, I was supposed to start attending Mass every Sunday, to live my life according to the sacraments, and to have Marti serve as an altar boy as soon as he was old enough. So far, I had stuck to my promises, and I fully intended to keep doing so.

The Virgin had compelled me to take stock of my life, and figure out my priorities. It took me two days, but by the end my mind was clear. The most important person in my life was Marti, and now the baby joined him. My own wishes and desires had to be secondary to my children. I had to acknowledge that my own selfish desires had gotten me into this mess, and that it was time for me to truly think about someone else.

Once I understood this, everything else fell into place. Although I had been unfaithful to Ariel, I felt that his conspiring against me to get me pregnant matched, if not exceeded, that betrayal. All the extra lovemaking we indulged in during those weeks hadn't been compelled by his passion for me, but merely to increase the chances that we would conceive. I knew, though, that there was no point getting angry. I was carrying a child, and I believed that harboring negativity and bad energy would be unhealthy for it.

Suddenly, I felt someone touching my neck and shoulders. I opened my eyes and saw that the nurse had returned and was wrapping cotton sheets around me. I could barely coordinate my mouth to form words, but I somehow managed to mumble a *"Gracias"* before closing my eyes again. The blankets soon made me feel warm and cozy in the cold, sterile room. I had no idea what Dr. Kennedy was doing down there at the foot of the operating table. I glanced down and saw the top of his head, but that was all.

I drifted off again. This time, I conjured up the scene when I confronted Ariel about switching the birth control pills. I could also visualize the scene at Luther's apartment when I told him I would not be seeing him anymore. Both had been equally painful. In my drug-induced haze, I kept going back from one scene to the other. Soon they had merged and become one.

"Margarita," someone said to me.

I almost said Luther's name, but stopped myself.

"Margarita, meet your daughter," Dr. Kennedy said. And he showed her to me, just before handing her off to a nurse who was waiting next to him with an open blanket.

I lay back and smiled.

"We're going to call her Caridad," I said, just before I passed out.

 My time in the recovery room passed in a haze, though I vaguely remembered a nurse coming in and pushing down hard on my stomach to expel as much fluid as possible after the birth. Later she told me I encouraged her to push down as hard as she could because I didn't want to struggle to lose weight once I left the hospital.

Hours later, back in my private room, I finally felt awake enough to receive visitors. Before I allowed anyone to see me, I bribed the Haitian nurse's aid to help me take a shower and wash my hair. At first she told me it was strictly against hospital rules, and that I had to lie down quietly in bed. I was so desperate that I told her I was an immigration attorney, and that I'd help anyone in her family if they were having problems with their legal documentation. I felt as though I'd run a marathon, and I was in no shape to see anyone in my present condition. Finally she held me up as I lathered myself in the shower stall, moving the I.V. stand around so I didn't yank the needle out of the top of my hand. After the shower, despite how difficult it had been, I felt like a new woman.

Ariel was my first visitor. Although most couples these days have the spouse in the delivery room during birth, I felt no such need. There was no percentage in having Ariel watch me in pain. I hadn't let him witness Marti's birth, and I didn't want him there for Caridad's. Besides, I wasn't even sure if he was the father, another reason for keeping him out. Although Ariel didn't know about the latter rationale, he was happy to spend the hours of my labor and delivery waiting in the lounge down the hall.

The nurse's aide was a jolly middle-aged woman whose mood had picked up considerably after my offer of free legal work. She helped me towel off my hair and pull a nightgown over my head. She even held up the mirror so I could apply makeup, then a squirt of Chanel No. 5.

Ariel knocked softly before entering the room.

"How are you?" he asked in a soft voice. He bent over to kiss me, then sat on the corner of the bed and held my hand, careful not to disturb my I.V. "I just came from the nursery, Margarita. The baby's beautiful. She's already driving the nurses crazy with her screams!"

Ariel chuckled, then turned serious. "Thank you for our daughter," he said. "I know she didn't come into the world under ideal circumstances and, believe me, I still feel terrible about that. But thank you."

Ariel's sincerity was touching, and I almost weakened and let him off the hook. But I told myself I had to be strong, and to hold on to our agreement no matter what happened.

"I only saw her for a second in the delivery room," I said. "But they should be bringing her in for a feeding pretty soon."

As though the nurses had read my mind, a moment later there was a soft tapping at the door. Ariel got up and opened it.

"Mrs. Silva? I've brought your daughter to you."

The nurse pushed the door open wide and came in carrying the baby in her arms; Caridad was wrapped in a pink blanket and wore a little cap on her head. I sat up as straight as I could and held out my arms to receive her.

"She *is* beautiful," I said to Ariel as I took off her cap to examine her more closely. "Our little Caridad."

Ariel frowned. "Caridad?" he asked. "What's that?"

"It's her name," I replied. "And I think it suits her perfectly."

"That's not one of the names we discussed," Ariel protested.

I think it's a beautiful name for a beautiful little girl," I said. "She's named after our patron saint, Ariel. Surely you don't object to that."

Ariel thought for a second, then decided to agree with me.

"Caridad is beautiful," he said.

I picked up the tiny bottle of milk the nurse had given me, and began to feed the baby with it. I had had physical problems nursing Marti the first time around, and decided to avoid the trial and heartache with Caridad.

The baby took the nipple eagerly and began to suck the milk. Watching her, I tried to banish a mental image of Luther. Now was the time to remind Ariel of the deal we'd cut when I confronted him with conspiring with Mamá to switch pills on me.

"Pay attention," I told him. "Remember, you're going to be doing this for her in a few weeks."

"You don't have to remind me, Margarita," Ariel said, smiling, trying to put a good face on the situation. "I'm a quick learner."

When I first confronted Ariel about the pills, I was prepared to leave him and told him so. The idea of my leaving with Marti was more than Ariel could bear, so we had come to an agreement. Ariel would stay at home with the kids for two years while I went back to work. That was the price for his betraying me. I knew we had more than enough money for him to quit work for a couple of years without affecting our standard of living. I worked the numbers out and was confident of my argument, so he really had no defense.

I pointed out to Ariel that he had wanted this baby so much that he had been willing to lie, manipulate, and coerce in order to bring her into the world. And now he could care for her, and Marti, too.

I took Caridad home from the hospital two days after her birth. She was a good baby, good natured and pleasant. We both recovered from the difficult birth quickly. Family and friends came by to visit, and the house was so filled with flowers it reminded me of Caballero's, the Funeral Home, when one of the politicos of Miami passed away.

Vivian and Anabel visited daily. Twice Vivian brought her daughter, and I was both pleased and surprised to see the child was behaving herself and minding Vivian. It had not been an easy road, but from all appearances, Vivian seemed content with her role as a mother. Well, at least she was getting her hair highlighted regularly, and she was going in to work, both reliable barometers of her state of mind. Anabel still dressed in her usual outlandish outfits, some combinations so frightful that I was grateful that Caridad's eyes were barely opened for her visits so she could not see them.

After ten days, on a spectacular, beautiful spring day, I decided we had to pay a visit to a very special lady. So after Caridad had woken up from her afternoon nap, I dressed her in her best baby outfit, and carefully placed her in the car seat in the Escalade.

We drove across the MacArthur Causeway from Miami Beach to the mainland and, once there, headed south on Bayshore Drive. On the street just north of Mercy Hospital, I turned left toward Biscayne Bay. I drove to the Ermita de la Caridad and parked the car as close to the building as possible.

Even though it was a warm, sunny day, the wind off the Bay was blowing hard. I stepped out of the car and opened the back door to take out the baby, who was sleeping peacefully in her carrier. Gently, so as not to disturb her, I picked her up and held her tight against my body. Carefully, I closed the car door and began walking toward the building.

There was someone inside I wanted to show Caridad to—her namesake. We slowly made our way up the aisle toward where the statue of the Virgin was. As we stood there, I could have sworn I saw the little Virgin wink at me. I winked back. To me, that sign meant that the Virgin knew I was there, and She was with me. I looked down at my baby, and thought I saw her eyelashes flutter as well. My heart began to pound as I reflected on what that meant. It was all I could do to keep from yelling out that I had had a sign from the Virgin.

Not wanting to break the spell, I walked back toward the first row of pews and sat down directly in front of the Virgin. I knew that pew well: it was the same one where I had spent all those long hours consulting with the Virgin. As I looked down at the face of my daughter in my arms, I could not help but think back on the long road that had led us here.

And so, after my one-year leave of absence, I went back to Weber, Miranda, et al., and resumed working there. Upon my return I told my partners I would require a six-week maternity leave, after which I would be returning full time. Maria told me that the possible deal with the other immigration attorney had been quietly dropped, and I was welcomed back into the fold at the firm.

I lay there in the nursery at home, watching Caridad sucking on the nipple of the bottle of milk, amazed at how well things had turned out. Now the only problem would be if Caridad was tall, blond, blue-eyed, and athletic.

Then I would have a lot of explaining to do.

But I wasn't worried about it. I would just take Caridad to visit her namesake at the Ermita de la Caridad, again. Before then, I would try to brush up on my lip reading.